HAUNTED: PERRON MANOR

LEE MOUNTFORD

FREE BOOK

Sign up to my mailing list for free horror books...

Want more scary stories? Sign up to my mailing list and receive your free copy of *The Nightmare Collection - Vol 1* as well as *Inside: Perron Manor* (a prequel novella to *Haunted: Perron Manor*) directly to your email address.

The novel-length short story collection and prequel novella are sure to have you sleeping with the lights on.

Sign up now.

www.leemountford.com

1

BACK, after all these years. Back to Devil's House.

Chloe Shaw took a breath and held it as she looked around the entrance lobby of Perron Manor. She had lived here for close to a year when she was a child, but had never set foot inside since. And now, after the passing of her uncle, it was hers.

Well, hers and her sister's. And it would be the perfect family home, history be damned.

The space around her was impressive, and much different than she was used to. A marble-tiled floor was firm underfoot, and just ahead of her was a grand set of oak stairs. The bannisters and spindles were a deep brown, and the timber treads had discoloured slightly over time. The stairs ran up to a half landing, which then split off both left and right before they turned back on themselves, creating walkways that gave access to the corridors upstairs.

Given the lobby was a double-height space, it made the entrance feel suitably majestic. The walls were covered with oak panelling up to mid-height, and after that cream wallpaper—which had peeled and yellowed over time—took over.

As majestic as it was, years of neglect were apparent. The wall panelling had scuffed and cracked in areas, and the varnish on the wood had stained. The air was stuffy as well, and the smell of something rotten permeated the air. Rectifying that would be only one of the many jobs that lay ahead of them.

'Cosy,' said her husband Andrew, making no attempt to hide his sarcasm. He held on to Emma, their eighteen-month-old daughter, who was asleep in his arms and had her face snuggled into his upper chest. Andrew was not as enthused about the place as Chloe was. She had known that ever since they had made their first visit up here to view the house, when his face had been a persistent frown. But, he'd agreed to move here—albeit a little reluctantly—and this was their home now.

'Cosy isn't the point,' Chloe said. 'Not with a place like this.'

She was still a little in awe of her surroundings. When they had first come up here, Chloe had not been able to remember much about Perron Manor, given she'd been only six years old when she'd left. But now, after being back inside for a little while, pangs of recognition had started to bloom: the intricate carvings of the stair balustrades, the ornate ceiling high above with detailed coving around the edges, and the pattern of the marble floor—overlapping squares and rectangles, a mixture of greys, whites, and dull yellows. They all hit home and pulled some long-forgotten memories back to the surface. She remembered running through here a lot, and had always loved the pattering echo her feet made on the tiled floor.

She turned back to Andrew and couldn't help but smile. 'Honestly... what do you think?'

He paused, looked around, and then scratched at the stubble on his chin with his free hand. The grey in his facial hair had long since spread to the receding hair atop his head. Andrew's normally serious blue eyes again settled on Chloe. He shrugged.

'Workable, I suppose,' he replied, then added with a grin, 'though it smells like someone died in here.'

She shot him a scowl. 'Don't push it,' she warned. Chloe knew he was only teasing, but she didn't want him going down that road. He was well aware that people *had* died in this house.

Her estranged uncle, for one. Though that was just the tip of the iceberg.

But that didn't matter, it was all in the past. And the past couldn't hurt them.

Andrew held up his free hand in mock supplication. 'Fine, fine,' he said. 'Not another word. I guess it has... potential.'

'It's got *huge* potential,' Chloe corrected. And it did. Perron Manor, for all its history, was a massive property, far too large for Andrew and her to have afforded on their own. And yet it had been gifted to her and her sister, along with a not-insubstantial inheritance.

The grounds around the house alone made her giddy with excitement, and the possibilities about what she could do with them were endless. Sure, the gardens and lawns all looked shabby and overgrown now, but with a little tender loving care, they could be transformed into something beautiful—just like the house itself.

It was a project Chloe could not wait to get started on. First, however, she knew they would need to get the important things in order. A transit van full of their essential belongings was parked outside, and two more trucks from a removal company were due to arrive later that same day. And then, of course, there was her sister.

'So, when is Sarah due to get here?' Andrew asked, as if reading her mind.

'Later today.'

'Well, then,' he went on, 'shouldn't we get to work claiming the best bedroom before she steals it?'

Chloe laughed. 'That sounds like a good idea.' Andrew started to walk over to the staircase before them, but she stopped him. 'Not so fast. Let's take a look around the ground floor. We have a little bit of time.'

Andrew glanced at the sleeping child in his arms. 'This one will be waking up soon,' he said. 'I think we should at least get her crib set up, first.'

'It'll be fine,' Chloe said with a dismissive wave of her hand. Her excitement to take in their new home was simply too great, so the unpacking could wait a while. It would do them good to explore the house a little and take a moment to savour their new home.

With Andrew following behind, she made her way off to the left of the entrance lobby to one of the heavy-looking oak doors. Chloe pushed it open, and it creaked horribly. A hallway was revealed beyond, the floor of which was lined with a faded patterned carpet of predominately reds and blacks. The walls, like the main foyer, were half-height wood panelling and the same cream wallpaper above. There were no external windows here, so most of the space was cloaked in darkness. Chloe hit the brass light switch to her side, and the single light fitting in the corridor—a black, iron chandelier—sputtered to life, casting a dull yellow hue not quite powerful enough to fill all the corners.

That will need to be replaced, Chloe thought.

The corridor was not a long one, and turned ninety degrees to their right just up ahead. She knew that by following the hallway, it would bring them out into what was called the great hall.

I own a house with a fucking great hall!

And from there they could look out into the rear courtyard.

I own a house with a fucking courtyard!

Chloe was giddy, there was simply so much to get excited about.

Straight ahead, set in the wall before them at the point where the corridor snapped to the right, was a door that led into a good-sized dining room. That door was open, even though Chloe was certain she had closed all of them during their last visit. *Obviously not.* The darkness of the room looked heavy. Chloe poked her head inside as they passed and saw that the thick curtains had been pulled closed. *Weren't they open when we left?*

'Something wrong?' Andrew asked.

Chloe shrugged, deciding she was simply misremembering in her excitement.

'No, let's keep going,' she replied. Chloe was just about to turn away and pull the door closed, when something in the dark caught her attention. She had to squint, and it was hard to make out, but when she looked toward the far wall, Chloe could swear there was a humanoid shape within the black, little more than a shadow itself. She stared more intently, taking in the unmoving form but unable to make out any firm details. A slight chill worked its way up her spine. However, the more she stared, the harder it was to see, and eventually she realised there was nothing there at all.

Chloe quickly reached her hand inside the room and felt for the light switch. The illumination was slow at first, but soon flickered to life.

There was nothing. No shape. No figure.

'What is it?' Andrew asked from behind her.

Chloe shook her head. 'Nothing,' she replied, deciding her mind was playing tricks.

Faces in the fire.

She switched the light off and pulled the door shut again. 'Come on, let's keep going.'

Her excitement returned. This place was going to be perfect for them. She just knew it.

2

THE TASTE of the coffee was almost as delicious and comforting as the smell itself. It was a hazelnut roast, and the fragrance the drink cast off from the plastic carry-out cup was divine.

Sarah Pearson smacked her lips together after taking another long slug of the hot liquid. Chloe would no doubt turn her nose up at the taste, given the woman—for some crazy reason—detested hazelnut.

'Good?' the barista asked.

Sarah smiled and nodded. 'Better than good. It's perfect.'

She hadn't expected to find such a good coffee shop in a place like Alnmouth. Though, in truth, she had no idea what to expect, really. Sarah knew it was a small town, but that was about all she had found out before travelling. For some reason, she had expected it to be a little... backwater.

Instead of heading straight to Perron Manor—her new home, and a place she hadn't even seen yet—Sarah had wanted to make a quick stop in the local town first and pick up a few bottles of alcohol to celebrate moving-in day. After all, if she couldn't celebrate being given a Goddamn mansion, then when *could* she celebrate?

And the first thing Sarah had seen after parking her car in the quaint town centre was a shop named *Hill of Beans*. Evidently a coffee shop and cafe. It had a plate glass frontage that was surrounded by sleek black framing, and actually looked quite modern. The smell from the shop pulled her inside immediately, calling to her—especially since it had been over two hours since her last cup.

It was quite busy inside, but not bustling, and the atmosphere was nice and calm. The only sounds were that of the chattering patrons and the hissing of the coffee machines. Sarah had feared the worst from Alnmouth, but her first impression was a good one.

Sarah took another sip of her coffee. 'Is there anywhere around here I can grab a few bottles of wine?' she asked.

The barista was a young woman with dark hair, which was mostly hidden behind a black cap embossed with the shop's logo. The girl couldn't have been much older than twenty, but seemed so quick and efficient at her job that Sarah guessed she could have worked there for years. She was shorter than Sarah, who herself stood at five-foot-seven, but had similar blue eyes.

'Sure,' the barista said. 'A few places, really. There is a convenience store just across the road that will have a good selection. It's directly opposite this place. You can't miss it.'

'Cool,' Sarah replied, but immediately regretted saying it. Even though she was only thirty-seven, the word sounded forced coming out of her mouth.

That's a young person's word, Sarah, and you aren't young anymore. You've only old age to look forward to now.

It was a sobering thought, and one that had tended to plague her more and more as the years advanced.

The barista smiled, but it was almost condescending. *Oh, look at that old person trying to be hip. Bless her heart.*

Or maybe that was just Sarah being paranoid.

Sarah thanked the girl for her drink and left the shop, stepping outside into the crisp, clean air. Her shoulder-length dark and wavy hair blew across her face, forcing her to tuck it back behind her ears.

The centre of Alnmouth was quaint, and Sarah guessed it was the kind of town people moved to when retired, given the average age of the people seemed to be around fifty or so. The architecture was predominantly Victorian, with lots of terraces and mismatching facing materials: bricks, stone, and even some renders. A small church sat on a lush green field, surrounded on one side by neatly kept trees. The stores in the vicinity seemed a mix of local companies and more well-known commercial chains. Hell, behind the church, a few hundred yards away, Sarah could also make out a small lake with a stream running off from it. It was very picturesque.

Whatever preconceived notions Sarah had about this place, she realised she had been wrong. She wasn't against roughing it, given the career and life she had just left behind, but Alnmouth seemed rather more upmarket than Sarah had first feared.

As hard as it had been, leaving her old life was the right call. The thought of staying after what had happened to Tania was far worse than leaving the military behind.

Sarah wanted something different out of life now. Trouble was, she didn't know what that was.

The trip to the convenience store was a quick one, and she grabbed a few bottles of red for her and Chloe to share, as well as a bottle of whiskey for Andrew. There was also a section of child's toys, and she chose a stuffed bunny that looked cute. The animal wore an endearing, dopey grin, and held a bright orange carrot, which was stitched to its paws. She hoped Emma would like it.

Sarah had never considered herself very maternal, so perhaps this was as close as she was ever going to get. Being the cool aunt. She was okay with that.

The drive to her new home—something she could still scarcely get her head around—took about fifteen minutes, the road bringing her out of the centre of Alnmouth and to the outskirts. Here it was all fields and trees, and the only pocket of civilisation she could see was in the town centre in her rear-view mirror. A small, country lane led her up a hill, between more trees, and then, eventually, to Perron Manor itself.

It took her breath away a little.

This is the place I've inherited?

Sarah had previously done a little digging about the house, of course. She knew a bit of the history, and found a few photos online, but they didn't give much away. Chloe, who had been here once before already, had previously given Sarah a description, but it was nothing like seeing the place in person.

Sarah was still a distance away, but the road ahead was a straight one, flanked by hedges and trees, and she could see the open, wrought-iron entry gate set into a high stone boundary wall. Beyond that lay the house itself.

She could make out a little of the detail, such as the steps up to the front door and the angled canopy above that, which ran the full width of the front elevation. But at this distance it was the floors above that were more visible, given they stood proudly over the top of the wall.

The external walls were constructed from buff stone blocks, built up in a random pattern with no uniform mortar joints to speak of. The windows—four to the middle floor and three to the top—all had arched heads, and thin white frames. One of the most distinct features Sarah could see was the three peaks to the roof at the head of the building, the central one being the most prominent. They all cut into the normal eaves line of the building's main roof facade, which ran in a perpendicular direction.

Central to the building—and lining up with the middle peak—was a shallow outward step in the building's footprint, one that brought a sense of character to the symmetrical design.

And the house was *big*. Sarah had never in her wildest dreams thought she'd own a home of this size. It just wasn't in her future. She wasn't sure what the technical distinction of a mansion was, but if Perron Manor wasn't actually classified as one, then it had to have been close.

Sarah carefully navigated her vehicle through the open gate and entrance pillars, then onto the property's grounds. She had no idea as to the age of the house, or how many modifications had been made over time, but it didn't strike her as an aesthetic that was from any one particular era. At least, none that she could discern. Not that Sarah was an architect or anything, but she did have a passing interest in building design and history, given she had been seriously considering following a career in that field before joining the military instead.

Was it too late to rekindle that interest and push for a new kind of career?

You're thirty-seven. Of course it is.

Not exactly old, but not young enough that the world was her oyster anymore.

Now that she was within the confines of the grounds, Sarah could see more of the ground-floor canopy. Its angled roof was slate, and the central section of it came together to form a ridge, with a smaller peak mirroring the larger ones above. Two grand columns ran down either side of the entrance door, and the windows lined up with the ones on the floors above it, making the front elevation seem very ordered, and almost simplistic in design. Had it not been for the canopy, slight central outcropping, and the three ridges at the head, the building might have looked quite boring. As it was, it had just enough character to be interesting without being chaotic.

As she drove down the gravel driveway, Sarah noticed that the grounds around her were clearly uncared for, but impressive in their size, with garden areas as well as long stretches of lawn.

Up ahead, she saw a few transit vans near the house, where the gravel driveway opened out to a considerable parking area. Sarah also saw Chloe and Andrew's metallic-blue SUV. A much bigger car than her own, and Sarah was happy with what she had. Her Mini had less bulk, but with that came more pull and speed, especially given the sports engine.

Sarah's own possessions, the ones that weren't packed into the small car with her, would be coming the following day. But it was a fraction of the amount Chloe and Andrew had to unload. Being in the army, and away from home most of the time, meant that Sarah hadn't really built up much in the way of material possessions. She liked that. It was easier to pack up and move on if needed.

She pulled her car to a stop away from the cluster of other vehicles and got out, leaving her bags, cases, and boxes inside for the time being. She could unpack everything later, after she'd greeted her family. The only thing Sarah did grab was Emma's stuffed toy.

A bulky man with a flat cap, his face glistening with a sheen of sweat, flashed her a polite smile as he trudged his way over to the tall removal van and hopped in the back. Sarah walked up the stone steps that led up to the entrance door, taking it all in. The house towered above her, and looking up at it made her feel dizzy and somehow... unworthy.

A lot of the steps beneath her were cracked, which was yet another sign that Perron Manor had not had the required love and attention needed over the years. That then begged the question: would the three of them—she, Chloe, and Andrew—be able to maintain it any better than her uncle had?

Sure, three people could do more than one, but with a place like this it seemed a whole staff would be required to keep the house in good order.

Chloe had previously assured Sarah that it would be fine. Her specific words being, 'It does need a lot of work, I won't lie, but it's manageable. And it can't hurt to try. Worst comes to worst, we just sell it.'

Sarah had agreed with her sister. In truth, she was actually looking forward to diving into a project, as it was something she could focus on to occupy her mind. She hadn't seen the inside of the house yet, of course, and she knew it could be in an even worse state of disrepair than the outside. But it was something to work on together.

Even if it was only temporary.

Sarah knew that she couldn't live here with Chloe, Andrew, and Emma forever. They were a family, but eventually both she and they would need their own space.

For now, however, fresh out of the army and with no other calling in life, it happened to come about at the perfect time.

As she reached the top step, Sarah briefly thought about the man who had left all of this—the house, and a quite generous sum of money—to them. It had been a gift from an uncle she had never even met and never would.

Vincent Bell.

To say the whole situation was surreal was an understatement. But Sarah was, in a way, used to the surreal. Being dropped into the harsh landscape of Afghanistan, knowing each day could be her last, had certainly been surreal.

And scary.

So living here, even if there was hard work ahead, would in truth be a luxury.

From the porch area, Sarah peered inside of Perron Manor for the first time and took in the sight of its entrance area, seeing the staircase rise up and then split off both left and right from a half-landing.

Very grand.

She also noticed the double door—which was currently open—that was made from heavy-looking stained oak, with glass panels to the top sections of each door leaf. On one, Sarah saw a brass knocker: a frowning lion's head with a circular ring hanging from its mouth. It wasn't quite to her tastes—too old world—and something she would quite happily get rid of in the near future. Sarah took hold of the brass ring and lifted it. It was heavier than she had expected. There was a squeaking of metal, and Sarah let it fall. A sharp *clank* rang out as the ring struck the door's brass fitting.

Quirky.

Sarah then stepped inside, and the fresh air outside was immediately replaced with something heavier. A distinctly damp smell caught her off guard. She heard slapping footsteps approach from a corridor to her left. Then, her sister appeared through an open door. Chloe paused at first, then a huge smile broke out over her angular face.

She was taller than Sarah, more lithe—she always called herself bony—and was certainly beautiful. She was blessed with gorgeous, long dark hair and hazel eyes, though she always had the appearance of looking slightly tired, something Sarah had noted could be common amongst mothers. At the moment, Chloe was dressed in a purple t-shirt with a light grey cardigan over the top with her sleeves rolled up to the elbows, as well as tight-fitting jeans and flat, black shoes.

'Hey, Sis,' Sarah said, returning Chloe's smile. She then made a show of looking around their surroundings. 'Does this make us upper class now?'

Chloe laughed and shook her head. 'I don't think any amount of money could get us into high society.'

'Speak for yourself, commoner,' Sarah shot back. 'I could get used to the high life.'

Maintaining her smile, Chloe strode over and the two embraced in an affectionate hug. Sarah could smell Chloe's lavender shampoo, which was a scent that she always associated with her sister.

'It's going to be great here, Sarah,' Chloe said to her. 'I promise.'

3

'WELL, look what the cat dragged in,' a male voice called out.

She pulled away from her hug with Chloe to see Andrew enter the room. He was dressed in a simple light-blue t-shirt, jeans, and trainers, and Sarah could see developing sweat patches beneath his armpits. Given how fastidious Andrew was about his appearance, and how professional he always tried to present himself, the sweat was a clear sign he had been hard at work.

Andrew came towards her with a friendly smile and arms out for a hug. This was now their normal way of greeting—which Sarah had insisted upon, knowing it had initially made him uncomfortable. Now that he was more at ease with it, though, it had lost its appeal to her.

This time, however, she held up a hand, stopping Andrew in his tracks.

'We can hug after you shower,' she said, pointing to the patches beneath his arms. He frowned, confused at first, then looked down. 'What happened, Andrew?' she asked with a playful smirk. 'You always used to take such pride in your appearance.'

An embarrassed smile spread across his lips. 'Working hard getting things unpacked, I guess.'

Sarah laughed and pulled him in for the hug anyway. 'Sure, sure, sweaty boy.' She pulled free of him and turned to Chloe.

'So, where's Emma?' Sarah held up the stuffed rabbit and shook it.

'Oh that's adorable,' Chloe said. 'She's just down for a nap.' Chloe then took out a baby monitor from her pocket and showed it to her sister.

The image was a mix of black shadows in the distance and a blue hue that illuminated little Emma as she lay in a large cot-bed with side railing. It had been over half a year since Sarah had last seen her niece, and the child had been less than a year old then.

'Look at how big she is!' Sarah cooed. She had seen photos that Chloe had uploaded on social media, of course, but it still hit home just how long it had been since she had last seen and held Emma.

'She's been down for a while,' Andrew said. 'We could wake her if you want?'

'No,' Sarah said, shaking her head. 'There will be plenty of time to make a fuss of her. Let her wake up in her own time. I don't want to be the reason she's all grumpy.'

'Strange,' Andrew said, raising his eyebrows. '*You're* usually the reason the rest of us are grumpy.'

'Hilarious,' Sarah replied before sticking out her tongue and shooting him the finger.

'Do you have any stuff with you?' Chloe asked. 'Or is it all coming tomorrow?'

'I have a little of it with me. Not much, though.'

'Should we fetch it?'

'Later,' Sarah said. 'I want a quick tour of our new house first.'

'Sounds good,' Chloe agreed, wearing a big grin. 'Might wanna prepare yourself, though. This place is something else.'

'You got that right,' Andrew said. 'Wait till you see the basement.'

'We have a basement?'

'Yeah,' Andrew replied. 'A really creepy one. Used to be used as a prison, apparently.'

Sarah paused for a moment. 'No way.'

He nodded. 'The cells are still there.'

Sarah turned to Chloe for confirmation. Chloe rolled her eyes, though she nodded as well. 'He's making it sound worse than it is. There aren't any iron bars or anything. Only the old walls. It's just a cool little feature.'

'The furnace is down there too,' Andrew added. 'When it starts up it sounds like a bloody—'

'Enough, Andrew,' Chloe cut in with a polite yet stern smile.

But Andrew went on. 'Oh, and there is a whole section on the top floor that is completely locked off and we can't even access. Don't forget that.'

Chloe's expression turned to a scowl.

'Wait, really?' Sarah asked.

'We just haven't found the right key yet, is all,' Chloe told her. 'But we will. It'll be around here somewhere. If not, we just take the doors off the hinges. No big deal.'

'Alright, then,' Sarah said with a laugh. 'Anything else I should be aware of?'

'Mobile phone signal is spotty at best,' Andrew told her. 'So, until we get the internet sorted and installed, you're not gonna be very connected to the outside world. Oh, there's also the whole history of the house, of course.'

'Andrew, please!' Chloe shot back. It was clear to Sarah that Andrew wasn't as enamoured with the house as Chloe was.

'That's no problem,' Sarah said. 'I think I know as much as I need to about the house's history, anyway.'

'Fair enough,' Andrew answered, holding his hands up in defeat.

It was fair to say the house they now owned *did* have a checkered history—at least the small amount Sarah knew of it, which basically consisted of the events that took place in October of 1982. Chloe had been present for those events, though Sarah's older sister didn't remember anything of the chaos that took place back then. Sarah missed everything, of course, as she hadn't been born until the following July.

If it didn't bother Chloe, and she was excited about living here, then it sure as hell wasn't going to concern Sarah. All places had history. With her role in the army, Sarah herself had been to many countries that had violent and bloody recent pasts. That didn't mean they were inherently bad.

'Come on, then,' Chloe said, taking Sarah's hand. 'There's loads to see.'

Sarah was initially shown the ground floor as they first headed through a short corridor. The walls of the hallway were lined with cream wallpaper above wooden panelling, and patterned red carpeting lay over the floor. A dining room and a storage room were accessed off that corridor, which took a ninety-degree turn, and then led to a large, open area that caused Sarah to gasp.

'This is the great hall,' Chloe said, sweeping her arm grandiosely in an arc.

And 'great hall' wasn't a bad description of the area. While it wasn't the size of something out of Hogwarts, it was still impressive for a stately home. A long dining table with twelve seats was dwarfed by the free space around it. The walls in the room were covered with a deep green wallpaper lined with golden patterns. Hung on the walls were oil paintings and a large mirror with an ornate, gold frame. The ceiling above was plaster with intricate and detailed panelling, and solid white columns that ran from ceiling to floor added to the grand ambience of the hall. Lastly, stone-tiled flooring underfoot lent the space an almost medieval feel.

The only natural light that spilled in was from the large, glazed double-door that sat in the centre of the rear wall. It looked out into a courtyard space, which was in itself flanked by the two rear protruding wings of the house's rear, forming a rough 'U' shape. There were doors on either side of the rectangular great hall as well, and Chloe informed Sarah that the one to their left opened into the kitchen and the ones to their right accessed a toilet. There were also some steps that led down to the basement as well. The damp odour had lessened in this large area, yet it still smelled very musty.

'This is unreal,' Sarah said, unable to hide her smile. It was so far beyond what she was used to—either bunking down in barracks, or her old, rented flat—that it made her head swim.

Also accessed from the great hall were the two wings at the back of the property, and each consisted of two bedrooms off a short corridor. It was clear that, while still old, these wings were definitely newer than the main house.

The group of three then looped around, taking a different door off the great hall on their way back. They passed a living room and library before ending up again in the entrance lobby, accessing it from the opposite side from which they had left. They then took the stairs up to the middle floor, which consisted of a maze of corridors, bedrooms, storage rooms, and bathrooms. Chloe made sure to point out the rooms they had claimed for themselves and Emma.

'You'll have to pick your room as well,' Chloe told her. 'Sorry we jumped in and nabbed ours before you were here, but we needed to start putting stuff away.'

'It's fine,' Sarah said. 'I'm sure one of the many, *many* others will work for me.'

The top storey was accessed from a different set of stairs, and consisted mostly of bedrooms, though this time they were set into the roof space, so there were sloping ceilings, and windows cut into the main roof. The views this high up allowed Sarah to see for miles beyond the house's boundary walls. Sarah was then shown one of the two locked doors set in the looping corridor, both of which blocked off the same area.

This door, and the cross wall it was set into, did not match the quality of materials and construction workman-ship elsewhere in the house. It looked strong, certainly, but it was plain, with only a basic wood veneer finish and nothing in the way of panelling or detailing. A brass handle and lock were the only distinguishing features.

'We have no idea what is beyond here,' Andrew said.

Chloe shrugged. 'Probably just more bedrooms, like everywhere else.'

'Then why lock it off?' he asked.

'I don't know,' Chloe admitted. 'We can find out when the key turns up. It's no big deal.'

'Can you remember if it was locked like this back when you lived here?' Sarah asked.

Chloe paused for a moment, clearly trying to remember. She shook her head. 'I don't know. That was a long time ago. To be honest, I don't remember a great deal of that time. Now it's just more feelings of nostalgia than anything actually specific.'

That made some sense to Sarah, as she herself couldn't remember a thing about being six years old.

'So the only thing left is the cellar, right?' Sarah asked. 'Definitely looking forward to seeing that.'

But then the baby monitor that Chloe was carrying crackled to life, and Emma's cries came through the speakers.

Chloe sighed. 'Doesn't look like I'll be joining you for this one.'

'That's okay,' Sarah said, 'I'd rather go see my niece anyway. The basement can wait.'

The trio then descended the stairs to the level below and entered the room that had been designated as Emma's, sitting right next to Chloe and Andrew's.

The inside of the room was very stately and traditional in appearance, with blue wallpaper on one feature wall. The others were painted an off-white, with cream carpet, decorative coving around the perimeter of the high ceiling, and a window that looked out over the front of the property. White cupboards, drawers, and a change unit had been placed against one of the walls, but there was little else in the way of furniture, other than the cot-bed Emma lay in. It made the room feel a little bare. And it seemed cold inside as well, with a distinct cabbage-like smell emanating from one corner in particular, next to the door. But almost as soon as Sarah had moved farther into the bedroom, the temperature seemed to return to normal, and the offending smell gave way to a more pleasant scent given off by an air freshener plugged in at the wall.

Sarah looked down at her niece, who was now standing up in her bed with her hands wrapped around the top bar of the side railing. Emma's hair was a dark, fuzzy, and untamed mop, and she had the same big brown eyes as her mother. The same pale complexion as well.

Emma gave Sarah a big, toothy grin.

'Oh my God, she has most of her teeth now!' Sarah exclaimed.

Chloe smiled. 'She does. It wasn't a whole lot of fun while she was getting them, though. Lot of sleepless nights.'

'I bet,' Sarah replied. Emma then balanced herself and held out her arms in Sarah's direction.

Chloe looked at Sarah expectantly. 'Well, aren't you going to pick her up? She seems eager to see you.'

'I'm surprised she remembers me. It's been a while,' Sarah replied.

'She'd never forget her cool aunt Sarah,' Chloe told her. Sarah reached down to scoop Emma up, giving the little girl a great big hug and nuzzling her cheek against her niece's hair.

'Oh I've missed you, baby girl,' Sarah said. Then, she detected another sharp odour that made her pull her head away.

'Someone needs changing!'

Chloe laughed. 'You up for that?'

But Sarah just shook her head and handed the child back. 'Cool aunty duties end with cuddles and snuggles, I'm afraid.'

Chloe shook her head and took Emma from Sarah before walking over to the change-table.

'I'll need to feed her next. Andrew, why don't you show Sarah the basement now?'

'I could,' Andrew replied, 'but think I should probably help the removal guys out a little more. We kinda just left them to it.'

'That's fine,' Sarah cut in, 'I need to get my stuff anyway. I'll check the creepy cellar out later.'

'Want a hand with any of your things?' Andrew asked.

Sarah shook her head. 'Thanks, but there's not much to get. I can handle it.'

'Might wanna claim a room first,' Chloe told her. 'And let us know which one you pick.'

'Given how badly Andrew snores, it'll probably be one over on the other side of the house,' Sarah responded. It was now Andrew's turn to shoot her the finger.

'Fair enough,' Chloe said, laughing. 'A lot of the rooms on this level have en-suites, and a private bathroom is always nice.'

'Noted,' Sarah said. 'I'll catch up with you three when I've gotten settled in.'

And with that, Sarah and Andrew turned and left, letting the door click shut behind her.

'Good luck finding anywhere nice,' Andrew whispered. 'All the rooms are pretty much the same. Old and cold.'

'Not thrilled to be here, I'm assuming?'

He shrugged. 'I'll give it a chance, like I promised.' And with that, he then strode off down the corridor before turning out of view.

Trouble in paradise, Sarah thought to herself. She then looked down the hallway to the many doors set into its walls.

'Now,' she said. 'Which one of you is going to be mine?'

4

'Kid, you have more of this smeared across your face than you do in your belly.'

Chloe ran a wet-wipe around Emma's mouth, cleaning away the mashed strawberry that clung to the child's skin, making her look like a freaky infant-zombie that was mid-feast. Emma pulled away as her face was cleaned, cranky at being fussed over.

'Well you shouldn't make such a mess, then,' Chloe told her, smiling, as Emma continued to squirm in her high-chair and babble angrily.

Andrew walked into the kitchen, carrying a large and heavy-looking box with him. He dumped it on the counter and took a few deep breaths. Chloe's husband always kept himself in shape and had an athletic physique, but it was clear he was pushing himself hard to get as much done as possible today.

'Have a quick break,' Chloe said, feeling a little guilty. Taking care of Emma was the priority, of course, but she really wanted to throw herself into it and help out as well.

Andrew turned and leaned back against the kitchen countertop. 'Maybe a couple of minutes,' he said.

One of the removal men, Tony, entered the room shortly after. He was a stocky young man with a shaved head and goatee, and was carrying a box full of kitchen utensils.

Emma turned her eyes to him, then pointed. 'Man!' the infant said through a mouthful of food. Tony smiled.

'Don't mind her,' Andrew said with a chuckle. 'It's a phase. She does it with most men she isn't familiar with.'

'Yeah, every now and again she just blurts it out,' Chloe added.

'It's no problem,' Tony said, then raised the box up a little and gently shook it. 'Anywhere in particular I should put this?'

'Anywhere,' Andrew said, and Tony set the box down on a countertop and left the room, giving Emma a little wave as he did. Emma chuckled and waved back.

Chloe turned to Andrew and noticed his eyes wander around the kitchen, taking it all in. This was a change for him, she knew. He was used to modern ways of living: town centres, big flatscreen TV's, energy-efficient light fittings, and solar panels. That was what they had left behind. And he had agreed to that... for her.

The kitchen itself summed up just how different Perron Manor was to their old place, with block walls that were painted an ugly and sickly shade of yellow, high windows, rustic stone-slab flooring, and a kitchen table that was long and well worn. The table could well have been as old as the house. The cooker was huge and wrought iron, looking like it had been installed many years ago with the intention of feeding scores of people—which made sense, given the size of the property. But, apart from the horrible yellow that would have to be changed, the features were precisely what

Chloe loved about the house. It just screamed history and character, something that could stand the test of time, as opposed to the generic, small boxes contractors were now throwing up and calling them houses.

But to make this work, compromises would need to be made. Andrew had done his part by moving here in the first place. It was many miles from where they used to live, so she couldn't accuse him of not trying. Thankfully, the move wouldn't interfere with his business, where he acted as a consultant in the construction industry, helping professionals and contractors acquire the health, safety, and sustainability qualifications they needed. He'd built his business from the ground up, and worked from home when he wasn't out visiting clients. Given his clientele were dotted around all over the country, his base of operations didn't really matter.

Chloe knew that many of the features she liked in Perron Manor—such as some of the old, classical wallpaper, and the patterned carpets—would eventually need to give way to more modern decoration.

'You'll get used to it, you know,' Chloe told Andrew as he continued to look around.

He smiled. 'I know. It's just bigger and colder than I'm used to, you know? It feels empty. It'll just need an adjustment period.'

'Trust me, once Emma gets older, it might not feel big enough.'

'Maybe not if she has a little brother or sister.'

Chloe paused. 'Is that in the cards?'

Andrew shrugged. 'Maybe. I'm not getting any younger. So it's something I've started to think about.' He was smiling as he said it.

Chloe didn't know what to say. It was true they were

both advancing in years, with him being forty-three, and her a year older at forty-four, but they were still young enough to add to the family if they acted quickly. The thought of it made Chloe happy.

But her heart quickly sank.

'Do you think we would get so lucky again?' Chloe asked.

They'd not spoken about trying again due to the problems they'd had conceiving Emma. The fact was, the couple hadn't expected her to come along at all, given the news they had received from the doctors many years ago.

You can keep trying, but given the low sperm count, the odds are against it happening naturally.

Andrew's smile faltered. 'Well, if we both want it, we could consider other options.'

'And you would be okay with that?'

Chloe remembered all too well the issues Andrew had had back when they found out children were unlikely for them. How his mood had darkened and enthusiasm for just about everything had waned. He blamed himself, and his pride had been dented. It took a couple of years before he seemed himself again. But he was never comfortable with any *outside help*, as he put it. A sperm donor was not an option for him, and the cost of IVF was prohibitive. Then, years after that, the miracle happened.

But the chances of that happening again, and quickly, were stacked against them.

'I don't know,' Andrew replied. 'Maybe. Just been thinking a lot recently that if we don't do it now, it'll never happen. I know it might not anyway, but if we don't even talk about it, then any chance we *do* have will just pass us by. And... I don't know if we would regret that.'

'Okay,' Chloe said, still searching for the appropriate

words. The whole conversation had blindsided her. 'Well, we can talk about that.'

He walked over to her and placed a gentle kiss on her forehead.

'I'm going to try with this place,' he said to her. 'I know I complain a lot, but I will give it a proper shot. I promise.'

She looked up at him. 'Thank you.'

Both Chloe and then Andrew jumped as an electronic noise sounded from the table. She whipped her head around to see the baby monitor was active, and the noise they both heard coming from it sounded like a long, distorted exhalation.

'I thought I switched that off,' Chloe said, picking up the small, rectangular monitor. The image was the normal blue and black, and showed Emma's empty bed.

'Strange sound,' Andrew said. 'Interference or something?'

'Must have been,' Chloe agreed, still staring at the image. Nothing moved, so she eventually switched it off.

'Right, I'm going to get back to work,' Andrew said, and kissed her on the head again. 'I'll leave you with this little monster.'

'Thanks,' Chloe replied with a laugh. 'I'd be happy to swap with you, if you want?'

'Nah, I got this. Your job looks more stressful.'

Chloe looked to Emma again. Though her mouth was now clean, the meal of cut cucumber, strawberries, blueberries, a little cheese, and some ham had been half-devoured and half-smeared around the highchair's table, as well as up Emma's arms and across her bib.

'You got that right,' Chloe agreed as Andrew left the room. 'Come on, then, little monster, let's get you cleaned up.'

5

SARAH'S UNPACKING WAS COMPLETE, so she took a moment to lie down on the four-poster bed in her chosen room. The mattress was firm beneath her, which she liked, though she knew she was lying on a bed that was likely older than she was, and it had kicked up a small cloud of dust when she settled into it. God knows when the thing had last been used. The sheets and blankets would need replacing, at the very least.

The descending dust particles that fell onto Sarah didn't bother her, even though she knew there was likely dead skin mixed in with the particles. During her time in the army, she had been covered in far worse than just a smattering of dead skin.

She paused briefly and thought of Tania, then quickly shook it off. She didn't want to succumb to sadness, guilt, or nausea. Not now. Today was supposed to be positive.

Sarah was pleased with her choice of the room— number fourteen—figuring if things didn't work out with it she could easily enough switch to a different one. It wasn't like there was a shortage of spare rooms in the house.

And even though she had joked with Andrew about picking one well away from him due to his snoring, that was actually what happened, with her choosing one directly opposite and on the other side of the manor. If Sarah opened her door, she could see the other occupied rooms at the far end of the corridor.

And there wasn't much between the two rooms other than distance, either. Midway down the joining corridor was a window on one side that looked out over the rear court-yard, and opposite that was the stairway that led up to the floor above.

Sarah was initially going to pick either a front-facing or a rear-facing room, figuring the views would be better. However, she'd ultimately decided on one on the side of the house, picking one that had an en-suite and was one of the largest on offer.

She had seen a lot in the world, and taken in views that had stolen her breath, but living in luxury would be new to her. She wanted to try going all in to see how it fit.

One thing she hadn't chosen the room for, however, was the current decor, which would need to be changed as quickly as possible. That, however, was true of most rooms here.

The wallpaper, for one, was hideous. An overwhelming mix of patterned reds, yellows, and whites that was so jarring it made her feel dizzy. It might have been slightly more bearable if the timber floor had been left exposed, but instead it was covered with a rug that had a similar pattern to the wallpaper, only a deeper shade of red. The whole decor just felt rather oppressive.

But that would only give her the impetus and drive to get it refurbished to her liking in short order. And, in truth, it didn't need a whole lot: throw out the bedsheets and rug, strip off the wallpaper, a new lick of paint to the walls... and that was pretty much it.

One thing she did like, though, was the fireplace. It was very ornate, with an oak mantelpiece. Most rooms in the building seemed to have a fireplace set in them, which was evidence of how the house used to be heated before the black, cast-iron radiators had been fitted.

The other thing Sarah liked was the furniture that had been left. On the opposing side of the room to her bed was an oak display unit, which was the height of a wardrobe and had glass set into its doors. Inside, Sarah could see shelves that held ornaments and old pictures of people she didn't recognise. The pictures were creepy, to be sure, but the oak unit itself was very nice, with intricate carvings cut into the frame. In the glass, she could see her own faint reflection from her position on the bed.

There was also a small dressing table in the room, which seemed to have been crafted with as much care as the display unit, and a set of drawers and two large wardrobes. Sarah figured the furniture alone could have been worth quite a bit of money. Though, given the inheritance she had just received, plus what she had saved from being in the army, she was in the fortunate position of not having to worry too much about her finances. At least not yet. However, Sarah knew she couldn't just loaf around for the rest of her life.

The problem was, she didn't know what direction to take beyond this adventure at Perron Manor. But, she reasoned, at least she had time to figure all that out.

She took a deep breath and was about to heave herself from the bed, when three quick and hard knocks on the door startled her.

'Hello?' she said, snapping her head over to the door.

There was no response.

'Chloe? Andrew?' she called, but again got nothing back.

Sarah sighed, got to her feet, and walked over. However, when she opened the door an empty hallway was all that greeted her. She poked her head out farther, then looked left and right. Nothing.

'What the hell?'

She was baffled. The noise sounded like someone had rapped on the door, but there was clearly no one around to have done so.

'Weird.'

Sarah shook her head, knowing there were likely going to be lots of strange noises and quirks to get used to in a building as old as this one. Since her unpacking was done for the moment, it was time to rejoin the others and help out if needed. Or, preferably, indulge in a cup of coffee. She grabbed a packet of hazelnut beans from her bag and headed downstairs.

6

'CAN'T BELIEVE YOU DRINK THAT,' Chloe said, making a face. 'Even the smell is revolting.'

'You're such a weirdo,' Sarah shot back. She then took another sip of her drink. 'It's divine.'

Chloe felt like she might vomit. The thought of that flavour was awful enough. But Sarah seemed to be enjoying it, taking yet another gulp and smacking her lips in satisfaction.

Chloe was pleased to see that her sister seemed happy and healthy, and Sarah's most recent deployment had left her with a healthy tan. For the most part, the Pearson family —Chloe *definitely* included—were generally pretty pale in complexion, but Sarah didn't seem to suffer from the same affliction, and years on deployment in sunnier climates had only helped in that regard. It was something Chloe envied her sister for.

'You have odd taste, Sis,' Chloe told her.

She then saw Sarah look back over to her with a cocked eyebrow, before she gestured towards Andrew with a nod. 'You're one to talk,' Sarah said.

'Thanks,' Andrew added sarcastically. 'I always could count on you to raise my spirits.'

Chloe set the snacks she had prepared down on the kitchen table, which was one they had brought with them. Though the actual dining room and great hall both had existing tables, gathering in the kitchen had always been something of a tradition with Chloe and Andrew.

It had been a whirlwind of a day, but their work was now done. The removal men had finally left, and as much unpacking was finished as was going to be. Chloe didn't want to push things too quickly. There was still plenty of work ahead, but no reason not to pace things out sensibly.

The family were all seated around the table, with Emma in her highchair again, and they picked at the assortment of nuts, crisps, and dip that Chloe had laid out.

'Just something to keep us going,' she said. 'We should order take-out later. Put Emma down for the night then have a nice big feast to celebrate.'

'And wine,' Sarah added. 'I brought alcohol, so we can *really* celebrate.'

Chloe chuckled. 'One or two glasses couldn't hurt.'

'And I even brought whiskey for the unrefined neanderthal over there.'

Andrew grinned and raised his cup of tea in a gesture of thanks.

There were a few moments of silence between the three of them, and Chloe sensed the other two were reflecting in their own way. She could definitely see Sarah's mind ticking over about something.

'Okay,' Sarah began, 'I know we've talked about it before, but... you really have no idea why this Uncle Vincent left us the house? I mean, he never even met me, and hadn't seen you since you were, what, six?'

Chloe shrugged. 'No idea at all. The only thing I can think is that we are his only surviving relatives, so if he had no one close to him, who else would it have gone to?'

'I guess,' Sarah replied. 'Did you know much about him?'

Chloe shook her head. 'Nope. Like I said, I don't remember too much from back then. And Mum and Dad didn't really speak about him.'

'That's true,' Sarah said. 'All they said was that he was an odd man who liked to keep to himself. Did you ever speak to Mum and Dad about Perron Manor?'

'No. I tried to when I was in my teens and I found out what happened here in '82. Crazy to think it all happened while I lived here.'

Andrew cut in. 'How many people died that night?'

'I don't know exactly,' Chloe admitted.

'Wasn't that the night the house got its nickname?' Sarah asked. Then, as if as an afterthought, she said, 'Devil's House.'

Chloe nodded. 'It was. A newspaper ran a story about what happened and named it that. And it just stuck, apparently, even though it was a hotel at the time, not a house.'

Sarah let out a disbelieving laugh. 'I still can't get over the fact we live in a place called Devil's House. It's crazy.'

'Tell me about it,' Chloe agreed. 'Whenever I brought it up with Mum or Dad, they always evaded the subject as best they could. Said something terrible happened, but not to worry about it. Not my problem. Dad once told me that, 'Bad things happen, but sometimes it's best to leave things in the past.' And I never got much more out of them.'

'I remember him saying that,' Sarah chimed in. 'He told me the same when I started asking about it. Must have been his go-to response.'

'And your parents had no idea you two were in Vincent's will?' Andrew asked.

'It would appear not,' Chloe answered.

Andrew crossed his arms over his chest and leaned back in his chair. 'You know the locals are going to think we're weird as hell for living here, given what happened.'

'Let them think that,' Chloe replied with a shrug. 'Besides, no one really knows *what* exactly happened. Yes, a lot of guests died—'

Andrew cut her off. 'They didn't just 'die' from what I read, Chloe. It was almost like they were... butchered.'

'Fine, whatever. The owner back then was a crank, anyway, obsessed with the occult. The most likely theory is that it was some kind of ritualistic thing, and everyone who attended was in some kind of cult. It was horrible, of course, but sometimes shit like that happens.'

'It happened while you were there, Chloe,' Andrew went on. 'I don't mean to belabour the point, but are you sure you're okay living here knowing that?'

'How many times do I have to repeat myself?! Yes, I'm fine with it!' Chloe snapped, feeling exasperated by the turn the conversation had taken.

It was one she'd already had with Andrew, so it had been adequately covered in her mind. There shouldn't have been a need to go over it again.

But, apparently, that wasn't the case.

'Look, I don't remember a thing,' she went on. 'I was asleep the whole time, and Dad carried me out of the house. I didn't wake up until I was outside with him, Mum, and Vincent, I think. Then we left. I didn't see anything bad happen, and didn't find out about it all until years later, because they had kept it hidden from Sarah and me. It doesn't matter. Sure, I'd prefer it if this place didn't have baggage, but does that really affect anything? We've gotten a *huge* house for nothing. Something we could never have dreamed of affording has literally been dropped into our laps, along with a nice little chunk of money.' Chloe noticed Andrew's face turn into a scowl at the mention of the money, but she went on, 'It would be stupid to turn it all away.'

'I know,' Andrew said, crossing his arms over his chest.

'So why keep going over old ground? Nothing is going to change what happened or how I feel.'

'I...' Andrew paused, then sighed. 'Fine. I'm sorry.'

Silence resumed. Chloe knew it was awkward, especially with Sarah here, but she was starting to get frustrated with her husband, as he just wouldn't let anything go, even after agreeing to move here.

And yet, only a few hours ago, he'd promised he was going to make a go of it. Even spoke of having another child.

As if sensing the atmosphere in the air, Emma began to squirm in her seat and held her hands up to Chloe.

'Out,' she said.

Chloe lifted her daughter out of the highchair and set her down, letting Emma toddle around the floor.

'So... this is fun,' Sarah said, draining her coffee. 'If you two could try not being at each other's throats for the rest of the day, that would be great.'

Chloe looked at Andrew, waiting to see his response to this.

He looked back at her. 'I already said I'm sorry.'

'Fine,' Chloe eventually replied, knowing it wasn't really fine, and the issue was not settled. But it could wait.

'Worst make up ever, but okay,' Sarah added. 'So, which room was Uncle Vincent's anyway?'

'Room 6,' Chloe said. 'Same floor as ours, but towards the back, in one of the rear wings.'

'You been in there much?'

'Once. Poked my head in to have a look. It's small. Not sure why he settled on that one, especially if he lived here alone. But there you go.'

'Does he have much stuff to get rid of?'

'Not sure. Didn't look to be a lot, since the room was really basic, but I guess we'll have to clear out his wardrobes and the like. Why do you ask?'

'Just curious about the man that used to live here. I think we should go check out his room a little more.'

'Now?' Chloe asked, raising an eyebrow.

'Why not? You at least met him, but I don't even know what he looked like.' Sarah then got to her feet.

'Why don't we do it tomorrow?' Chloe asked.

'Because I want to make a start on my room tomorrow. And there will be loads to do. We don't have anything pressing right now.'

'I have an engineer coming out tomorrow as well,' Andrew added. 'He's going to look at that furnace downstairs. See if we can't get it working a bit better.'

'See,' Sarah said, gesturing toward him. 'Andrew has an engineer coming out. That could take all day... wait.' She turned to him. 'Tell me we still have heating. The furnace *does* still work, right? I mean, I imagine this place gets pretty cold at night.'

'Oh the heating works,' Andrew said. 'We tested it before you got here. It's just... well, I'll put it on later and let you hear for yourself.'

'Sounds ominous,' Sarah said, then turned back to Chloe. 'So, why not now? Not like we have anything else to do.'

'Fine,' Chloe said. 'I'll run Emma's bath while we're up there, then put her down for the night.'

'Awesome,' Sarah said, clapping her hands together. 'But, if we find any hidden gold or jewellery, I have dibs.'

Chloe laughed. 'You'll have to fight me for it.'

7

'THIS IS... FUNKY,' Sarah stated.

Vincent's room, just as Chloe had said, did not have much in it at all. There was a single metal-framed bed, with a thin, red quilt, a set of drawers sat opposite the bed, a window on the side wall, and a full-height black cupboard.

And that was it.

There weren't even any pictures on the walls. The dirty-white wallpaper was peeling, and the hardwood floor was stained and a little sticky underfoot.

'Told you there wasn't much here,' Chloe said. 'He seemed to keep it pretty basic.'

'And didn't bother cleaning,' Andrew added.

Given the size of many of the other bedrooms in Perron Manor, it was indeed odd that Vincent had chosen one of the smaller rooms to sleep in. With the three of them all inside, plus Emma in Chloe's arms, the space felt extremely cramped.

Sarah began looking through the drawers, working from the top down.

'Anything of interest?' Andrew asked.

'Just a few clothes. I was hoping he'd have a picture or something. I wanted to see what he looked like.'

'Doesn't this feel like snooping?' Chloe asked as Sarah moved over to the wardrobe. 'A bit disrespectful?'

'Of course not, we need to sort through all this stuff anyway, so we aren't seeing anything we wouldn't see eventually.'

Sarah then pulled open the doors on the black-painted wardrobe, and inside she saw a few hanging clothes: a frayed jacket, some shirts, and three pairs of trousers. Above the clothes was a high shelf, which contained a few small boxes. However, it was what was on the back of the wardrobe that drew Sarah's attention.

Scratches.

She slid the hanging clothes out of the way to get a better view, and Chloe and Andrew crowded round as well to look inside. 'Did an animal do that?' Chloe asked. Sarah wasn't certain, but doubted it.

Frantic claw marks had been cut into the back face of the wardrobe, mainly around the centre of the panel, though many pulled down closer to the ground. The natural, creamy colour of the timber showed through where the paint had been scraped away. While an animal could indeed have done that, Sarah was quick to spot something that made her think otherwise.

She didn't want to touch it, so instead pointed at the remnant of a fingernail stuck in one of the gouges.

'Oh that's disgusting,' Chloe said, backing up.

While in the army, Sarah had been shot in the arm, which had certainly hurt. A *lot*. However, potentially getting shot again, while unwelcome, never really unnerved her too much, nor did it get under her skin. But the thought of a nail being torn out, exposing the raw nerve endings beneath made her shudder.

'Creepy,' she said. 'What the hell got into him to claw at this like a dog?'

'No idea,' Andrew answered. 'Maybe he was mentally ill.'

'It doesn't matter,' Chloe added. 'We'll throw that wardrobe out. Chuck away everything in here. Decorate the room and make it nice. It'll be like... that,' she gestured to the markings, 'never happened.'

'Fine,' Sarah said, 'It's just strange, is all.'

'Well, like Andrew said, he could have been ill. We don't know what happened here, so let's just ignore it.'

Sarah caught Andrew's attention, and raised an eyebrow. Andrew, in return, rolled his eyes.

'We'll ignore it, then,' Sarah said, before looking up to the shelf above. The boxes on it were covered with dust, and she pulled out the first one she could reach—which was a box not much bigger than the palm of her hand. She opened it.

'It's a key,' Sarah said, retrieving the metal object and holding it up for the others to see. It was long, and made of black iron, with decorative spirals at the head.

Chloe looked at it, then shrugged. 'So what?'

'Well, if it's a key, then surely it...' She trailed off as something clicked, suddenly making sense to her.

She knew of a lock that could be a perfect match. With a grin, Sarah said, 'I think we have a way to see what's been locked away upstairs.'

8

'LET'S just check it out tomorrow,' Chloe said. 'I need to bathe Emma, and it's getting late.'

But Sarah shook her head. 'No way. I can't wait on this until tomorrow. It's too exciting!'

'How is it exciting?' Chloe asked. For her, the whole thing was annoying and an inconvenience—especially what they had found in Vincent's room. But to Sarah, it seemed like some kind of childish adventure.

'Oh lighten up, Sis,' she replied. 'Aren't you even the tiniest bit intrigued?'

Perhaps part of Chloe was, in truth, but mostly she was worried about what might be uncovered up there. She knew Andrew's hesitation with the house would only grow every time an unexpected issue was thrown up. They'd already had to deal with things like the furnace, the hideous decor, the poor mobile phone reception, and those scratches at the back of Vincent's wardrobe. All things Andrew could no doubt use as an excuse if he ultimately decided this place wasn't for him. Chloe didn't want anything else added to that list.

'I'm too busy to be intrigued,' Chloe eventually replied. 'I have Emma to take care of.'

It was just an excuse, of course. Emma could wait a few more minutes—it wasn't particularly late for the child—but she *really* didn't want to go up there.

'Then I'll go up on my own.'

'I'll go as well,' Andrew added.

Chloe sighed. The two of them going without her was an even worse prospect.

'Fine,' she said. 'But let's make it quick.'

They all made their way up to the top floor. Sarah first, then Chloe with Emma, and Andrew bringing up the rear. The area was decorated similarly to the floor below, and directly to their left after coming up the stairs was the first locked door, which barred entry to the corridor beyond. If they had turned right at the top, they could have followed the hallway round in a loop, and would eventually reach the other locked door to the sectioned-off area.

Chloe watched as Sarah slotted the key into the lock before her. It fit perfectly. Sarah beamed and turned the key and heard the faint clunk of sliding metal. With a turn of the handle, the door drifted open.

'Ta-da!' Sarah exclaimed.

The way ahead was dark, the only illumination coming from the artificial light that spilled in from the hallway they were currently in.

The now-opened door revealed another corridor beyond, or rather a continuation of the one they were in. Sarah tried a nearby switch, but it was clear that the light fixtures here were not working. And with no external windows, the way ahead would be tricky.

In response to the problem, Sarah quickly flicked on her phone's flashlight feature. The newly opened area was a lot more ominous than the other hallways of the house. Though decorated in a similar fashion, the wallpaper here peeled heavily, and a thick layer of dust lined the bare, untreated timber floor. There were cobwebs aplenty, and Chloe knew there would be scores of scuttling spiders running loose up here. She smirked. Arachnids had never bothered her, but she could already sense Andrew tensing up.

Yet again, Sarah led the way, and they moved into the dark hallway with the torch from her phone lighting their path. Up ahead, the corridor branched off both left and right. To the left, they could see the other locked door that would take them back out into the main area. There was also another door close to it that, if it repeated the layout of the floor below, would give access to a bathroom. To the right were two doors, both of which looked like bedroom doors, but neither had numbers on them.

'Shall we?' Sarah asked. Chloe rolled her eyes and hugged Emma a little tighter, as it was noticeably colder here than elsewhere in the house. Sarah didn't wait for an answer, and pushed open the nearest door, one that looked like it led to a bedroom. She cast her light around the room, allowing the beam to highlight the area.

'Are you fucking kidding me?!' Chloe asked through gritted teeth, momentarily forgetting her rule about not cursing in front of Emma.

'Oh my God!' Sarah exclaimed as well, but there was a hint of humour in her voice. She clearly found this more than a little funny. 'This is wild.'

Though it was difficult to take in the full details of the room, Chloe could still make out its purpose.

It was a study, of sorts. And a spacious one.

As Sarah's light moved steadily around the area, Chloe

saw that it was actually two rooms converted into one. She also realised, given their location on the right-hand side of the building, that they were directly above the bedroom Sarah had chosen.

While joining two rooms together and having a space used as a study was far from odd or noteworthy, it was the *contents* of the room that caused Chloe to bristle.

Firstly, there was the thing on the floor, which Sarah's light had illuminated first. A faint symbol, drawn in something white—possibly chalk—on the timber floorboards. That was the reason for Chloe's initial outburst.

An honest-to-God fucking pentagram.

Old candles stood at each of the symbol's five points, rising up from puddles of hardened wax. And smeared across the marking was a dark stain that had discoloured an area of the flooring.

But there was more to the room beyond the pentagram: display cabinets, bookshelves, chests, and desks all filled the space. Each was a dark oak, matching the panelling on the lower section of walls.

The bookshelves were packed with old-looking leather-bound tomes, and even glass jars filled with small animal bones. And the display cabinets had within them all kind of strange artefacts and parchments, and even some daggers. With the pentagram linking all of these items and artefacts together, it didn't take a genius to work out the occult theme that ran through the room.

Chloe heard the click of a light switch, and she turned to see Andrew trying the brass fitting on the wall next to the door. However, like those in the corridor outside, the lights in the room refused to work, with the bulbs obviously having long since given up.

Sarah began inspecting some of the books that filled a

shelf, and Chloe again felt the cold. Emma began to shift in her grip, and let out a discontented whine. The child then shook her head and snapped, 'No!'

Emma clearly didn't like it up here.

That makes two of us, kid.

'Can we go?' Chloe asked. 'It's cold in here and creepy as hell.'

'It's amazing,' Sarah argued, like she was a kid looking around a toyshop. She moved over to a prominently positioned, waist-high display cabinet with a glass top. Even from her position on the other side of the room, Chloe could make out a single book, set against a plush red and cushioned interior. The cracked leather of the book's cover looked extremely old—even ancient—and it bore a title that was etched in faded gold. However, the words made no sense to her.

Was that Latin?

There was no author name that Chloe could see, but in each corner of the cover were odd-looking markings.

'How old do you think this is?' Sarah asked in something approaching wonder.

Andrew walked over and gazed through the glass. 'God knows.'

Emma's frustration grew, and she began to cry.

'Right!' Chloe snapped, having seen enough. She then grabbed Andrew by the arm and pulled him towards the door. 'Enough of this. Emma needs her bath.' She turned to Sarah. 'You finished here? How about you come and spend some time with your niece.' Chloe's tone was firm and annoyed.

Sarah's eyes widened a little in surprise. 'Calm down, Chloe. I was just looking around, for God's sake. And don't try and guilt me with my niece. I swear, you're such a control freak.' Sarah then shook her head and stomped past Chloe, walking out into the corridor.

Chloe immediately felt bad, and knew that Sarah had a point.

But then, Chloe had a point too. It *was* cold and dusty up here, and not a good place for Emma to be in for too long.

Chloe locked the room up, and then did the same to the door in the corridor, closing off the whole area again. Then, they all proceeded downstairs without saying another word.

The little spat between Chloe and Sarah would need nipping in the bud. Given things between her and Andrew seemed to be a tad up and down at the minute, Chloe didn't want things to be frosty with her sister as well—especially not when it was supposed to be an exciting time for them all.

Chloe got the chance to put things right not even a half-hour later. Emma was splashing happily in the bath when Sarah came into the room. As she entered, Chloe flashed her a small, apologetic smile.

'Sorry,' she said.

Sarah just rolled her eyes. 'If this is gonna work, Sis,' she began, 'then you are going to have to loosen the reins a bit. You know that, right?' She then moved over to them, kneeling down next to Chloe to watch Emma in the bath, who was laughing as she dunked a plastic duck under the water.

'I know,' Chloe admitted. 'It's just, well, I really want things to work here. Andrew is on the fence about it, at best, and I don't think it'll take much to push him the wrong way. That room we found upstairs... well, let's just say that isn't going to help matters.'

'Really? I think it's cool as hell,' Sarah said. After a slight pause, she then went on to ask, 'So, what is it he doesn't like about the house? The history? Or that it's old?'

'A bit of both, maybe,' Chloe said. 'But I don't think either of those is the main issue.'

'Then what is?'

She paused, but then went on. 'It's that *he* didn't provide the house for us.'

Sarah cocked an eyebrow. 'What do you mean?'

Chloe just shook her head quickly. 'Nothing. I shouldn't have said anything. But, if we get this place just how we like it, he might come round. I know we could be really happy here.'

'Can I ask...' Sarah went on. 'What makes you so sure? I mean, don't get me wrong, it *is* an amazing place, but it's also kind of a novelty. Do you actually think it'll make a good family home?'

'Of course I do,' Chloe replied, turning to her sister. 'Why wouldn't it?'

'Oh, it *could*. But isn't it a little... big, for just us?'

'Not really. I think you get used to the space around you. It will be odd at first, but it'll soon become normal.'

'Fair enough,' Sarah replied. 'So what is the draw for you? Just that it's big and not the norm?'

'Not really. I think this place made an impression on me when I was little. I don't remember too much, but I do know that I was happy while I was here. It always felt so rich with history. Beyond the obvious, anyway. I think houses like this just have more charm and character.'

'Oh yeah,' Sarah said with a grin. 'I remember that old Victorian dollhouse you used to have. You loved it.'

'Exactly,' Chloe replied. 'I never thought I'd actually get to live in a place like that, and then one just fell into our laps. Plus, imagine all we could do with it!'

'How do you mean?'

'Well, Emma isn't going to need this much attention forever, so in the future we could... I dunno... turn it into a guest house or hotel or something. It would give me a project to focus on, I guess.'

'Running a hotel? Really? Given what happened here last time—'

'Don't,' Chloe said sternly.

Sarah laughed and held up her hands in defence. 'Fair enough. But running a hotel... really?'

Chloe shrugged. 'It could be nice. I mean, I love being a mother, I do, and I wouldn't swap it for anything. And I also don't regret leaving the corporate world behind. But sometimes, with Emma, it's sort of... all-encompassing, you know? It's like, this is your role and your life, you're a wife and a mother... and sometimes I feel like that other part of myself, the one with the ambition, kind of gets drowned out. I suppose that's why I'm so eager to get started fixing up this place. It gives me something else to focus on except being a mum.'

'I get that,' Sarah said after a brief moment of thought.

'Really?' Chloe asked, then looked at Sarah a little sheepishly. 'It doesn't sound like I'm being a little selfish?'

'Fuck no! It doesn't make you a bad mother just because you want to focus on yourself from time to time.'

Chloe smiled, feeling a little relieved. 'Thanks.'

Logically, she knew there wasn't anything to feel guilty about in the first place, but that didn't stop her feeling that way sometimes, or questioning herself endlessly.

'So... I take it there are no plans to give this little one a sibling?' Sarah asked as she looked down at Emma, who continued to splash the duck around in the water. 'Cos that could derail your plan of a guest house pretty quickly. I mean, I know you two struggled with Emma, but you never know... wait, why are you smiling?' Sarah frowned in confusion.

Chloe chuckled. 'It's just... Andrew actually mentioned that earlier today.'

'Really?'

'Yeah.'

'Bloody hell. So, are you guys gonna try?'

Chloe shrugged. 'Not sure, we didn't go into much detail.'

'Well, that would *definitely* put the whole hotel thing on ice.'

'It would,' Chloe agreed. 'But who knows what's gonna happen. Nothing is decided or anything. Plus, you know, even if we wanted to, it might not happen. But that's all for the future, I guess. All right, time to get this little one dried, fed, then put to bed.'

'And then we get drunk!' Sarah announced, holding her arms up in celebration. Emma looked up at the sudden movement and giggled.

'*You* can get as drunk as you want,' Chloe said. 'I'll just have a couple of glasses of wine.'

Sarah stood to her feet. 'Aw come on, Sis, cut loose. You only live once.'

'Maybe three glasses, then.'

'Wow,' Sarah said, completely deadpan. 'Wild.'

Chloe gave her sister a playful bat on the leg, then lifted Emma out the bath, quickly carrying her over to the change-table and laying her on the already placed towel. She wrapped the infant up in a bundle to keep her warm, then began drying her off. Once Emma was changed, Sarah left the room, and Chloe carried Emma to the child's bedroom. As Chloe entered, a sudden surge of cold ran through her, and she made a mental note to check the furnace in the basement. It was an old heating system, but the only one they had. Why Vincent had never had it replaced was beyond her.

However, almost as soon as she had felt the chill, and after taking a few more steps inside, Chloe's body temperature quickly normalised. Which, she guessed, was one of the problems with living in an old house: lots of air leakage and cold spots.

Chloe then walked over to the rocking chair they had set up in the corner of the room closest to the window, took a seat, and began to feed Emma. The child's eyes grew drowsy as she suckled. And it was just as the little girl slowed her feeding, and was about to fall asleep, that a sudden and awful odour assaulted Chloe's senses. Something... rotten. Once again, a cold draft drifted down onto the back of her neck, causing the hairs there to stand on end.

Chloe quickly stood up, holding Emma carefully, and turned to look over her shoulder, but could see no reason for the draft. The seat was close to the window, but not so close as to allow a breeze that strong to reach her, unless it had been open. And besides, the closed curtains weren't moving or blowing either, indicating no draft was coming through. Also, the feeling of cold had seemed to emanate directly behind the chair she had sat in, right in the room's corner.

She felt Emma's little body slacken in her grip, and Chloe looked down to see her daughter start to gently snore. Chloe then lifted her head back up and realised that smell had disappeared, as had the feeling of cold.

Suppose I gotta get used to that, she told herself. The scope of the work ahead started to seem a little daunting.

Chloe then set Emma down in her cot-bed, checked the

baby camera was still in position on top of the wardrobe, and then picked up the accompanying portable monitor. She whispered good night to her daughter, then left the room, turning off the light as she did.

Sarah's previous idea of getting drunk was starting to sound a bit more appealing.

9

AFTER CLEARING AWAY the last of the plates and throwing out the rubbish, Sarah poured herself a hearty measure of wine.

The meal, while not mind-blowing, had certainly been good. Enough to fill the emptiness in their stomachs, at any rate. Once they had decided on Indian food, the actual ordering process had been a chore, given the lack of consistent phone signal in the house. Sarah was forced to go outside to order.

But, it had all worked out in the end.

Sarah, Chloe, and Andrew all sat around the kitchen table, enjoying a well-earned drink, with Sarah and Chloe on the red wine and Andrew indulging in a glass of the whiskey Sarah had bought him.

After taking her first sip, Sarah was pleased to discover the brand she had chosen was delicious, with a smooth taste, long finish, and slightly peppery undertones. She was far from a wine connoisseur, but had drunk enough in her time to know the good from the bad.

And this one was definitely good. Chloe appeared to

agree as well, letting out a long moan of satisfaction after her first mouthful.

'So, you all set with your room, Sarah?' Chloe asked. 'I mean, as much as you can be?'

'Yeah, I guess,' Sarah replied. 'I swapped out the sheets with some I brought with me. But, other than that, and packing away some clothes, there isn't much more I can do just yet. Are you guys all set?'

Chloe nodded. 'Enough for tonight, anyway. But plenty to get through tomorrow.'

'Let tomorrow wait,' Sarah said. 'Tonight, we drink!' She didn't want the fun to be derailed by any worries of the future. And, on that note, she raised her glass. 'A toast, to Perron Manor—our new home. It may be weird as hell, but shit... what an opportunity.'

Chloe raised her glass as well, and was reluctantly followed by Andrew. 'Here, here,' Chloe said. She then twisted the baby-monitor around to glance at Emma.

'She okay?' Sarah asked.

'Fine. Sleeping like a... well, you know.'

Andrew took a sip of his amber-coloured drink, then looked up to Sarah. 'So, you've left the army for good now?'

Sarah nodded. 'Yup. All done. No more tours.'

'Aren't you going to miss it?' he asked. Sarah knew he wasn't prying, or being insensitive as to what happened. He was genuinely curious.

'Oh yeah, of course I'll miss it,' Sarah told him. 'But it was the right time.'

'We were really sorry to hear about Tania,' Chloe added.

It was a nice sentiment, and it came from the right place, especially since Chloe and Andrew hadn't seen her since it all happened. However, Sarah still felt her body tense up at the mention of her best friend. Thinking about what happened in Afghanistan wasn't what Sarah needed at the moment. She just wanted to forget.

'Thanks,' Sarah eventually said, more dismissively than she had intended. 'But I'm okay.'

Chloe gave a sad smile and nodded before changing the subject completely.

'So, what time is that engineer coming tomorrow to look at the furnace?'

'Sometime in the morning,' Andrew replied. 'Don't have an exact time. Hopefully he can at least figure out what's wrong with it. I'll see if he can quote for a completely new system as well, strip that old thing out.'

'What was the deal with the furnace, anyway?' Sarah asked, recalling the earlier conversation about it.

Andrew laughed. 'It screams when you start it up.'

Sarah paused. 'It fucking *what*?' She looked to Chloe, fully expecting it to be a joke, but Chloe gave an embarrassed nod.

'Well,' she added, 'it doesn't *actually* scream, but when you light it up and the steam starts running up through the pipes, it does sound a little like it.'

'A screaming furnace? For real?'

Andrew nodded and got to his feet. 'I need to go down and have a look at it now, actually, since it's starting to get cold in here. The bloody thing might have gone out again. Come with me, if you want. I'll show you.'

'You don't have to—' Chloe began.

'Fuck yeah,' Sarah said, cutting her off and quickly standing up. 'This I gotta see.'

'Why doesn't that surprise me?' Chloe asked. 'Well, I've seen it, so I'll let you two run along. I'm warning you though, Sarah, if you don't hurry back, I'm finishing this wine on my own.'

Sarah laughed. 'Fair enough. We'll be back before you know it.'

10

'JESUS, THIS PLACE IS CREEPY,' Sarah said, looking around.

The basement was partially illuminated by dirty-yellow lighting from fittings in the ceiling above, but there were deep pockets of shadows where the light could not reach.

They'd had to use light from their phones to guide themselves down, as the light switch was, frustratingly, at the bottom of the steps.

The floor around them consisted of old and uneven stone slabs, and the walls were bare stonework with some areas of water leakage. Sarah guessed the size of the basement was probably half the area of the storey above.

To her right, Sarah could see internal stone walls which formed a line of small rooms, each no bigger than a tiny bedroom. While there were no doors, Sarah knew what they were. Or, rather, what they used to be.

The cells.

The other main feature down in the basement was set against the far wall: a large, industrial-looking furnace. It was made from strong black iron, and was far larger than she had expected it to be.

'Bloody hell,' she said. 'We could both fit inside that thing.'

'Not what you were expecting?'

She shook her head. 'I'll say. It's huge. Though I guess that makes sense, considering the size of the house.'

The furnace stood taller than both Sarah and Andrew, and was split vertically into two sections. The top was a little wider, and the bottom had three hatches to the front, with two adjacent to one another and the third centrally below them. It gave the impression of a rudimentary face, with eyes and a mouth. Given their size, any of these hatches could be used to gain access if someone so wished. And each hatch had a door to it that would conceal the heat inside when closed. The furnace was also longer than it was wide, with thick, ribbed fins that ran along its side.

Thick and circular metal ducting—made from the same rusted-black metal as the furnace itself—ran off the large unit, snaking up the wall behind it before disappearing through the floor above. In addition, there were piles of black coal mounded close to the huge appliance, as well as a few smaller piles of chopped wood. Sarah could also see that some of the old cells were piled up with coal as well, leaving pools of fine black dust on the ground around them.

'Not the most efficient system, is it?' she asked, pointing to the coal. 'Bit of a bitch having to load it up just to get the house warm.'

'Tell me about it,' Andrew agreed. 'Not like it was back home, where we just flipped a switch.'

Sarah sensed the frustration in his voice, and remembered the conversation she'd had with Chloe up in the bathroom earlier. Though it wasn't her place to get involved, she did feel a duty to help out her sister.

'I know it isn't easy,' Sarah began, 'but this is all fixable. The furnace can easily be replaced.'

'Yeah, but at what cost? This house is huge, so any new heating system is going to cost an arm and a leg.'

'But we have the inheritance,' she said. 'I'm sure we can easily cover the cost of it.'

Sarah saw him tense up at the suggestion, and he didn't respond. Instead, he opened one of the three hatches in the front of the furnace, peeked inside, then grabbed a nearby shovel that lay on the ground. He scooped up a mound of coal and thrust it through the opening.

'It's definitely stopped working again,' he muttered. 'Fucking thing. I'll have to start her up.'

The level of rust on the once-black metal gave an indication of just how infrequently the furnace had been cleaned during its lifetime.

Andrew continued to shovel coal inside. He was depositing it in the lower, central hatch, which made it look like he was feeding some kind of giant, metallic infant. Andrew stopped after only six loads.

'Will that be enough?' Sarah asked.

'It will for now,' he replied. 'I'm just topping it off.'

'So... how does it work?'

'Basically, the coal burns, and that heats up the top unit,' he pointed to the higher, wider section now. 'That one is full of water. The water turns to steam, and the steam is then fed through the house via these pipes to the various radiators.'

Sarah watched him turn some of the valve handles on the side of the main unit, as well as a circular wheel on the main ducting that protruded from the top of the furnace. The wheel was quite high up, and he had to climb to reach it. Lastly, Andrew threw a piece of chopped wood inside before grabbing a strip of old, dry cloth, from the pile on a stool close to the furnace. There was a box of matches with the cloth, and Andrew lit one, using it to ignite the end of the rags he held. Sarah could smell the burning material, and Andrew then carefully held the flaming cloth in through the opening for a while until some of the wood and coal inside began to take.

'Should work,' he said, dropping the material inside and closing the door. 'But we won't know for a little while.'

The furnace was truly a fascinating piece of equipment, one that gave a brief glimpse into a prior way of life. Sarah could certainly understand Chloe's obsession with things like that. However, having to go through all that work just to get the heating going was certainly going to be a chore.

'And that's all there is to it?' Sarah asked, trying to make her sarcasm obvious. Andrew laughed. They then stood in silence for a little while, just waiting.

Eventually, Sarah heard the crackle of flames getting stronger inside the iron unit, and the temperature gauges started to slowly rise.

'Getting there,' Andrew said.

'Do we have to wait around for it?' Sarah asked.

Andrew shrugged. 'Probably not, but I just like to make sure the water is at least boiling. I've read that these things can go out pretty easily if you don't watch them carefully.'

'Fair enough,' Sarah replied. She felt the wine upstairs calling her, but it didn't feel right just leaving Andrew alone down here on his own. As the crackling inside continued, Sarah soon detected another sound, one that was faint and almost intertwined with the sounds of burning coal.

It almost sounded like... a moan. However, it quickly faded, and Sarah thought herself stupid—only to then hear it again.

'Is that just my ears playing tricks?' Sarah asked. 'Or can you hear something inside of there?'

Andrew looked puzzled. 'All I hear is the burning. But that isn't what's special. Just wait until the water starts steaming, and then you'll see.'

It didn't happen straight away, and Sarah continued to pick up what she thought was intermittent groaning within the metal furnace. Then, when the temperature and pressure gauges were higher, she could tell the liquid in the top section had started to boil. It quickly turned to gas and was then pushed through the ductwork.

It was at that point a sudden and horrible sound caused Sarah to jump.

Andrew began to laugh. 'Catches you off guard, right?'

'You're fucking right it does,' she replied, still reeling. *It does sound like a fucking scream!*

'It's just the steam forcing its way through the pipes,' he said. 'There is air inside that is pushing its way along. Some of it is no doubt getting out through a crack or some gaps in the pipework. That's all it is, like the sound old kettles used to make. But it's pretty freaky.'

In all honesty, Sarah didn't need the explanation; her mind had quickly formed a similar conclusion itself. But she had to admit that just as Chloe and Andrew had told her earlier, the sound did indeed initially resemble a sharp and sudden scream.

'That is freaky,' Sarah agreed after the noise had completely dissipated.

'Not a bad feature, is it? A screaming furnace. Think we could get people to pay to listen to it?'

Sarah laughed. 'Probably. Ghost hunters and the like would have a field day with it. With the house in general, I suppose.'

'You might be right. Anyway, things *should* start to warm up now, but we'll need to see how it goes. I want to make sure it doesn't kick out too much heat during the night.'

Sarah nodded.

She wanted to go back to her point about having enough money for a replacement, and tell him this was all just a temporary issue. That they were family, all in it together, and that the problem would quickly get resolved.

But she also remembered Chloe's words about why Andrew hadn't been overly enamoured with the house in the first place.

Because he didn't provide it.

That wasn't an issue she wanted to deal with right now. It was for Chloe and Andrew to work out between them.

'Come on,' Sarah said. 'It's dark and depressing down here, and there is alcohol waiting for us upstairs. Let's go.'

Andrew gave her a thumbs up, then followed her back upstairs.

11

THE THREE OF them spent the rest of the night drinking and talking, and the mood was a positive one.

Earlier, Sarah had briefly raised the topic of the weird study on the top floor, but Chloe had made it clear that wasn't something she wanted to discuss at the minute. That was fine for Sarah, who was happy to move onto a different topic, but she knew it could not be ignored indefinitely.

And Sarah certainly had questions.

For one, whose study was it? Obviously it would have belonged to Vincent, the whole house had, but was he the one responsible for the weird collection? Or had he just been the most recent custodian? Could it have maybe been the man who owned Perron Manor when the events in 1982 occurred? Sarah remembered his name from an article she'd read online: Marcus Blackwater.

At eleven-thirty, Chloe suggested they call it a night. Sarah could have easily continued, but Andrew agreed with his wife and Sarah did not want to keep on drinking alone. So, they all went up to the middle floor together, said their goodnights, and entered their respective rooms.

Given it had been a long day of driving and carrying boxes around, Sarah felt a little grimy, so she decided to wash before she got into bed.

The room's en-suite housed a deep metal bath, which stood on four legs, all of which were shaped like lion paws. There was no shower—which was a shame, given it would have been quicker—so instead Sarah started to draw a bath. She figured her room was far enough away from the others for the noise not to disturb them.

Thankfully, the heating in the room still seemed to be working, and the water ran hot. Once Sarah had the bath full enough, she undressed, leaving her clothes in a pile on the floor. She then dipped a toe down through the surface of the water. It was hot.

Not quite scalding, but just right for her. Her skin would no doubt be bright red when she got out, but that didn't bother her in the slightest. Sarah then stepped fully inside and carefully let herself slide down, submerging herself up to her shoulders and leaning her head back into the curved rim of the bath.

The room around her swirled with a layer of building steam, which was exacerbated by the lack of a window. There didn't seem to be an extractor fan either—something else that would need to be rectified when Sarah eventually got a shower fitted in the room.

The en-suite wasn't huge, but it was certainly big enough, and housed the bath, a vanity unit with washbasin, and a toilet. The walls were clad with simple white tiles, and the floor was similarly tiled as well, though with a light grey finish. Nothing fancy, but the decor worked. There was a large mirror above the vanity unit as well, that had completely misted up.

The aches of the day began to melt away, seeping out

from her bones and into the hot water around her. A welcome feeling of relaxation started to consume Sarah. She was well aware she'd consumed a reasonable amount of alcohol, so didn't want to relax too much and fall asleep. Even now, after only a few minutes of stewing in the water, Sarah felt her eyes grow heavy. She let them close for a moment, enjoying the warmth around her. But it was getting late, and she knew she should make this quick, especially given there would be another full and hectic day tomorrow. Her bed was calling her.

She opened her eyes and poured some shower gel into her hands from the bottle she'd set on the bath's edge. Casting a look to her side and towards the vanity unit, she paused, seeing an unclear dark mass in the mirror's glass surface. It appeared to show something on the opposite side of the bath, but after turning her head Sarah saw nothing behind her at all. She again looked back to the mirror. Whatever the figure-shaped mass had been, it was no longer there. Sarah frowned, unsure if she'd even seen anything in the first place.

She then proceeded to wash, finishing off with her hair. After completely submerging to rinse off the suds, Sarah felt a sudden cold between her legs and gasped and pulled in a mouthful of water. She quickly sat up, coughing and spluttering, heaving out the warm water she had swallowed. Panic seized her, and she frantically looked around.

But there was nothing that could explain the sudden sensation of intense cold beneath the surface of the water that had settled over Sarah's crotch. It had felt like someone with ice-cold hands had roughly grabbed her groin.

Despite the warmth of both the water and the room, goosebumps formed on Sarah's arms. After she got her coughing under control, and wiped the water from her eyes, she looked around the bathroom. Whatever had caused the sensation, it clearly hadn't come from anyone's hand, given she was still alone.

Sarah sat in the water for a little while longer, letting herself calm down and forcing her breathing into a slow and steady rhythm. She would not let irrational fear get the better of her.

During her career, she had been in situations that were truly terrifying—and life threatening—and she'd come through them by forcing her mind to focus and push the fear away.

This was nothing. *Literally* nothing. Just her getting spooked by something that was likely very explainable— even if she couldn't actually explain it at the moment. And yet, she still felt anxious.

Get a grip, you fucking idiot.

She stood up and grabbed her towel, then wrapped it around her shoulders. Sarah used her toes to fish around under the water, snagging the chain between them, and released the plug. She then stepped onto the bathmat and began to dry herself off. After brushing her teeth and using the toilet, Sarah gave the bathroom another glance over— seeing nothing out of the ordinary—before flicking off the light and closing the door. She was finally feeling a little more relaxed, and it wasn't long before she fell asleep.

That night, however, she slept fitfully, and her dreams continued to replay her final moments with Tania.

The wrong step. The explosion. Sarah thrown to the ground from the blast. And then feeling the hot mush that was once her best friend coat her.

Something was different, however. Through it all, Sarah could hear an odd whispering. It wasn't in a language she recognised, but she still somehow understood the intent.

The whispering got louder and louder and louder, and then the dream changed. She was falling... no, being dragged down into the ground...

When Sarah snapped her eyes open, there was only darkness around her. It took a few seconds for her mind to pull itself from the horrible dream—being pulled through a hole in the earth, into an existence of agony. All the while, horrible, taunting whispers echoed around her. And for a moment after waking, that insidious whispering was still present.

Soon, however, everything grew quiet, and Sarah started to fully wake up, even if she was still tired. She reached for her mobile phone, and the screen showed it was only three-thirty.

After rolling back over, Sarah stared through the dark at the ceiling above her, remembering her vivid dream. Remembering Tania.

Sarah had been supposed to take point that day. But she didn't. And Tania had died because of it.

Sarah cried, and didn't sleep any more that night.

12

OLIVER TRIPP WAS a local heating engineer Andrew had found online, one who had mostly positive reviews. He arrived mid-morning, and Andrew greeted him at the door. The man was well into his fifties, heavily balding, and had a thick, grey moustache under a pronounced nose. He was also rake-thin, and had fingers that had yellowed and stained, no doubt caused by years of smoking. Dressed in navy blue trousers, and a matching polo-shirt that had his company name embedded in gold across the upper-left side, he looked professional enough as well. Andrew immediately liked Oliver, as he seemed amenable and friendly.

However, after showing the man the furnace, Andrew could tell that fixing it was beyond Oliver's skill.

Andrew had switched it off early that morning, so that he could show Oliver exactly what they were dealing with. As expected, the noises that came from the furnace had startled him. Regardless, Oliver had taken a good look around, but did so with constant shakes of his head and a confused rubbing of his chin. Finally, they moved back upstairs to the kitchen.

'I've never heard anything like it before,' the engineer said as he took a drink of his coffee, which Sarah had made for him. Oliver, Andrew, and Sarah were all gathered around the kitchen table, while Chloe had left them to go up and get Emma, who had just woken from her nap.

'Takes you by surprise, doesn't it,' Sarah stated.

Oliver nodded. 'Just about shit myself,' he said, causing Sarah to chuckle.

'So, can you do anything with it?' Andrew asked Oliver. 'Even if it's just to check and see if everything's running okay?'

The engineer rubbed his chin again and shook his head. 'Sorry to say, but the system isn't something I'm familiar with. It's just too old, and I wouldn't really know what to look out for. Not much I can do beyond what I already have in checking the seals and everything. Wasn't anything too in-depth, to be honest.'

'Fair enough,' Andrew replied just as Chloe reentered the room with Emma in her arms. The child looked around, spotted Oliver, then pointed.

'Man!' she exclaimed.

'Yes,' Chloe responded to her. 'It *is* a man.' She then looked apologetically over to Oliver. 'Sorry, she keeps doing that.'

Oliver just laughed. 'Don't apologise, she's just curious. Isn't that right, little one?' He then gave her a playful wave, but Emma just turned away and began to play with the small plastic car she had with her.

Andrew wanted to turn things back to business. 'Hopefully what you've done will help for the time being,' he said. 'What if we were to look at replacing the whole thing, and putting in a more modern system? Is that something you can do?'

Oliver's eyebrows raised excitedly. 'Sure is,' he said. 'I'd need to pull in some help, given the size of the house. Also, I suppose you know it wouldn't just be a standard boiler that you'd need. House this big would need a commercial-sized system. But I could get it designed for you and install the whole thing. Only trouble is,' Oliver's enthused expression dampened a little, 'it would cost a pretty penny. I don't say that to dissuade you, and I'd keep my price as keen as I could, but I want you to be aware of that upfront.'

'No, I understand that,' Andrew replied. 'But it certainly needs doing. It's just no good having to fire the old thing up and wait an age just to get warm.'

Oliver nodded, his smile returning. 'Then yeah, I'd love to price it up for you. I'll need to pop back at some point to get a full measure of the house, if that's okay? Don't really have time to fit it in today. That way I can get a designer I know to come up with a full system, and get a cost back over to you.'

'And how long would that take?'

Oliver rubbed his chin yet again as he pondered the question. 'I could get back out in a few days to measure up. Say a couple of weeks or so to get the design done, then I'd need to cost it. Given a job of this size, and the labour I'd need to pull in, I'd make it a priority, but it would probably be a month or two after we agree on price before I could start. Would that work?'

Andrew looked to Chloe and Sarah, who in turn cast each other a glance before turning back to him and nodding.

'Okay,' Andrew said. 'Get the price over and I will consider it. We can go from there.'

'Sounds good!' Oliver said. He then took a look around

the kitchen, drinking it all in. 'You know, I never thought I'd be working up here at Devil's House.'

Andrew had to fight to stop from cringing at the man's words. 'You know about this place?'

'Of course, everyone in town does. My uncle actually came up here once. He was a plumber. Saw something that spooked him pretty badly, I heard. Never said much about it to me, but my cousin said he was really freaked out.'

'Really?' Andrew asked. 'Well, I'm not sure what he saw, but I can assure you there is nothing here that—'

'Oh, don't worry,' Oliver cut in. 'I don't put much stock in stuff like that. All a bunch of nonsense.'

Andrew smiled. 'Glad you think so. Wouldn't want you getting spooked about working up here.'

'Don't worry about that,' Oliver said before he downed the last of his coffee. The man then got to his feet. 'This would be a hell of a job for me: putting a full new system in a place as big and famous as this house. It'd be a hell of a thing for my business.'

Andrew shook his hand. 'Sounds good. Get the price over, first and foremost. And hopefully we can get things moving.'

'Will do,' Oliver said. He then turned to Sarah and pointed to his now-empty mug. 'Hazelnut roast, you say?'

Sarah nodded, smiling. 'That's right. Did you enjoy it?'

'Loved it!' he replied. 'I'll have to get me some of that.'

Andrew saw Sarah turn to Chloe and stick out her tongue. He then stood up and ushered Oliver towards the exit. The engineer waved to both Chloe and Sarah as he left.

Just as Oliver stepped over the threshold at the main door, he turned back to Andrew.

'I'm assuming you will be seeking alternative quotes as well?'

Andrew nodded. 'Probably,' he admitted. 'No offence, but I'd be silly not to.'

Oliver shook his head and held up his hands. 'No need to apologise, I totally understand and would do the same in your situation. But, can I ask: if you get something comes in cheaper, can you let me know and give me the opportunity to shave a bit more off? It's not like my price would be high, or anything, but I'd certainly look again at areas I could save, if it meant getting the job.'

Andrew didn't answer straight away, as he wasn't sure how comfortable he was with that. In his head, the price should just be the price—no second bite of the cherry if you missed out the first time. 'I'll consider it,' he eventually said, then held out his hand.

Oliver looked down for a moment, clearly expecting a different answer. However, he still shook. 'Thank you,' Oliver said. 'I'll be in touch soon about coming back out to measure up.'

After he'd gone, Andrew walked back to the others in the kitchen and sat down. 'What do you think?' he asked Chloe and Sarah.

'He seemed nice,' Sarah said.

'Think the job may be too big for him, though,' Andrew added.

'Suppose we won't know that until he starts and it all goes wrong,' Chloe added. 'But he seemed to know his stuff. Although... would he be okay stripping out what's here if he isn't familiar with it, do you think?'

'I think so,' Andrew replied. 'Ripping stuff out is a lot easier than maintaining it. I just don't know if we would be better suited getting a larger company in. A commercial one. But that would cost us a lot more.'

'I think we'd have enough to cover it,' Sarah offered, and

Andrew felt himself bristle. Just because they had money now didn't mean they had to waste it. Besides, that money wasn't earned, anyway. But he tried to keep his annoyance in check.

'No reason to let costs spiral, though,' was all he said.

'So let's get some other prices in, then,' Chloe said. 'That way, we'll know where we stand. Can't hurt to look around a little.'

Andrew nodded. 'I agree.' He then looked to Sarah for her confirmation as well. It was every bit as much her house as it was Chloe's, so she had a say.

Even more so than Andrew did, in truth.

'Yeah, I'm okay with all that,' she agreed.

'I'll arrange for us to get some other quotes,' Andrew said. 'Hopefully, I can get them here before I go away.'

Sarah frowned. 'You having a holiday without us or something?'

'Nothing so fancy,' Andrew replied. 'I need to get back to work, I've taken enough days as it is. I have to head down to London to meet with a client, so I'll be out and about for a few days.'

'The Big Smoke? Nice,' Sarah replied. 'But have you even set up an office yet?'

Andrew shook his head. 'No, that's next on my list. I also need to get the bloody internet sorted out, though I don't think that'll be done before I leave.'

'I can't believe Vincent didn't even have any kind of connection here,' Chloe chimed in. 'Imagine not being connected all those years.'

'Sounds like that's the way he wanted it,' Sarah offered. 'Besides, we've lived without the internet before, when we were kids, and it didn't do us any harm.'

'I guess,' Chloe replied. 'Still feels like we are cut off a little bit.'

The sound of the doorbell ringing brought the conversation to a close.

Sarah stood. 'I'll get it.'

13

Upon opening the front door, Sarah was met with a smiling man whose grey eyes—which widened upon seeing her—sat behind black-framed glasses.

'H-hello,' he said, his tone uneven and slightly nervous. He then thrust his hand out to be shook, but moved so quickly as to make Sarah flinch. 'Sorry,' the stranger quickly said. 'My name is David, David Ritter.'

There was an awkward pause, and Sarah waited for him to give a little more information. None was forthcoming.

'Okay, David Ritter,' she said. 'Is there something you need?'

He pursed his lips and looked to the ground. 'Well, what I am going to say may come off as a little... strange.'

Sarah wasn't surprised to hear that, as he seemed a little bit strange himself. However, she wasn't unnerved by him in the slightest. More amused at his uncertain demeanour.

The man before her had brushed-back grey hair that framed a square face. However, though his hair was grey, he only looked a similar age to Sarah herself. He wore a black jacket over a dark shirt, as well as blue jeans, old scruffy trainers, and a backpack slung over one shoulder. He had a certain nerdish quality to him, and if Sarah were to guess at his job, she'd have gone with some kind of role in I.T.

'Go on,' she said, somewhat intrigued.

'Well, I live in the area... and I'm a paranormal investigator.'

'No fucking way!' Sarah blurted out, unable to help herself. Then, she quickly brought a hand up to her mouth. 'Sorry,' she said. 'I just... really didn't expect that.'

He gave a nervous laugh as his cheeks flushed red. 'Not the sort of thing you tend to hear when a stranger knocks on your door, I guess.'

'No, it isn't. Certainly not something to open with, anyway.'

He gave an embarrassed nod. 'Fair enough, I suppose. But it was relevant.'

Sarah smiled politely, but crossed her arms over her chest. 'Okay, David Ritter, paranormal investigator, I'm gonna have to ask you to start from the beginning here.'

'Understood. It's about the house you now own. See, it is a place I know a lot about.' David reached into his backpack and pulled out a pristine-looking paperback book, then handed it over to her. She looked down at the cover and the title: *Inside: Perron Manor*. And the tagline read: *Investigating Britain's Most Haunted House*. Sarah's eyes widened. *He* was the author.

'Wow... you wrote a book about my house?'

He nodded enthusiastically. 'I did. A few years ago now. You can keep it if you want.'

'Thanks,' Sarah said, trying—and failing—to find a tone to match his enthusiasm. She imagined that he likely had boxes and boxes full of unsold copies of this book at his home.

'It's well researched, and goes into a bit of detail about the history of the place. I like to think I uncovered quite a lot.'

'Okay. So are you here to tell me my house is haunted, David?' Sarah gave a playful smile.

'Erm... kind of,' he replied.

Sarah laughed. 'Is that so? Well, sorry to burst your bubble, David, but I really don't think it is. I haven't seen any ghosts or heard any clanking chains in the night.'

'Well, it doesn't really work like that. It's more—'

'David,' Sarah cut in, rather sternly, but she still couldn't hide her amused smile. The exchange was odd enough to almost be endearing, but she still had no clue what the hell this strange man wanted. 'Can we get to the point of the matter, please?'

'Yes, of course. See, if you read that,' he pointed to the book in Sarah's hands, 'you will see it also details an investigation I carried out here with my team in 2013. The results blew us away. I mean, the things we saw... it was phenomenal.'

'Is that so?'

'It is. Honestly, please read the book. It's all true. And it will amaze you, I'm sure.'

'So... what? Is this a warning about my new house, then?'

'Excuse me?'

'Have you come here to warn me the house is haunted?'

'Well... kind of. But, you see, after my initial investigation, the prior owner never let us back. I don't know why, but he just cut us off.'

'Wait... you mean Vincent Bell?'

'That's right,' David said.

'You knew him?' Sarah asked, suddenly interested in what the man had to say.

'Not quite. I met him, of course, and we spoke a few times when he let me and my team stay here for a weekend.'

'What was he like?'

'Mr. Bell?' David paused for a little while. 'Cranky,' was his response. 'Sorry,' he added quickly. 'I don't mean to speak ill of your deceased uncle, it's just—'

'How did you know he was my uncle?'

David shrugged. 'It's public record who inherited the house, if you know where to look. That's how I found out it was willed down to his surviving nieces.'

Sarah took half a step back. 'This is getting a little stalkery, David.'

'No!' he said, and his hands came up defensively, palms facing her. 'It's not that. I just have a great interest in the house. I researched what happened here in '82, and I know that your parents, and uncle, all escaped. And... are you Chloe?'

'Chloe is my sister.'

'Ah,' he said. 'So that would make you...'

'Sarah,' she finished for him.

'Sarah, right. Pleased to meet you, Sarah.'

He offered his hand again, no less awkwardly than the first time. Sarah didn't take it.

'As fun as this has been,' she said, wanting to bring everything to a close, 'I really am very busy.'

'Oh, of course.' His face fell. 'Can I just ask you to consider something for me? I would be eternally grateful.'

'Care to get to the point?'

'Yes. Certainly. See, Vincent never let us back in here, and I'd like to ask if you would consider allowing me and my team back in, at some point? To, you know, carry out another investigation.'

Sarah was momentarily lost for words—a rarity for her. She soon found her voice. 'Are you serious?'

'Yes, of course.'

She laughed. 'We've *just* moved in, David. Couldn't you have at least waited a few months to ask?'

'Oh... I didn't mean—'

'Look,' she said firmly. 'That isn't something we'd be willing to accommodate, to be honest. This is our home, not a public attraction. So I'm going to have to say no. But, thanks for asking.'

Sarah saw a look that boarded on heartbreak cross his face, and she couldn't help but feel bad for letting him down so abruptly.

'I see,' he replied, sounding like a child who had been told he couldn't have his favourite toy. 'Is there no way...'

'Sorry, David, but we don't believe in things like that, and letting people run around our house hunting imaginary ghosts would just be intrusive. I'm sure you understand.'

He nodded slowly. 'Okay. Please, though, keep the book. It might be of interest.'

'I will,' Sarah said with a smile, waving the book in her hand. 'But I've got to go now. It was nice to meet you, David.'

'You too,' he replied, 'but one more thing. If you do see anything in there, and ever need any help... please let me know.'

Yet again, his hand thrust forward. This time, however, it was holding a small rectangular piece of card. Sarah sighed, but took it, and read what was written on the front: *David Ritter, Paranormal Investigator.*

He has an honest-to-God business card. 'Okay, I promise I'll call you if I see anything. But I really have to go now,' Sarah said, trying not to laugh. She still couldn't get over the fact he had gotten business cards made up. She waved, then closed the door on her strange new acquaintance.

Sarah quickly walked back through to the kitchen and saw Chloe fixing up dinner. 'Where's Andrew?' she asked.

'He's gone to start setting up his office. Who was at the door? And what's that book?'

Sarah pulled her sister away from the food she was preparing, moving her over to the kitchen table.

'You are not gonna fucking *believe* the conversation I just had.'

14

---

3 Days Later...

'Why the hell are you reading that thing?' Chloe asked her sister.

The sisters were curled up in the living room, which was situated at the front corner of the house and looked out over the front lawn and driveway. They were seated on the leather sofas Chloe had brought with her, with Chloe on one and Sarah on the other.

Sarah had a blanket wrapped over her legs, and she sipped at a hazelnut coffee. The television was playing a documentary about Orca whales, but Chloe felt distracted and found it hard to concentrate. Her own cup of tea was close to being empty. And while it wasn't exactly late in the evening—a little after eight—Chloe still felt tired.

'Actually, it isn't too bad,' Sarah told her, looking up from the pages she had been so engrossed in. 'If half of this is true, then Perron Manor has one fucked-up history.'

Chloe just chuckled. 'We already knew it had a fucked-up history. I was here for some of it,' she said, before adding, 'whether I remember it or not.'

'No, I mean before that,' Sarah replied, '*Way* before that. It was built back in the 1200s as a monastery, apparently, and the stuff that has supposedly happened since is... unreal.'

'I'm not sure I even want to know,' Chloe said, turning back to the television.

'Really? It's fascinating. Though it's definitely not something I should share with Andrew. Don't need to add more fuel to his fire about this place.'

Chloe nodded. 'Agreed.'

Fortunately, Andrew wasn't with them that night and was down in London on business, leaving Chloe, Sarah, and Emma alone for a few days of quality girl time. Chloe was used to him going away every now and again, but still missed him every time he did.

'Does it say anything about why we have Satan's study upstairs, then?' Chloe asked.

Sarah laughed but shook her head. 'No, but I haven't gotten into modern history yet. Still covering the 1800s, so no mention of it.'

'That book you're reading could all be bullshit, you know.'

'It could, I suppose, and I'm sure the stories of ghosts and the like *are*. But I think a lot of the events it covers are factual.'

'I still can't believe that creepy guy turned up on our doorstep and wanted to use this place to hunt bloody ghosts. It's weird.'

'I know,' Sarah said with a chuckle. 'Harmless enough, though.'

Chloe's attention was turned to the side-table, where the baby monitor sat. The sound of Emma mumbling in her sleep was coming through the speakers.

Chloe watched her daughter, bathed in blue, as she rolled over, then quickly settled down again.

'I just don't want our house becoming some kind of freakshow,' Chloe said.

'I get that,' her sister replied. 'But come on, it's known as Devil's House. And bad shit happened here. It's always gonna have that stigma, and there isn't much we can do about it. If this is going to work for you, I think you need to come to terms with that and accept it.'

Chloe didn't like that notion, as true as it was. 'It just feels like a black stain on what we're trying to do. This place would be perfect, otherwise.'

'Yeah, but it's a small price to pay for getting a free mansion, Sis. If that is the only drawback—that, and the ungodly amount of work that needs doing—then it still isn't a bad deal, is it?'

'I guess,' Chloe admitted, but still wished she could snap her fingers and make everyone forget about the irrelevant past. Had she been naïve in thinking a history like that would have no bearing on their lives here?

'You'll get used to it,' Sarah said. 'Just don't let it get you down.'

'Easy for you to say, you seem to love it all,' Chloe replied, pointing at the book. 'When we found that study upstairs, you were practically giddy.'

'Of *course* I was,' Sarah exclaimed. 'It's as far from normal as anything possibly can be, so why wouldn't I be interested in it? One thing I'll say about this place: it certainly hasn't been boring so far.'

Chloe sighed. 'Boring would have suited me fine.'

But Sarah just stared over to her sister and narrowed her eyes. 'That's a lie.' Chloe had no response to that.

More noises from the baby monitor caught her attention

again. Emma was now standing up, hands resting against the side rail, and was chattering to herself.

'She's awake, then, I take it?' Sarah asked.

'Yeah. I'll give her a minute, see if she settles back down.'

Then Emma paused, and Chloe saw her point to something out of view of the camera. It wasn't unusual for her to point at things, but something had clearly gotten Emma's attention.

'Man!' the child said.

Chloe paused and felt a small chill run down her spine.

Sarah looked over to her. 'Did she just say...?'

'Yeah,' Chloe confirmed with a frown. 'Probably just jabbering.' Even so, Chloe felt the need to go up and check. She grabbed the monitor and got to her feet.

'Want me to come with you?' Sarah asked, but Chloe shook her head.

'Nah, it's nothing. You enjoy your book.'

Although in all likelihood it was indeed nothing, Chloe still kept a close eye on the monitor as she made her way upstairs. Emma continued to stare off-camera, standing in silence. Chloe put on a burst of speed, and practically jogged all the way to Emma's room.

Upon entering, she saw her daughter was still standing, but there was no one else present. However, it was cold, and that horrible odour Chloe had previously noticed in the room again lingered for a few moments. She quickly checked the room over, to satisfy herself there was nothing to worry about.

Chloe then laid Emma back down and ran a hand through her daughter's fuzzy hair. 'Kindly do me a favour, kid, and stop freaking me out like that.'

Giving one last look around, and realising that the nasty smell had dissipated completely, Chloe turned the radiator up a touch and left Emma alone, closing the door behind her.

She knew that fixing the smell in Emma's room would need to be a priority.

As Chloe walked back downstairs, she kept stealing glances at the monitor. Thankfully, Emma remained lying down and settled.

'All okay?' Sarah asked as Chloe re-entered the living room.

'All okay,' Chloe confirmed, and took her seat again.

The sisters then sat in silence for a little while, with Sarah still engrossed in her book and Chloe watching the whale documentary. Chloe's hand kept wandering to her phone so she could check social media or surf the internet. However, given the Wi-Fi wasn't yet installed, and the signal in most of the house was terrible, it proved futile.

Over the last few days, she had found that annoying desire to idly waste time on her mobile phone had begun to wane, which was a good thing. Chloe, like so many others in today's world, had definitely developed an annoying habit of having her face constantly buried into the screen, letting social media devour every spare moment she had.

That was something Chloe respected about Sarah, who obviously still owned a phone, but never seemed to get drawn into the time-sucking loop of browsing and scrolling.

They remained in the living room for a couple more hours, until Chloe started to feel tired. She yawned and stretched. 'I'm done,' she said. 'Going to turn in.'

Sarah closed her book. 'Yeah, me too.'

The two women double-checked the ground-floor doors to make sure they were all locked before moving upstairs and bidding each other goodnight. Chloe then looked in on Emma again, who was still sleeping soundly.

She then went into her room and readied herself for bed, quickly paying a visit to the en-suite in order to brush her teeth and answer the call of nature.

Just as she got into bed and pulled the covers over her, Chloe heard something that startled her.

While it wasn't particularly loud, the noise was still very audible. And it caused an instant pang of anxiety to rise up from her gut.

She sat up in bed and checked her phone, seeing it was a little after ten at night.

And then she heard it again. A knocking—no, a banging —on the front door downstairs.

What the hell?

She climbed out of bed, feeling a sense of building dread, similar to the apprehension experienced when getting a phone call late at night: it could never be good news.

Who the hell could be knocking at this time of night?

Chloe slung a dressing gown around herself, then grabbed her keys, as well as her phone, just in case an emergency call was needed. She then quickly stepped out into the hallway, wondering if she should find something to arm herself with.

When she looked down the corridor, Chloe saw that the banging had obviously disturbed Sarah as well, who was now standing outside of her own room dressed in a blue tank top, grey jogging bottoms, and was barefoot. She had, however, armed herself with a baseball bat.

Chloe had no idea that her sister had packed a bat, but in that moment, Chloe was grateful for her having it.

Bang, bang, bang.

The two sisters ran to each other. 'Who the hell could that be?' Chloe asked, trying not to let the panic she felt come through in her voice. She had images of going down to see police officers standing outside. *'Ma'am, I'm afraid it's about your husband.'*

'Maybe it's my new friend coming to get his book back,' Sarah joked.

While her dilated pupils indicated she was far from relaxed, Sarah did still exude a level of calm Chloe could not match. Not surprising, given Sarah's training.

'Should we answer it?' Chloe asked.

Sarah nodded. 'I think so. Just follow me.' She then held up the bat. 'If you see me start to swing, run up to Emma, then call the police. Got your phone?'

Chloe raised and shook it as confirmation. 'I have my keys to unlock the front door.'

'Me too,' Sarah said.

The pair then navigated the hallway to the upper section of the entrance lobby. They quickly looked over the rail, and down to the front door. Chloe was not able to make anything out through the glazed panels, as there was only darkness beyond. That in itself was strange, given Andrew had installed security lighting. If someone *was* outside, then it should have tripped the sensor.

Unless the visitor had already run off.

But that idea was quickly disproven, as three more quick bangs sounded out. They were hard enough to rattle the solid door on its hinges and loud enough to make both Chloe and Sarah jump.

Though the glass in the door was frosted for privacy, Chloe still couldn't make out any movement beyond it. Sarah then started to walk towards the staircase.

'We need to answer it,' she said, 'otherwise they're just going to keep banging on the fucking door and wake Emma.'

Chloe didn't like it, but Sarah had a point. So the two sisters slowly made their way down, each step causing an ominous creak underfoot. Once at the bottom of the stairs, they approached the front entrance, with Sarah taking the lead.

She moved to the door, drew in a breath, then yelled, 'Who is it?'

Silence.

'Maybe they've gone,' Chloe offered, hoping it was true but not really believing it.

Sarah slowly moved her face closer to the glass panel and peered out.

'Can't see anyone,' she said. Then, she called out again, 'Hello?'

Nothing.

'Let's just ignore it,' Chloe said. 'Whoever it was has obviously left.'

But instead, Sarah retrieved the keys from her pocket and slid the correct one into the lock. There was a click as it opened, and Chloe felt her breath catch in her throat.

Sarah slowly pulled the door open a crack and peeked outside. For Chloe, the silence as her sister looked about felt like an eternity. Sarah then pushed her head farther out and the security light flicked on, illuminating more of the outside space and pushing back the shadows. After scanning the area thoroughly, Sarah pulled her head back inside and closed the door.

'Well?' Chloe asked.

Sarah shook her head. 'No one.'

Chloe felt a wave of relief wash over her. *Thank Christ for that.* Though the thought that someone *had* been there was still hugely unnerving.

'Who the fuck was it, then?' Chloe asked.

'No idea, but it might be an idea to get a security camera fitted.'

'Yeah,' Chloe agreed. 'I like the sound of that.'

'I'm going to check the back door as well,' Sarah said. 'You can go back upstairs if you want.'

Chloe's heart was still beating fast, and thoughts of sleep seemed a million miles away. 'No, I'll come with you.'

The two women then walked from the entrance lobby through to the great hall. From there, the rear glass doors that looked out into the courtyard could be seen. The security light there remained off. They walked up to the door and peered out, but no one could be seen.

'All clear,' Sarah confirmed.

'Do you think we should call the police?' Chloe asked. 'I mean, we still don't know who it was. I don't like the idea of someone creeping around out there. It's a long trek for someone to make without a good reason.'

Sarah seemed to be considering it, but then shook her head. 'It's stopped, so whoever it was has likely gone. If it happens again, then maybe.'

'But how do we know they've gone?' Chloe asked. 'They could still be on the grounds somewhere.'

'Then let's check,' Sarah replied.

Chloe was confused, and a little worried that meant actually going outside. But instead, Sarah led the way upstairs into an unused and rear-facing bedroom. There, they both looked out of the window to see the courtyard and rear gardens. The view was bathed in darkness, but they could just about make out the edge of the property, close to the boundary wall.

'Can't see anyone,' Sarah said. They then checked a few more rooms as well, looking out either side of the house, as well as the front.

There was no one.

'I honestly think we are okay now,' Sarah said.

'Fine,' Chloe conceded, though she still would have felt safer calling the police.

'Try and get some sleep,' Sarah told her. 'We can discuss it more in the morning, maybe file a report or something then. Pointless dragging anyone out here now.'

'Fair enough,' Chloe replied. The two sisters hugged, and said their goodnights for the second time. Chloe then checked Emma again before finally getting into bed herself. She let out a long sigh.

Bang, bang, bang!

Her eyes went wide and her body locked up. Another banging, again from the front door.

Bang, bang, bang!

Chloe was quickly up again and out into the hallway, pushing herself forward despite the fear she was feeling. As expected, Sarah was just leaving her room as well.

'This has got to be a fucking joke!' Sarah seethed, marching towards the stairs. Her face was twisted into a look of pure anger, and the bat was again in hand. 'I am not having some fuckwit mess with us like this. Come on!' she called to Chloe.

Chloe had her phone in hand, ready to call the police, feeling her heart hammer in her chest. But her screen showed no signal. Chloe jogged along in order to keep up with Sarah, though she didn't like the idea of going back down again.

The house felt colder now, somehow.

Bang, bang, bang.

Bang, bang, bang.

Sarah gripped the bat tightly in two hands as the sisters

emerged again onto the walkway of the entrance lobby. They both again looked over the side railing.

Like before, the security light was still off, and they couldn't spot any shapes or movement beyond the privacy glazing in the door panels.

Sarah quickly ran down the stairs.

'What about the police?' Chloe shouted, following her sister on shaking legs.

'Later,' Sarah snapped. 'First, I'm going to wrap this bat around their fucking heads, whoever the hell they are.'

She strode over to the door, took in a breath, set herself, then yelled out, 'I'm giving you one last warning, you fucking creeps. Get the hell out of here before I rip your Goddamn lungs out!'

Chloe's eyes went wide. She had never seen such aggression from Sarah before, and from the expression on her sister's face, Chloe didn't doubt Sarah intended to follow through with her rather graphic threat. Aggression had been part of her job, of course. But still, for Chloe to see her little sister unleash it in such a way was unnerving.

Sarah was still slow and steady, however, as she reached a hand towards the door handle and once again pulled open the front door. She had the bat cocked back, ready to strike, and she slowly inched her way outside while checking left and right. Once fully out, and her bare feet planted on the paving stones, Sarah stood ready, bat still poised. Just as she stepped outside the security light above her clicked on, washing Sarah in a cold, white light.

'I don't believe this,' she muttered.

'No one there again?' Chloe asked, realising she was hugging herself—both from the cold and the anxiety.

Sarah looked around, but her body started to relax, and the bat lowered.

'I don't understand it,' she said. 'The light is clearly working. So how come it didn't go off when we heard the knocking?'

Chloe shrugged. 'I have no idea. But, can we please call the—'

Bang, bang, bang.

The quick, hard banging this time came from somewhere else in the house. It was duller this time, like a strong thumping on thick glass.

'The back door!' Sarah exclaimed.

'Sarah, wait!'

But it was no use, and Chloe yet again had to follow her sister while experiencing an ever-growing feeling of panic. Chloe checked her phone, but there was still no signal. The only place she'd been able to consistently get any inside of the house was up on the top floor, towards the front of the building.

The two women ran into the great hall and flicked on the light. Sarah once again readied the bat, but no one was outside.

This time, however, the security light above the door *was* on, washing the courtyard out back in a yellow hue that reached to the end of the two protruding rear wings of the house. Though it was not quite enough to see the back of the boundary wall.

Given the light from both outside and within the great hall, Chloe saw their own reflections in the glass door as they approached it. Hers specifically looked tired, with messy hair in a loose ponytail, and brown eyes so wide they looked like they were about to pop out of their sockets. Despite being a quite tall five-foot-ten, she looked more like a scared child, especially next to her shorter but more determined-looking sister.

'Sarah,' Chloe whispered, trying to find some steel in her voice, 'I really want us to call the... oh my God!'

Sarah quickly turned to Chloe with a frown of confusion, but Chloe kept staring straight ahead. Sarah then whipped her head back around, and a gasp of surprise indicated she had seen it, too.

A person was standing outside, just beyond the illuminated area and mostly covered in shadow.

'Who the fuck is that?' Sarah shouted, taking a tentative step closer to the door.

It was hard to see much of the stationary figure that stood at the edge of the light. From what Chloe could see, it was a man, based only on the fact he was very tall—easily over six feet. They could also make out that he seemed to be wrapped in dark robes, but had the hood pulled down.

'What... what the hell is up with his face?' Chloe asked, feeling a sudden increase in her anxiety.

Though it was difficult to make out, the face in question seemed... off... somehow. As well as being deathly pale, the man's nose was bent and twisted, and there looked to be painful sores and scars on the skin. The eyes were lost in pools of shadow.

The man, whoever it was, did not move an inch. He just continued to stare at them.

Sarah dug one of her hands into her pockets and pulled out her phone.

'Police?' Chloe asked, relieved.

'Picture,' Sarah replied, unlocking the screen. 'And I wanna use the zoom on the camera to see—'

But when they looked up, the figure was gone.

'What the hell!' Sarah growled.

Chloe looked around frantically, but could not see him. The only explanation was that he'd stepped back into the darkness, because now all they saw was the empty court-yard, and their own reflections in the glass.

Then, the security light clicked off.

'Enough,' Chloe stated, shaking her head. 'We are calling the police right the fuck now.'

Thankfully, Sarah agreed. 'Yeah, I think that's a good idea.'

The two women then quickly moved up to the top floor again, and Chloe grabbed Emma on the way. The little girl cried incessantly, but there was no way Chloe was going to leave her daughter when a stranger was lurking around outside.

Once on the top floor, Sarah managed to find enough signal in one of the front bedrooms to make the call.

15

IT ONLY TOOK the police car fifteen minutes to show up.

'Well, we've had a good look around,' the policewoman said, her thumbs hooked into her black, standard issue stab-vest. 'But can't find anyone on the grounds. They must have run off.'

Sarah wasn't surprised. Even if the stranger had been hanging around, the police arriving surely would have scared him away.

She was a little ashamed of herself for getting so spooked, but there was something about the man—a feeling she got after looking out at him which she couldn't quite place, yet had truly unnerved her.

Sarah had been in war zones before, so a man creeping around outside should have been way down on the list of things that should get under her skin. But after seeing him, she couldn't deny that sneaking fear quickly overrode her previous desire to confront him.

Something about the whole thing just felt wrong.

Sarah, Chloe, and the two police officers—PC Andrea

Taylor and PC Terry Rollins—were all gathered in the great hall, with Emma asleep in Chloe's arms. After arriving and speaking with the sisters, the officers had checked the full exterior of the property before coming back inside to speak to them.

'I'd recommend getting a security camera installed,' PC Andrea Taylor said. She had blonde hair pulled back in a tight bun, a square-set jaw, and a stocky build.

'Yeah,' Chloe replied. 'It's on the to-do list, now. But who do you think it was? Just someone trying to fuck with us?'

'We can't be sure,' PC Terry Rollins replied. He was taller and thinner than his female counterpart, and had a neatly trimmed black beard and brushed-back hair. 'We could only speculate. However...' he trailed off, seeming to consider his next words.

But Sarah had an idea what he was going to say. 'It's the house, isn't it?'

PC Taylor raised an eyebrow in confusion. 'How do you mean?'

'It's pretty well known in the area, so it's not a stretch to think it could attract a bit of attention.'

'It could be,' PC Rollins confirmed with a nod. 'Most people around here know of this place—'

'They do?' his colleague cut in.

He smiled. 'Well, those of us who aren't new to the area do, yeah.' He then turned back to Sarah. 'I've seen a few cases of people coming up here just because they're intrigued by it, in all honesty. Mostly youths, but it has never been anything sinister.'

'Well, this guy definitely wasn't a kid,' Chloe said. 'Not from what we could make out.'

'And he was wearing robes, you say?' the female officer asked.

Chloe nodded. 'Yeah. Not exactly normal clothing when out exploring at night, is it?'

'No,' PC Rollins admitted. 'But, if I may, the house doesn't always attract people who are *normal*.'

Sarah and Chloe looked at each other, then turned to him with a frown.

'Oh God,' he said, holding up his hands. 'I didn't mean you two. You live here. I'm talking about the people who want to come up and see the house where people have died. They're sometimes a little... eccentric.'

Sarah thought of David Ritter, and realised the officer had a point.

'So... nothing to worry about?' she asked.

'I don't think so,' he replied. 'But, I'd obviously advise you to stay vigilant. Think about getting some cameras installed, like we said, and if you do see anyone else, don't hesitate to call.'

'Be *very* vigilant,' PC Taylor added. 'Sorry, but if someone is running around knocking on doors when they *know* someone is inside, that isn't just a person curious about a building. That's deliberate. Probably messing around or for kicks and actually *trying* to scare you.'

'I guess,' the other policeman conceded. 'Maybe they thought they were being funny. I still don't think you are in danger, but like my colleague says, best to keep an eye out.'

Not very comforting, Sarah thought. But the policewoman had certainly made a good point, and Sarah was glad of her candid advice.

However, she knew there was little more the police could do now.

After finishing up, the officers bade Sarah and Chloe goodnight, and then left. The sisters watched the police drive their squad car down the long, gravel driveway.

When they were gone, Sarah took a step forward. 'I'm gonna follow them down and close the gate,' she said.

'Are you sure?' Chloe responded.

'Of course. You can't take Emma down there. Go ahead and put the kettle on. I don't feel like sleeping at the minute.'

'Why don't we leave the gate until morning.'

Sarah turned to her, and forced a smile. 'Honestly, Chloe, it's fine. I had to walk down there to open it for them in the first place. And that didn't bother me.'

However, that wasn't necessarily true. The long walk in the dark so soon after seeing that stranger had certainly been an unsettling one.

What the fuck was it about that man that freaked me out so much?

The lack of explanation was infuriating Sarah. Perhaps it was the way he had looked—so pale and... *unnatural?*

Was that the right word?

Just thinking about him and those pools of shadows over his eyes caused a creeping feeling of cold to work its way up her spine.

Push it out of your head.

Sarah didn't give Chloe any further chance to change her mind, and set off down the driveway, the gravel crunching under her now-slippered feet. She called back over her shoulder.

'Hazelnut coffee for me. Feel free to make one yourself, Sis.'

She could only imagine the face Chloe was making at the suggestion.

'You sure you want coffee this late?' Chloe asked. 'You won't sleep.'

'I'll be fine,' she replied and kept walking.

Though Sarah tried to force all thoughts of the watcher from her mind, it was difficult, and as she got farther and farther away from the safety of the house, the more she felt isolated and exposed. She half expected to suddenly see the man in the shadows—or worse, to turn around and see him right behind her, following her up the driveway.

That didn't happen, of course, and Sarah reached the security gate without incident. She pulled the gate shut, replaced the padlock, and dropped the bolts that slotted into a concrete base-pad. It was an old gate, which would also need replacing at some point, preferably with an automatic one so they wouldn't need to open and close it on their own.

The return trip to the house was equally creepy, especially when she heard her crunching footsteps in the otherwise dead silence, but also equally uneventful. Sarah was grateful when she eventually got back inside to the relative warmth of Perron Manor. She headed straight to the kitchen and found Chloe sitting at the table with two drinks.

However, the coffee had been ignored, and two glasses of red wine sat ready.

'Perfect,' Sarah said approvingly. 'Did Emma go back down okay?'

'Yeah, she was asleep anyway. Just hope this doesn't cause her to be tired and grouchy tomorrow. I did the right thing getting her, didn't I?'

'Of course,' Sarah replied, taking the glass that was offered. 'Better to risk her losing a bit of sleep than anything bad happening. We didn't know what was going on.'

'I guess,' Chloe said, and took a long drink. Then she shuddered.

'Not good?' Sarah asked.

'What? Oh... no, it's not that. The wine is delicious. It's just... you know, thinking about that guy.'

Sarah took a gulp of her own drink. 'Try not to dwell on it,' she said.

'Easier said than done,' was Chloe's reply, and it was one Sarah fully understood. Though Sarah's advice had been good, it wasn't exactly something she could keep herself from doing either. Her mind was especially drawn to the way he had just stood there, totally unmoving.

Watching.

After each sister took a few more sips in silence, it was Chloe who went on. 'What the fuck am I going to tell Andrew?'

'What do you mean?' Sarah asked.

'Well, if I tell him what happened, then that's it for this place, isn't it? He's not going to entertain staying here if it's dangerous.'

Sarah considered her answer, as she knew Chloe had a point. If Andrew wanted a way out of this place, and he wanted an excuse where he couldn't be blamed for not giving the house a fair shot, then this was it.

Andrew would no doubt decide that strangers showing up in the middle of the night was sufficient to get out.

But, then again, it *was* a valid reason.

Sarah saw disappointment etched on her sister's face as Chloe stared at the ground while sipping her wine. Sarah's heart ached for her a little. It was clear just how much Chloe wanted this to work.

'Look,' Sarah eventually said. 'We can't hide this from him, it wouldn't be right. But, we can... I don't know, maybe... *frame* it a certain way.'

'What do you mean?'

'Well, we tell him what happened, but we play it down. Just say some idiot was knocking on our door then running away, being a nuisance. Don't let on that we were a little freaked out.'

'A *little* freaked out?' Chloe asked with a smile.

'Well, maybe more than a little. But, you have to make sure you're happy with that.'

'Happy with what?'

'I mean... would you still feel safe here? Do you think it's safe for Emma? Is staying here the right thing to do?'

Chloe paused for a moment. 'I... I don't know.'

Sarah understood the uncertainty. She was feeling it herself, but the more time that had passed since the incident, the more she'd started to think the whole thing ridiculous.

'Then let's think it through. What really happened here?'

'Some creepy guy tried to scare us.'

'Probably,' Sarah agreed. 'But no more than that. He knocked on our door. Is that really worth us losing a house like this over? I do think the history is something we need to keep in mind, as it might attract a few oddballs. But once we get some cameras set up, and maybe look at improving the boundary walls, electric gate... hell, even more security lighting on the grounds, that should stop strangers coming up here for a snoop around.'

'You think?' Chloe asked, and Sarah nodded. She *did* think that, more so now than earlier. It was a ridiculous notion to give up your home just because of the actions of an idiot.

Hell, harassment could happen anywhere. Even in the most populated of areas.

'We aren't going anywhere,' Sarah stated. 'Like I said,

you need to tell Andrew, since it isn't right keeping it from him. But, you know...'

'Frame it,' Chloe repeated with a laugh.

Sarah clinked Chloe's glass with her own. 'Exactly.'

16

1 Month Later...

Steam filled the room, and even the open window failed to adequately ventilate the air.

'Can't see why you just didn't want to leave it as it was,' Sarah said to Andrew while nodding towards the wall's covering. 'This wallpaper has character.' She then slid the edge of her scraper utensil under the paper and cut away another strip of it.

The hell it does, Andrew thought.

He was holding the steamer machine to a separate area, letting the heat and moisture seep into the fabric of the wall lining, which made it easier to pull away. It also turned the room into a makeshift sauna with the steam it was kicking out.

'I hate the wallpaper,' he replied. 'You can have it everywhere else, if you want, but if this is going to be my office, then I need it how I like it.'

And that was their task today: to strip the wallpaper and carpet, which would allow the room to be re-plastered in a few days. Then he could decorate as he saw fit.

Earlier that morning, they'd humped out all of his equipment—computer, desk, filing cabinet—and moved them into a temporary office. Next, they had ripped out the carpet. Now all that remained was the hideous wall coverings.

'You're only going to plaster the whole thing then paint every wall white,' Sarah said with a grin. 'That's so boring.'

'Well,' he replied, 'I might go crazy and have a feature wall. You never know.'

'Oh, what colour?' Chloe asked.

Andrew shrugged. 'Probably some kind of pastel.'

Both Chloe and Sarah laughed. 'Absolutely *wild*,' Chloe joked.

They carried on stripping the paper and loading the rubbish into black bin-bags as the steam continued to clog the room. In truth, it was probably overcrowded with the three of them, but with Emma down for her midday nap, Chloe had insisted she wanted to chip in.

And, in fairness, the two girls had already set about fixing up the other parts of the house. Given Andrew had to work a lot, he'd expected the refurbishments to take an age, but he had underestimated just how much the sisters were looking forward to the monumental task ahead of them. With the help of sub-contractors and specialists, they had all managed to get a lot done. The internet was up and running—though it still tended to drop out quite a bit—and they had replaced the front entrance gate with an electronic one. Security cameras had been fitted to the front and rear doors, which also sent a feed to all of their mobile phones. Additionally, they'd finished the redecorating of their bedrooms, including Emma's. They had even started on renovating the garden and surrounding grounds.

The damn furnace still hadn't been replaced yet, but that

was hopefully in hand and they were just waiting on a start date from Oliver. Andrew desperately wanted that thing replaced. Only a few days ago he had tried tightening a pipe that seemed to be leaking in one of the rooms. The water that dripped steadily from the heating pipe must have been mixed with rust, as it had a distinct crimson colour to it. When he'd cleaned it up, it had smeared across his fingers and left them smelling like copper.

However, even though Andrew still had his reservations about Perron Manor overall, he did feel like things were looking up.

That hadn't been the case when he'd found out about Chloe and Sarah being harassed—some idiot trying to scare them, apparently—and that had made him see red. But in the end, Chloe and Sarah had put things into perspective.

Would they have left their last house because of the same thing?

The answer to that, he was forced to admit, would have been *no*. He and Chloe had then had a long conversation, where she again stressed her desire to make living here work. She also raised the point that he had promised to try, so his sniping and jibes at the house and the situation weren't helping. She also said that if he never intended to really commit, he should have never agreed to live here in the first place.

It took Andrew a little while to see things from her point of view, since he was initially defensive, but he'd eventually apologised.

She was right.

The truth was, he'd never *really* tried since moving in, and had just been going through the motions, waiting for an excuse to get out.

The possibility of another child had also been talked

about again. They'd agreed that Chloe would come off the pill, and then they would see what happened over the next few months.

Thankfully, there had been no more instances of trespassers on the property.

The baby monitor—which was set on the floor in the room—crackled over the hissing of the steamer. Chloe leaned over to inspect it.

'Nothing,' Chloe said to them. 'She's still asleep.'

They carried on with their work, but another bout of light static came from the device, again drawing their attention. This time, however, Andrew could detect something within the crackling noise, though he wasn't certain what it was.

Sarah laughed. 'Jesus, that sounded like someone was whispering.'

Chloe was staring at the monitor. 'It did a little bit, didn't it? Strange.'

While it was true there was an odd sound on the monitor, he certainly didn't think it was anyone whispering.

'Pareidolia,' Andrew stated.

The girls turned to look at him. 'In English, please?' Chloe replied with a raised eyebrow.

'It *is* English,' Andrew told her, grinning. 'It's when you see or hear things that aren't there. You hear something odd, and your brain makes a connection to explain it, likening it to something you understand.'

'Is that so, Doctor?' Sarah asked.

'Yes, that is so,' Andrew confirmed with a playful smile and nod.

'Sounds like something they'd yell at Hogwarts while swinging their wands around.'

'I wouldn't know about that. But the 'whisper' was likely

just more static, probably at a different frequency or something.'

'Scientist as well as a doctor, now?' Chloe teased. 'Full of surprises.'

Andrew chuckled. But then, all of their phones chimed at the same time.

It was the signal that indicated one of the motion-detection security cameras had been activated. Andrew pulled out his phone and saw an alert, then quickly checked the feed.

'Anything?' Chloe asked.

He shook his head.

'That thing is far too sensitive,' Sarah added. 'It goes off at the slightest thing. Probably just a bug flying past.'

'I'll have a look at it,' Andrew said.

The three of them managed to strip the last of the wallpaper before Emma woke, which then left Andrew and Sarah to bag up all of the remaining rubbish and take it out back. After throwing the last bag into the large bins outside, which were set within a timber bin-shed, Sarah let the bin lid drop shut.

She shook her hands off. 'Urgh, I definitely need a shower.'

'True,' Andrew replied. 'You stink.' Sarah flipped him the bird, but he ignored it and went on, 'How are you finding it here?' he asked her.

She let out an exhale. 'Where to start? It's certainly different.'

'Do you like it?'

She paused briefly, before giving a firm nod of her head. 'I do,' she stated, then narrowed her eyes at him. 'But you aren't a fan, are you?'

'It wouldn't have been my ideal forever home, put it that way' he admitted.

'I know that, Andrew, but Chloe—'

'I'm not about to start complaining again,' Andrew cut in, raising his hands in defence. 'Honestly, I'm going to make a go of it. I just wanted to know what you thought of it here as well. After all, there are three of us involved.'

'And are you okay with that?' Sarah asked.

'What? There being three of us?'

'Yeah.'

'Why wouldn't I be?'

'Well, I don't suppose you ever expected to have to share your forever home with your sister-in-law, did you?'

He laughed. 'No, I guess not. But the house is so big I don't think it will be an issue. Are *you* okay with it, though?'

'I am,' she said. 'For now.'

He frowned. 'What's that supposed to mean?'

'Meaning I'm well aware it can't stay like this. I might end up starting my own family one day. Hell, I've even been thinking about travelling for a little while. This place should just be for you guys in the long run.'

'Erm... have you spoken to Chloe about that?' he asked.

Sarah gave a guilty shake of her head. 'Not yet. I was going to, but she just seems so happy. I guess I didn't want to ruin that just yet.'

'Okay. But don't you think you need to have that conversation?'

Sarah nodded. 'Yeah. And I will. But there's no rush. It's not like I'm just going to pack up and go tomorrow. I think staying here for the foreseeable future will be good for me, at least until I figure things out.'

'What things?'

Sarah paused, then smiled. 'Life.'

'Life is a pretty big thing.'

'It is. I just... don't know what I want out of it yet. Everything was clear and straightforward in the army. And the future was always so far away. Now... it just feels like it's right on top of me and breathing down my neck.'

'Sneaks up on you, doesn't it?'

'It does! And soon I'll be old and grey like you. Then what is there to live for?'

He smirked and shook his head. 'Always a pleasure, Sarah.'

She did a curtsy, which looked strange coming from her. 'Thank you. Now come on, let's go. I need to get cleaned up.'

'Doing anything exciting today?'

'Nothing concrete, just going to head into town for a little bit. Been cooped up in the house for days and I want a break.'

'Just you?'

'That's the plan.'

'Take Chloe,' he said. 'That is, if you don't mind. I'll watch Emma.'

'Really? You don't have any work to do?'

'I *always* have work to do,' he said with a grin. 'But it's Saturday, and I've earned a day off. You two have a few hours out of the house together.'

'Cool,' Sarah replied. 'Sounds great. We'll bring back some food.'

'And some whiskey, if you don't mind,' he added. 'I'm running low.'

'I'll see what I can do.'

The two then walked back inside, with Andrew finally optimistic about the house.

17

'Well,' Chloe began as she sipped on her tea, 'we know Alnmouth has some nice shops, but for a proper shopping trip we're going to have to go farther afield.'

'Yeah,' agreed Sarah. 'It's good for the basics, and nice coffee, but that's about it.'

Chloe made a face as her sister took another large mouthful of that revolting hazelnut coffee.

They were seated in *Hill of Beans*, the lone coffee shop in town. Chloe liked the establishment. It was quaint, with a gentle stream of people moving in and out, and had a modern decor.

Sarah was facing the entrance, and Chloe's position gave her a view of the seating area and serving counter. The smell of coffee beans was strong and pleasant.

Chloe definitely felt better being out of the house for a little while, especially since the work there had overtaken all of their lives recently.

That had been expected, of course, but it didn't mean it wasn't tiring, with a rinse-and-repeat cycle of sleep, work, eat, work, eat, work, sleep. The only variable was Emma and the attention that she needed.

So this was a welcome distraction.

'We're making good progress with the house,' Sarah said. 'I mean, still a long way off from finishing, but the essentials are getting there.'

'Yeah. Hard work, though.'

'And how are you feeling about it all? Is it starting to seem like home yet?'

Chloe thought about that for a moment, before eventually nodding. 'It is. I think it's easier to settle into a smaller house, to be honest. The Manor is so big and it's hard to make it feel like a home. That will change, though.'

'Yeah, I get that,' Sarah added. 'Seems like a place you go for a quiet weekend away, like a retreat in the country or something.'

'Exactly. But it is getting more and more familiar. And I *do* love it. Every day I wake up and am excited that it's mine. Sorry... ours.'

Sarah laughed. 'That's right, Sis, *ours*. Remember to share.'

'You know what I mean.'

'I do.'

'And how do *you* feel about the house?' she asked Sarah.

There was a pause, but Sarah finally responded, 'I like it.'

Clearly there was something else to be said. 'But?' Chloe asked.

'No, no buts, I like it. Honestly.'

'Somewhere you can see yourself living, then?'

Sarah smiled at her, but it was almost false, as if disguising something.

'Sarah, just tell me if—'

'There isn't anything wrong with the house, Sis,' Sarah insisted with a smile. 'It's fine, I swear. It's just... I'm struggling to sleep, is all.'

'How so?' Chloe asked.

'I don't know,' Sarah replied with a dismissive shrug. 'I'm having trouble getting a full night. Odd dreams. I keep waking up in the early hours of the morning a lot of the time.'

'Strange,' Chloe said.

'Just adjusting, I guess. I've certainly slept in worse places.'

'I bet. Though, you've never really told me much about that side of your life.'

'Not a whole lot to tell,' Sarah said quickly, then a playful smirk drew over her face. 'You've seen Rambo, right? Same thing. I was just like him.'

'Of course you were,' Chloe said with a laugh.

'Anyway,' Sarah went on, and Chloe got the impression she was quickly changing the subject, 'there is something about the house we need to discuss.'

'Go on...'

'A certain room that we need to get sorted. One I think you're avoiding.'

'Vincent's?' Chloe asked.

'Okay... I guess there are two rooms.'

Chloe sighed. 'That fucking study.'

'Have you been back in since we found it?'

'No,' Chloe answered, shaking her head. 'You?'

'Briefly. I know you hate it and all, but I wanna go in there and take a good look. I mean, Andrew seems committed now, don't you think? I don't see any reason why we need to ignore the room like it doesn't exist. Some of the stuff in there seemed fascinating.'

'It looked macabre,' Chloe corrected.

'Those things don't have to be mutually exclusive. I'm just saying we can't keep ignoring it, unless you wanna keep that room as a kind of creepy museum forever.'

Chloe considered that for a moment, then rolled her eyes. 'Fine, we can move onto that one next.' Sarah gave an excited clap, and Chloe laughed before adding, 'You're so weird. And, *speaking* of weird, did you finish that book you were given?'

'Yeah,' Sarah said with a nod. 'It was really good. A little farfetched in places, obviously the whole thing about the ghosts is bullshit, but the history of the building is certainly cool. Wanna read it?'

'Nah,' Chloe replied. 'You can give me the highlights sometime. That man hasn't been back to the house again, has he?'

'No,' Sarah said with a grin. 'I'm pleased to say I haven't seen him since...' Then Sarah's face fell, and her jaw hung open.

Chloe frowned. 'What? What is it?'

'You know the saying: speak of the Devil and he shall appear?' Chloe's eyes went wide, and she turned her head as Sarah went on. 'Not that he's the Devil or anything, but that ghost hunter just walked into the fucking shop!'

Chloe scanned the entrance and quickly noticed the man that had just entered. He had grey, brushed-back hair, black-rimmed glasses, and was dressed in a black coat, jeans, and scruffy trainers.

'So that's the ghostbuster?' Chloe asked quietly.

'That's him,' Sarah confirmed.

David Ritter glanced around the shop after entering, and his gaze fell on the sisters. His eyes went wide. Both Chloe and Sarah immediately looked away, but the act was so obvious it had to have looked ridiculous.

'He's seen us,' Sarah whispered.

No shit.

'What do we do?' Chloe asked, looking down at her nails and pretending to inspect them.

'I... uh-oh. He's coming over.'

Chloe looked up again and saw that Sarah was correct. Though he looked nervous and moved awkwardly, the strange man was weaving between tables as he made his way over.

'Sarah?' he said as he reached the table and stood between the two sisters. Then, he looked down at Chloe and gave an uncertain smile.

'Hi, David,' Sarah said. 'Nice to see you again.'

'You too,' he replied.

Chloe braced herself, certain he was once again going to try and get inside their home to hunt his ghosts.

'I'm glad I bumped into you,' he said. 'I... erm... I think I owe you an apology.'

'You do?' Sarah asked, sounding as surprised as Chloe felt. That was not what she had expected to come out of his mouth.

'I do,' he confirmed. Then he cast his eyes down to the ground. 'I shouldn't have just shown up at your house like that, just after you'd moved in, to ask for access. It was insensitive. I... I tend to get carried away with things like that. And I'm truly sorry.'

He seemed sincere, and Chloe felt a little bad for branding him 'strange' without ever having spoken to him. It still might have been an accurate description, but even so...

'Thank you, David,' Sarah replied. 'I appreciate that.'

An uncomfortable silence fell, with no one seeming to know what to say next. David looked over to Chloe and his hand shot out, causing her to jump a little. She soon realised that it wasn't an aggressive move, but it had still caught her off guard.

Jesus, fella, don't move so suddenly!

'You must be Chloe Pearson,' he said. 'I'm David Ritter.'

She shook his hand. His grip was gentle, bordering on limp. 'It's Shaw now,' she told him. 'I married.'

'Oh, I see,' he replied, holding on for a little too long. It wasn't in any kind of creepy way, she knew, more that he seemed socially awkward and just didn't realise when to release. So Chloe pulled her hand away instead.

'David hunts ghosts,' Sarah said with a grin.

'So I've heard,' Chloe added, keeping her answer brief.

'Well,' David cut in, 'only in my spare time. My day job is an I.T. consultant.'

Chloe heard Sarah snigger a little, so she turned to see what was so funny. 'You were mentioned in David's book, you know,' Sarah said, pointing at Chloe.

'You read it!' David exclaimed with a big smile.

'I did.'

'Wait, what did it say about me?' Chloe asked, now interested, though 'concerned' would have been more accurate.

'Nothing much,' Sarah told her. 'Just that you, Mum, Dad, and Vincent were the only survivors back in 1982.'

'Oh,' Chloe said, still not comfortable with being discussed without her knowledge—and in a bloody *book* of all places.

'What did you think of it?' he pressed. 'If you don't mind me asking.'

'It was good,' Sarah replied. 'I found the history of the house really interesting.'

'I knew you would.' He seemed almost giddy. Then, he turned apprehensive. 'And... the end? The section about my investigation.'

Sarah then made a face, wearing a condescending smile. 'Well, that part didn't do it for me.'

'Oh,' he said, looking crestfallen.

'Don't take it badly. It's just, well, I really don't believe in that kind of thing.'

'Every word was true,' he insisted. His cheeks were now flushed red.

But Sarah, it seemed, was not about to simply humour him.

'Don't take offence, that's just my opinion. It's like if someone were telling me that Santa was real. It's the same thing.'

'It... it *isn't* the same thing, though.'

'To me it is,' Sarah insisted. 'But hey, I wasn't there. I'm just going on what I personally believe.'

David looked as if he wanted to debate the point farther, but instead gave a nod. 'Okay. That's fair enough.' He gave a short pause, before adding, 'But I'm not making anything up. Hasn't there been anything happen there that was a little... odd?'

Chloe turned to Sarah and gave her a death stare.

Don't you dare.

Chloe knew there was a plethora of weird shit Sarah could use by way of example: the smells, the noises, the creep who had knocked on their door in the middle of the night. And, of course, that occult study upstairs, which was a black mark that needed to be scrubbed away.

'Nope,' Sarah eventually answered. 'Sorry, but we haven't seen anything.'

Chloe breathed a sigh of relief.

'Well... that's good,' David replied, though he didn't look pleased with the answer.

'It is,' Sarah went on. 'Hell, Chloe has a daughter living there. Little Emma, my niece. And *she* is absolutely fine.'

David's face quickly darkened. 'There's a child living at the house?'

'There is,' Chloe stated firmly as she turned more towards him. 'Why is that an issue?'

David paused, his face twisting a little. He clearly had something he wanted to say, but was resisting. Or, he might have been trying to find an appropriate way to word it.

'Look,' he began, 'I know you don't believe in the things I'm telling you. And that is fine, I can totally understand that. And I'm not saying this to deliberately scare you or anything. But... you need to be careful. Especially with your daughter. It's dangerous in that house for anyone, but especially for a child.'

Chloe felt a pang of anger and quickly stood to her feet. 'Enough!' she snapped, loud enough to draw attention from all those around her. David visibly shrank back. 'You have no right to harass us like this.'

'I'm not harassing!' he stressed, palms held out and his eyes wide in shock.

'You pester my sister to run some kind of bloody ghost-hunting expedition. Then, when that doesn't work, you come over under the guise of apologising, only to use the safety of my child to... what... find an angle? Are we supposed to panic now that you've given us your warning? Are we to ask you to come save us?'

'Honestly, that wasn't my intention. I—'

'No!' Chloe snarled, cutting him off. 'You've said enough. Now leave us alone and don't ever bother us again.'

The man actually had the nerve to look hurt, almost

close to tears. But Chloe didn't care. She just wanted him gone.

He took a breath, looked her in the eye, and quietly uttered, 'I'm sorry.'

With that, he left, not even bothering to get whatever he'd come in for. After he'd gone, Chloe allowed herself to retake her seat. She was shaking a little, and had to keep from grinding her teeth together. She glanced up at her sister, who looked both shocked and amused.

'Wow,' Sarah said. 'You know, if we hurry outside now, we might actually see him cry. I'm guessing floods of tears, what do you think?'

'Don't,' Chloe said.

'Come on, Sis, don't you think you went a bit far, embarrassing him like that?'

'*I* went too far? Are you serious?'

Is Sarah really taking his side here?

'Look,' Sarah began, 'I know what he said was bat-shit crazy, but he wasn't nasty or anything.'

'Sarah! He brought my daughter into this. Tried to use her as a pawn to get his own way.'

Sarah held up her hands. 'Fair enough,' she said. 'Although, I honestly don't think he was looking for an angle. I think he believes the things he is saying.'

'Then he's an idiot,' Chloe snapped.

Sarah laughed. 'Probably. Anyway, come on. Let's get back before you make anyone else cry. Oh, and for the record, I totally guessed he would be an I.T. consultant.'

18

Emma's electronic cries came through the monitor on the nightstand, and Chloe slowly sat up in bed.

She wasn't ready to be pulled from a well-earned sleep just yet, and she felt her body protesting. There was a temptation to just lie back down and drift off again, but she knew she couldn't do that.

The room still smelled a little of fresh paint. It had been given a makeover recently where they had put in carpets, fitted wardrobes, and redecorated the walls, providing the room with a much lighter and airy feel.

Chloe yawned, stretched, then checked the monitor, already knowing she would have to get up and tend to her daughter. Chloe had learned quickly to distinguish between the different cries and mutterings that Emma made, and she knew which ones could be ignored and which ones required attention. These were the latter, and the child was clearly upset. On the display, Chloe saw that Emma was standing, propped up against the side of her cot-bed, and wailing. Chloe then looked at her phone to check the time.

Three-twenty-seven.

Perfect, she thought to herself with a hint of annoyance.

She glanced over to Andrew, who snored lightly, undisturbed by the sound of his daughter. Chloe then got out of bed and padded her way to Emma's room next door, shivering a little as she passed through a pocket of cold air in the entryway. The child, with tears running down her face, looked visibly relieved to see her mother.

'Come here, baby,' Chloe cooed, and lifted Emma up, bringing her in for a protective hug. She was surprised to feel the child clinging to her tightly. 'It's okay,' Chloe whispered, nuzzling her cheek into Emma's fuzzy hair. 'You hungry?'

Chloe took a seat in the wooden rocking chair in the corner of the room and brought Emma in to feed. Chloe then looked around the room in the dark, feeling pleased with its transformation. While it was true that she quite liked the traditional wallpapers and features found throughout the house, she agreed with Andrew that the room needed to be both more modern and more child friendly. The walls had been stripped, re-plastered, and painted, and Chloe had even added a hand-painted mural on one wall, showing some of Emma's favourite cartoon characters. It was basic—Chloe classed herself as a competent artist, though no more than that—but gave the room life. The other walls were a very light grey, and to complement that, there was a thick light-grey carpet on the floor.

The black cast-iron radiator certainly looked out of place, but that would have to stay until the furnace and heating system had been replaced. Hopefully, that would eradicate some of the random cold spots that seemed to pop up throughout the house with no rhyme or reason to them.

As Emma fed, Chloe felt her eyes grow heavier, and it was only when she felt a sudden chill from behind—almost as if an icy hand touched the back of her neck—that she jolted fully awake.

Emma grumbled for a moment, and then carried on feeding.

'Sorry, kid,' Chloe whispered, and shuddered, feeling warmth once again run through her.

Fucking cold spots.

It didn't take long for Emma's suckling to cease, and Chloe heard tiny, adorable snores come from her little girl. Gently, as to not wake her, Chloe got to her feet and set Emma back down into her bed. She then tiptoed from the room.

Once out into the hallway, she turned and moved back to her own room, but stopped just outside when she was suddenly hit with a feeling of being watched. Chloe turned to look down the long, dark corridor behind her. At the far end, she could see the door to Sarah's room, which was slightly open. However, she could see nothing inside, except for thick and impenetrable darkness.

Then, the door glided shut, punctuated with the audible *click* of the latch snapping into the mortise.

Chloe stood motionless for a moment, and a sudden and oppressive feeling hung over her. Had Sarah been watching her? If so, why close the door like that?

It struck Chloe as extremely odd. She did consider ignoring it and just going back to bed, but curiosity got the better of her. She began to make her way slowly down the hallway to her sister's room, deciding not to flick on any lights in fear of waking anyone.

A squeak of floorboards under her bare soles sounded after every few steps.

She arrived at the stairs that led to the top floor, then

glanced up. It was dark, and the shadows seemed even heavier up there.

Then she paused, and her body froze. For a moment, Chloe could have sworn there was a figure at the top of the stairs, merging with the darkness. But after staring for a few seconds, it became obvious that wasn't the case. There was nothing.

Pareidolia, she thought to herself as she moved on, soon reaching Sarah's room. She stood outside the door and listened, not really sure what to expect. If Sarah *was* up and awake, she would likely make some kind of noise.

At first, Chloe could hear nothing.

Then... whispering. Though the words themselves were unintelligible, Chloe knew the voice was Sarah's.

'Sarah?' she quietly called through the door. There was no response, just a short pause in the whispering before it quickly resumed again. Try as she might, Chloe could not pick out or understand any of the words being uttered.

It was then Chloe realised that her sister could just be talking in her sleep.

She had a protective impulse to check on her little sister, which was ridiculous, knowing the kind of person Sarah was; she certainly wasn't someone that needed protecting. However, Chloe was still the big sister, so she gently twisted the brass handle and pushed the door open.

It took a few moments for her eyes to adjust to the gloom and blackness in the room, but she was soon able to make out Sarah's form in her bed. Her sister lay still, eyes closed and breathing steadily—very clearly asleep. The covers looked like they had been kicked away, and lay crumpled and twisted around Sarah's lower legs.

The room, like Chloe's own, had been freshened up from its original state, but Sarah had elected to keep the same wallpaper as before, as well as most of the original furniture.

After a few moments, Sarah's mouth moved, and again those gentle utterances escaped, a kind of babbling Emma would have been proud of.

But... was it really babbling?

Chloe paused, and realised that it actually sounded more like a different language than random gibberish. She wasn't versed in anything other than English, but this had a certain familiarity to it, something she had at least heard before.

Perhaps Latin?

As Sarah continued to whisper, she began to slowly turn her head as it lay on the pillow, moving it right and left. Sarah scrunched her already closed eyes even tighter.

Whatever dream was taking place in her mind didn't seem a pleasant one. Chloe was tempted to wake her sister and relieve her of the mental torment, but decided against it. Fitful sleep was perhaps better than no sleep at all.

Instead, she walked round to the other side of the bed, took hold of the discarded sheets and pulled them, wanting to cover up her sister. However, she found resistance, which was confusing, given there was nothing there for the sheets to get snagged on. Chloe pulled again, and this time the duvet complied.

Chloe then dropped the sheet over Sarah and tucked the top up around her chin. Hopefully it would keep her warm, since the room had a noticeable chill to it. Chloe then sat on the bed next to her sister, and placed a comforting hand over her forehead, feeling a light layer of perspiration.

'Night, Sis,' she whispered. Chloe then detected a faint, but rank odour in the room, as if something were rotting and fetid. It came out of nowhere, and Chloe could only assume it was perhaps standing water in the heating pipes. An ongoing issue, and something else to fix.

Chloe sat back, ready to stand up, knowing there was nothing she could do about it now. However, as she leaned back, her gaze moved over towards the glass-fronted cabinet opposite Sarah's bed.

She froze.

In the dark reflection, Chloe was able to make out a terrifying sight. There was something else in the room with them. A woman. And she was on the bed, right next to Chloe.

Through the reflection in the cabinet, Chloe could see the woman was haggard and twisted, with dark hair that was pulled tightly back into a bun. Her face was lowered over Sarah's head, mouth to Sarah's ear, and she wore what looked to be a dirty, once-white cotton blouse, one that had a high neck and was form-fitted to the thin figure. The woman also wore a long black skirt that covered her legs, complementing an outfit that looked to be from a different era.

It was her horrifying face that truly scared Chloe. Pale skin was pulled tight over the skull, and it had thin purple veins running through it. The deeply sunken eyes looked blank, fully white, with no pupil to speak of. One eye sagged lower than the other, its lid half-closed. Any skin that had existed around the mouth had rotted away, leaving exposed, raw, and red flesh as the strange woman's mouth hung open.

The last detail Chloe took in was a gash of red across the throat, accompanied by a drizzle of crimson liquid that stained the neck of the woman's top.

And in the reflection, Chloe saw the hideous stranger move, slowly lifting her head up and bringing it millimetres away from Chloe's, who suddenly felt an even more intense cold radiate from the space next to her. The woman's head turned from Chloe, towards the reflection in the glass cabinet, and their gazes locked.

It was only then that Chloe was finally able to gain control of her body and cry out in absolute fear. She whipped her head around, expecting to see that horrible sight directly before her. But she did not.

Sarah sat upright in her bed, hair a mess and eyes drowsy.

'What... what the fuck?!' was all she managed to say.

However, Chloe couldn't concentrate on her sister at the moment, and she simply stared ahead of her, at where that horrible woman *should* have been.

But there was nothing.

She quickly turned back to look at the reflection again. But there was no woman.

The only reflections in the glass now were of Chloe and her sister.

'Chloe?' Sarah asked in a groggy voice, squinting through tired and confused eyes. 'What is it? Did you just scream?'

Chloe was unable to answer. Fear had resumed its grip on her voice, and she was shaking uncontrollably. She turned back to Sarah, whose face became a picture of concern.

'Sis?' she asked. All Chloe could do was break down and cry.

19

SARAH'S MIND WAS REELING.

Upon opening her eyes, she'd spotted Chloe sitting on the bed. Her sister had a look of fear on her face as tears rolled down her cheeks.

So, naturally, panic flooded through Sarah, too.

Something's wrong. Is Emma okay?

But that worry was mixed in with grogginess and confusion at having been woken so abruptly. A portion of her mind still swam in her dreams, and she still heard the echoes of that horrible voice.

Dede!

Soon, however, she was able to fully focus, and she sat up on the bed, taking hold of her sister's hands.

'What is it?' Sarah quickly asked, trying to keep calm.

Chloe's eyes turned and fell on Sarah. Her breathing was quick and ragged. 'I... I...' but she was unable to continue.

That did nothing to ease Sarah's rising panic. She had never seen her sister like this before, which meant that whatever had happened was serious. Sarah brought Chloe close and hugged her, hoping to calm her enough for her to explain what had happened.

'It... it can't have been real,' Chloe whispered.

'What?' Sarah asked. 'What can't have been real?'

It took Chloe a few moments to compose herself enough to speak, and she cast Sarah a desperate look. 'Please tell me you'll believe me.'

That caught Sarah off guard. 'Of course I will,' she quickly replied, surprised Chloe would even have to ask. There wasn't a thing in the world Sarah wouldn't believe her sister about—she trusted Chloe completely.

Then, Chloe told Sarah what had happened: about waking in the night, coming into Sarah's room, and seeing a strange woman crouched over her.

Sarah paused, unsure how to reply.

As it turned out, for the first time in her life, she *didn't* believe her sister. Well, perhaps that wasn't true; she didn't doubt Chloe believed what she was saying, but that didn't mean it was factually correct.

Because what she was saying was physically impossible. People didn't just vanish into thin air. Could it be possible that the altercation with David Ritter was simply playing on Chloe's mind and caused her to have a very life-like dream?

Sarah considered her next words carefully, not wanting to hurt or offend her sister, who was clearly upset.

'Wow, that's... unreal. Are you okay?'

Chloe shrugged. She had stopped sobbing, but was still visibly shivering. 'I just don't know what to make of it. It seemed so real. But it can't have been... can it?'

A wave of relief washed over Sarah. Sanity and reason, it appeared, had taken hold. Maybe she didn't have to hurt Chloe by dismissing her story. Chloe was already questioning the whole thing on her own.

'Well, no,' Sarah replied. 'But that's a good thing, because I *really* don't want some creepy ghost-woman watching me sleep, thank you.'

Chloe offered a small smile.

Progress.

'I guess not,' she said. 'Guess I'm just losing my mind.'

'Nah, you're just stressed. There's a lot going on, and this isn't exactly a normal situation we're in, is it?'

'True,' Chloe replied. 'To be honest, I've felt a little on edge here since that night a while back...'

'Ah, when the weirdo came a-knocking?'

Chloe nodded.

And it started to all make sense now: the pressure Chloe was putting on herself to make Perron Manor work for them all, the work involved in refurbishing it, Andrew not being a team player at first, the study of the Devil upstairs, David Ritter's ramblings and warnings, and the fright they both had a little over a month ago... how could it all *not* affect her?

A stressed mind could very easily play tricks on its host. Sarah was well aware of that. In the months after Tania's death, she'd woken up in the night more than once only to see her friend at the end of her bed, yelling, *'Your fault!'* before exploding into a sea of crimson mist. But Sarah knew it was nothing more than a guilty vision left over from her subconscious mind.

Perhaps it was the same with Chloe.

Sarah then relayed the story of seeing Tania—something she had *never* shared with anyone before—to Chloe. It wasn't something she wanted to do, but felt it might help provide clarity and perspective.

'Shit, Sarah,' Chloe said. 'I had no idea you were going through that. I mean, I know you and Tania were close, but I didn't know you felt so guilty about it. It wasn't your fault, though.'

Sarah took a moment. 'But it was.'

'What do you mean?'

'She was on point, and stepped on a mine. That was supposed to have been me. But I... something just felt *wrong* about the whole day. I hesitated after being selected, resisted even... I've never done that before in my life. Following an order was never an issue for me, dangerous or not. So, Tania volunteered to help me out. I didn't want her to, but...'

'Jesus,' Chloe uttered.

Sarah nodded. 'Yeah.'

'Why didn't you tell me that before?'

Sarah looked away and twisted up her mouth. 'Dunno. Haven't really told anyone about it. I'm not exactly proud of killing my best friend.'

'That isn't what happened!' Chloe stated firmly. 'It was a horrible situation, but it wasn't your fault. That's pretty clear to me.'

'It's hard to see it that way, Chloe.'

'But it's the facts, regardless of how it looks to you. It wasn't your fault, Sis.'

Sarah waved a hand dismissively, 'Anyway, it doesn't matter. I just wanted you to realise that, just because I saw her doesn't mean she was really there. The mind can be a funny thing, and it can fuck you up if you let it.'

'And make you believe things that aren't really true,' Chloe added. 'Maybe we both need to remember that.'

'Maybe,' Sarah said, though she knew the guilt over Tania would never go away. Nor should it.

20

'You sure you want to go up there?' Sarah asked, and Chloe nodded.

After how foolish Chloe had been the previous night, she felt like she needed to prove to herself there was nothing odd about the house.

Well, that wasn't the best way to put it, because there was plenty *odd* about Perron Manor. The room they were in was a prime example.

But she needed to convince herself that there was nothing more to it than that.

Sarah had mentioned that she wanted to go back up to the study, so Chloe had insisted she go as well, which was clearly a pleasant surprise to her sister.

Emma had been put down for her mid-morning nap, so Chloe, Sarah, and Andrew ventured up to the top floor.

They stood in the previously hidden section of hallway, with its discoloured wallpaper, dusty floors, and dark surroundings. This time, Andrew had come prepared, and set about replacing the old bulbs in the antiquated light fittings. After trying a switch, the darkness was washed away.

'Let there be light,' he said, waving his arm in a sweeping gesture.

'You're such a nerd,' Sarah said to him.

'A nerd who lit the way,' he retorted. 'These bulbs should work in the study as well, so we can finally get a good look at what we're dealing with.'

'Where do we even start with all of that stuff?' Chloe asked. 'Do we just throw it all out?'

'Hell no!' Andrew shot back. 'We don't know what's in there. Some of it may be valuable. Hell, the least we should do is donate it all to a museum or something.'

'First, we have to see what's there,' Sarah reasoned. 'It might all be junk.'

Chloe and Andrew both nodded in agreement, and they once again entered the bizarre study.

Andrew set about his task of replacing the bulbs, and was aided by the torchlight from Chloe's phone. There were four wall fixtures to replace, and two in the ceiling.

Once done, he flicked the switch and—just as it had with the hallway outside—dull light illuminated the area.

The first thing Chloe noticed again was that damn symbol on the floor, and the dark stain within.

Sarah was looking at it as well. '*That*,' she said while pointing, 'is fucking ridiculous.'

'It is a little... hokey,' Andrew agreed, clearly struggling to find the right word.

With more light at their disposal, Chloe could easily make out more of her surroundings, and was quick to move her attention away from the pentagram on the floor.

With more light, it was easier to see the wallpaper now, and

Chloe could now make out the odd, faded pattern of intermingling burgundies and creams, which actually meshed rather well with the dark oak panelling below it. However, all the colours still lent the room an overbearing and oppressive feel, only exacerbated by the amount of junk crammed in here.

The bookshelves were overflowing with old-looking tomes, all packed into any available space. Piles of cardboard boxes seemed to have been dumped haphazardly on the floor, and the display cases were laid out without any real thought or form.

It wasn't a space to showcase the items it held, and was obviously just a storage area.

However, one thing seemed to have been given both respect and room: the glass-topped, waist-high display cabinet Sarah had seen during their last visit. It drew her attention again now, and she stood before it, gazing through the glass.

Chloe walked and joined her sister in peering at the thick, ancient-looking book that lay on the red, cushioned base inside the cabinet. The gold title of the book, set against the black leather, read: *Ianua Diaboli.*

Chloe had no idea what that meant, and really didn't want to know. She watched as Sarah traced a finger down the glass lid that protected the book. Her eyes had a longing expression in them, which Chloe found odd.

'Piqued your interest, has it?' she asked.

Sarah blinked, then turned to her sister and her eyes slowly regained focus. 'I guess. Just looks interesting.'

Sarah had a point.

There were strange markings—all set within small, concentric circles—in each corner of the front cover. And while most of the leather looked aged and cracked, these golden symbols and the small areas around them somehow appeared to be pristine.

One of the markings was an eight-pointed star, and another a simple cross. The lower left was a triangle which had another inverted triangle set within it, and the final symbol, in the bottom right, resembled the eight lines on a compass, all pointing off to their respective directions.

Close to the book they were inspecting sat a beautiful, old-style mahogany writing desk. There was a large, brown-leather ledger upon it, and though it still looked older than Chloe, it could well have been the youngest item in the room. An elegant fountain pen was slotted into a metallic base next to it.

Chloe took a step towards the desk, but stopped as Andrew spoke up.

'So... should I state the obvious?'

Both girls turned to look at him. 'Which is?' Sarah asked.

'1982? I mean, look at this place. Pentagram on the ground, with what is quite clearly blood in it, and then items that are obviously occult in nature. I mean, Aleister Crowley would have been in his element here. Wasn't there a theory that what happened back then was some kind of cult suicide or something?'

'*One* of the theories,' Chloe said, having heard it before. 'But I don't remember the guests here being part of a cult.'

'Maybe they just hid it well. Or maybe someone went off on a rampage, fuelled by stuff like this,' he said, and cast an arm about the room.

Then Sarah threw in something else. 'What about Vincent? If that is true, do you think he was involved?'

Chloe shook her head.

Her memories of the man were limited, but their uncle had always seemed nice and genuine as far as she could recall. However, there was another person back then whose impression upon Chloe had been a little... darker. 'Maybe the owner, if anyone,' she said. 'Marcus Blackwater. He committed suicide that night, so it's a possibility, I suppose.'

'That's a lot of people to kill on your own, though,' Andrew replied.

'It doesn't matter,' Chloe snapped, feeling agitated. 'The police looked into it all, and it was up to them to figure out what happened. It's not our problem.' She then looked at the stain within the pentagram. 'They could have cleaned up the blood, though,' she added.

'Not surprised they left it,' Andrew said. 'Especially back then. Once they were finished with the house, I can imagine it was up to the owners to clean everything up.'

'Vincent inherited the house,' Sarah added. 'So he just left it all like this all these years?'

'I'd guess that he was the one who locked this area up, too,' Andrew said.

'Maybe he wanted to just forget about it all,' Chloe offered. 'I can certainly understand wanting to ignore it. Regardless, it doesn't matter anymore. We can clean it up now, and scrub it all away from history.'

'Agreed,' Sarah said.

Andrew nodded as well.

'So,' Chloe began, 'how do we start? Just sorting through all of this is going to take a *lot* of time. Do we put the rest of the house on hold until it's done?'

'I don't think we should,' Sarah replied. 'We can spend a little bit of time each day just working through it, I guess. Slow and steady, when we have any spare time. Start with the smaller stuff, and get it all boxed away, then stack it with the things that are already packed.' She then pointed towards the piles of cardboard boxes.

'Which is fine,' Andrew cut in, 'but wouldn't it be wise to get someone in to have a look at it all first? Just to see what the hell we're dealing with, and if any of it is valuable?'

'Do you know anyone who deals in this kind of thing?' Chloe asked.

'Hell no,' he replied. 'But I do know my way around the internet. I'm sure we could find someone.'

Chloe and Sarah cast a look at each other. Andrew had a point.

'Fair enough,' she said. 'We can pack away what we can for now, I guess, and get someone here to look through everything. But... Andrew?'

'Yeah?'

'Can you get someone here quickly? I'd like this stuff gone as soon as possible.'

Andrew nodded. 'No problem. In fact, I'll start looking today and try and have someone at least lined up before I go away.' Andrew gave Chloe a kiss on the cheek and walked from the room, shouting back, 'I'll be in my office.'

He was due to leave again in two days, heading up to Scotland this time.

Once he was gone, a dull clicking sound caused Chloe to turn around. She saw that Sarah had unlocked the display cabinet she had been looking at.

'What are you doing?' Chloe asked.

'Just having a look,' Sarah replied, and once again had the same longing look in her eyes. With the glass barrier released, she was able to run a finger over the leather cover of the book and trace around the title.

But Chloe didn't see the appeal. It was just an old book.

Sarah opened it and began to carefully leaf through the yellowed, fragile-looking pages. The handwriting within was written in block columns; the penmanship was extremely neat, with elegant curves.

And not a single word in English that Chloe could see.

On some pages were detailed sketches of things she could have done without seeing.

There were diagrams of the human form, such as the flesh, the skeleton, the muscle, even certain organs. In addition, inked on the pages were a plethora of other occult-looking symbols, along with drawings of things that appeared to be... inhuman.

Terrible things, clearly born from a terrible mind.

Sarah stopped flicking through the pages close to the centre, and then stared at the foreign text on the page. There seemed to be a title at the top: *Impius Sanguis.*

To Chloe, there didn't appear to be anything special about this section of the book, at least compared to some of the others.

'Something interesting, Sis?' Chloe asked.

'Huh?' Sarah responded without looking up. 'No... just...' Her voice sounded distant.

Chloe clicked her fingers before Sarah's face, causing Sarah to blink quickly and shake her head. She looked like she'd been pulled from a nap.

'What?' Sarah eventually asked.

'I was asking why you found this'—Chloe pointed to the words on the page before them—'so interesting.'

Sarah glanced down, then gave a confused look. 'I don't. I can't even read it.'

'Then why... Forget it,' Chloe said, rolling her eyes. 'Come on, we can make a start on this another day.'

'Okay,' Sarah agreed, but didn't move away from the book.

While it was an interesting artefact, Chloe wanted to

know why it had beguiled Sarah so much. She had an idea to quickly flick to the back and see if there was any information about the writer—though even if there was, she doubted she'd be able to read what was there. She moved next to Sarah and took hold of the book herself.

After turning through to the rear pages, she saw the last section was titled: *Claude Ianua*. It was similar to the other passages, and had accompanying sketches as well. One was of a mirror, and one of what seemed to be hideous reflections on a liquid surface. But, beyond that, nothing. The book just seemed to end abruptly.

With a shake of her head, Chloe heaved the full thing shut. She then closed the glass lid and turned the small key to the front of the cabinet, locking it once again.

Sarah followed Chloe from the room, though Chloe noticed her sister glance back once more as they left.

21

2 DAYS LATER...

'I could have just come on my own,' Chloe said, dropping the carton of baby tomatoes she held into the shopping trolley.

'Well, I can't just leave you to do the grocery shopping all the time, can I?' Sarah responded. 'Seems a bit lazy. Plus, I wanted to get out of the house for a little bit.'

The supermarket was large, which was surprising for a small town like Alnmouth. The aisles inside were packed with goods, and the trolley Chloe pushed squeaked across the laminate flooring underfoot. The high ceiling above them consisted of corrugated metal sheeting and exposed steel purlins.

Emma sat in the built-in child's seat at the rear of the trolley, happily looking through one of her sturdy board-books, one about a dog who had gone missing just before dinnertime. As they passed an elderly man, who walked on his own, Emma pointed at him.

'Man!'

Chloe gave the old man an apologetic smile, but he just

chuckled and gave Chloe a friendly wave. The girls moved on, browsing the isles.

For weeks, Chloe had taken it upon herself to fulfil the weekly task of shopping, but today Sarah had been keen to come along as well.

And Chloe was quick to notice that her sister looked tired.

'Still not sleeping too well?' she asked.

Sarah shook her head. 'Not really. It's getting a little worse now, to be honest. It seems like I'm waking up every single night.'

'Always at the same time?'

'Yup, roughly between three and four in the morning.'

'Well, don't take this the wrong way but... why don't you try speaking to someone?'

Sarah picked up a packet of chocolate bars and looked them over. 'What do you mean?' she asked before setting the chocolate back.

'Well, isn't not sleeping a symptom of going through some kind of trauma?' Chloe wasn't a psychologist, but it certainly sounded right to her.

Sarah whipped her head around and frowned. 'Dealing with trauma? What the hell are you talking about?'

'You know what I mean,' Chloe replied. 'What happened with Tania. Maybe something isn't sitting right, and talking about it could help.'

'I don't think so,' Sarah stated dismissively. 'I'm fine.'

'Fair enough,' Chloe said, deciding to drop it. For now. But she knew Sarah was not *fine*.

The two women then moved on to the frozen section, and the air around them dropped in temperature. Chloe was picking through the frozen meats when she heard a jingling tone emit from her phone.

Sarah's too.

It was the camera system they had installed at the house. Detecting movement was a regular occurrence, and nine-times-out-of-ten, it was a false alarm, set off by God-knows-what.

Both girls pulled out their phones and flicked on the live-feed application, which displayed the full-colour stream from the activated camera. It was from the rear door, and looked out over the courtyard of Perron Manor.

'Nothing,' Sarah said. 'I swear to God, that thing is so sensitive the fucking light from the sun could set it off.'

And that was true enough. They'd had an engineer check the system over, but all he'd said was that it was configured correctly. But the amount of notifications they were receiving, which showed nothing of interest, had definitely worn on them.

Only this time, Chloe spotted something that her sister had not. In the distance, standing close to a large hedge, was the form of a person peeking out.

It was little more than a dark mass, but Chloe was able to see the rough shape of a head and a body, which was covered in a thick-looking material. She felt herself seize up.

'Who the hell is *that*?' Chloe asked, showing her phone screen to Sarah and pointing to the figure. Sarah frowned, then looked to her own phone.

'Oh shit, I missed that.'

The coldness around Chloe seemed to grow heavier at the sight of this stranger and her thoughts ran back to the night they had been harassed by someone knocking on their door and running away.

Chloe hit the record button on the streaming application, so they at least had a record of what they were seeing.

'Is he just... covered in shadow or something?' Chloe

asked, feeling an ominous sense of panic start to emerge, like grass-shoots breaking through the soil above.

'Looks like it,' Sarah confirmed, though she sounded less than convinced. Chloe understood why: there didn't seem to be any other shadows near him. 'And it's definitely a person?'

'I... I think so,' Chloe said, but started to doubt herself. 'Can't be certain, since he's standing so far back. Could be a trick of the camera. Maybe.'

Sarah then clicked her touch screen, and cycled to the feature that allowed her to transmit her voice out of a speaker near the camera.

'Excuse me,' she said into the phone, 'care to tell us who you are?'

The girls stared at their respective phones, but the person—if it truly *was* a person—made no movement at all. They just continued to stare, and Chloe got the distinct impression the stranger was looking directly at *them* through the camera, like it knew they were there.

'We should call the police,' she stated.

'But we don't even know if anyone is actually standing there. It's kinda hard to make out.'

'Better safe than sorry,' Chloe stated, remembering the last time they'd needed officers there. She had regretted not calling sooner.

She clicked off the feed, knowing Sarah still had hers going, and made the phone call. Once connected, Chloe started to relay what was happening to the call handler. Sarah nudged Chloe and showed her the phone screen, which was still displaying the feed but with no sign of the shadowy stranger anymore.

Where is he? Chloe mouthed.

Sarah shrugged and whispered, 'Just vanished. I looked back at my phone and he'd gone.'

Frustration rippled through Chloe, but she carried on with the call, still wanting the police to get over to the house and check everything out. The woman she spoke to confirmed that a squad car would head over as soon as possible.

'We better get back,' Chloe said once she had ended the call. 'And meet them there.'

'Fair enough,' Sarah said, but pointed at the trolley full of food. 'Do we pay first?'

'No time, we should just leave it. Come on, let's go.'

Chloe drove them back to the house as quickly as she could without breaking the speed limit. She was certain the person from the video feed was the same one who had tormented her and her sister.

And she wanted the fucker caught. No more of this nonsense. Whoever this freak was, he would *not* scare them out of their home.

However, she couldn't deny how strange it had been that, the longer they looked at the image on the feed, the more the visitor seemed to almost dissipate. She started to question if he had even been there in the first place.

The police arrived at Perron Manor only moments after Chloe and Sarah, and the squad car followed the sisters down the long driveway to the house. They all disembarked, and Chloe recognised one of the two officers as the female policewoman who had attended last time.

The other officer was someone different this time: a short, clean-shaven man, with broad shoulders and thick frame.

'Mrs. Pearson,' PC Taylor said. 'I understand you have another unwelcome visitor.'

'Yes,' Chloe confirmed. 'We have a camera system installed now, and while we were out we saw someone out back on the video stream.'

The policewoman nodded. 'Now, am I correct in understanding the house is locked, and there should be no one inside?'

'That's right,' Chloe said.

'Okay, we'll check it out.' She then gestured to her partner. 'This is PC Walters. I'd like you two to get back in your car while the two of us have a look around the grounds.'

Chloe didn't particularly want to retreat back into her vehicle, and would have rather accompanied the two officers on their walk-around. She knew the police would never agree to that, though, so she and Sarah did as instructed.

Once they were back inside the SUV, they sat in wait.

'Should we show them the footage?' Chloe asked.

Sarah paused. 'Honestly, I'm not sure. It isn't exactly clear cut. They could say it's nothing, and I'd rather they kept taking us seriously, just in case this happens again.'

It was a fair point, so Chloe decided to keep the recording to themselves for now.

They waited for about fifteen minutes before the two police officers emerged from the other side of the house. Chloe could tell by the expressions on their faces that the officers had found nothing of note.

PC Taylor, on her approach to the car, shook her head, confirming Chloe's gut feeling. Chloe and Sarah disembarked.

'All clear,' PC Taylor said. 'We didn't find anything out of the ordinary.

'To be expected,' Sarah added. 'They probably ran when they heard the cars approach.'

The police officer nodded in agreement. 'Yeah, if not

before that. There were no signs of a break-in or forced entry, either. Obviously, you should take a good look around inside to make sure nothing has been taken. We can stay and help with that if you want?'

'You don't need to do that,' Chloe said, feeling her frustrations grow. She wasn't frustrated at the police, of course, but at whoever was hounding them like this. 'They didn't get inside. The alarm would have gone off.'

PC Taylor nodded, then paused for a moment before speaking. 'Look, I know this is an annoyance for you, given this is the second time I've been up here, but like I said before, stay vigilant. Call us if you need to. Don't let people like this scare you.'

'Oh, don't worry,' Chloe said, 'I'm past being scared now. Just angry.'

'Well, in that case, also remember not to do anything stupid. Let us handle what we need to. Don't go and get yourself in trouble, understand?'

Chloe nodded. 'Understood.'

Soon after, the officers left Chloe and Sarah alone again, and the two sisters—along with Emma—went inside. As they did, Chloe tried to keep a lid on her bubbling anger. After heading over to the kitchen, she started to make herself a cup of tea, and a coffee for Sarah, but set the cups down so hard on the kitchen countertop as to almost shear off the handles.

'It's okay,' Sarah said. 'I'm angry too. And that's good. Better to be angry than to be scared. But… just make sure it's channelled correctly. Otherwise…'

'Otherwise what?' Chloe asked.

'Otherwise you may end up breaking my favourite mug, and then I'd have to give you a beating,' Sarah responded with a grin. Chloe smiled. Sarah went on, 'And you'll drive yourself crazy. I'm willing to bet our little visitor is just someone obsessed with the house and its history. When we catch him, and we will, I'll make it clear to him that he isn't welcome here. And I guarantee he won't come back then.'

Chloe frowned at her sister. 'Didn't you hear what the policewoman said about not doing anything stupid?'

Sarah smiled. 'I won't do anything that gets us in trouble. But he won't bother us again, I promise you that.'

Chloe finished making the drinks and took a sip of her hot, bitter tea. 'You know,' she said, handing Sarah her drink, 'we keep referring to our visitor as a *he*. Could be a woman, for all we know.'

'I guess it's possible,' Sarah replied, 'but not likely. It tends to be men who play the obsessive stalker card.'

'Fair enough,' Chloe replied. Her mind quickly jumped back to the thing she had seen in Sarah's room a few days ago, the thing that had been crouched over her sister. That was a woman...

And that *was all in your head,* Chloe scolded herself. *Enough!*

Sarah let out a yawn and stretched her arms above her head. Chloe noticed just how tired her sister looked, with purple patches beneath sleepy eyes.

'Go take a nap,' Chloe offered.

'No, I'm not a napping person. I'll sleep tonight. The coffee will get me through.'

Chloe knew it was pointless trying to persuade Sarah to do something she didn't want to, so she left it.

Instead, she took out her phone and played back the footage from earlier, which showed the shadowy stranger standing outside in the courtyard. Chloe wanted to see the exact moment he disappeared. Then, a notion occurred to her.

'I'm going to check something,' she said, and walked from the room. Sarah followed, and they moved out to the great hall, then over to the glazed rear doors, which gave a clear view out over the courtyard.

Chloe played back the recording.

The stream showed the figure. Try as she might, however, Chloe could not make out any detail beyond a dark mass that was quite obviously humanoid in its shape. It was also tall, especially when actually looking at the hedge outside, which helped put things into perspective.

'Big guy,' said Chloe.

'Yup,' Sarah agreed.

'Still think you can put him in his place?'

Sarah just nodded confidently. 'It doesn't matter how tall a man is, if he gets kicked in the balls, he's going down.'

They continued to watch the footage, with the stranger not moving an inch. Chloe eventually speeded up the play-back a little, but even then there was no jerking or flickering from the black mass, no swaying of any kind, as would be natural from a person standing for so long.

Eventually, Chloe reached the section where the mass disappeared. She rewound, then watched it back in real-time twice more.

'That's weird,' Sarah said, stating out loud what Chloe was thinking.

The visitor on the footage didn't step out of the shot, nor did he just blink away. Over the course of several frames, the shadows around the mass seemed to fully consume it, then melt away into the surroundings.

'What the fuck!' Chloe exclaimed. 'That makes no sense.'

'Maybe it wasn't a person after all?' Sarah offered. 'Just a shadow that kind of disappeared as the sun moved, or maybe as some clouds had passed over?'

Chloe turned to her sister, with a look of scepticism.

Sarah shrugged. 'Do you have any other explanation?'

Chloe did not.

---

22

3 Days Later...

'Big job, but high profile,' Oliver Tripp said to Steve Davis, one of the plumbers he'd drafted in to help with the project. They stood outside of Perron Manor, where they were joined by the other three that would be helping, as well as the client, Andrew Shaw.

'Won't argue that,' Steve replied. 'Everyone around here knows this place. As kids, we used to come up here and dare each other to go inside.'

'Did any of you ever do it?' Andrew asked.

Steve—a painfully thin man in his mid-fifties with thin red hair and speckles of stubble—shook his head as he took a drag from the roll-up cigarette between his thin, chapped lips. 'Nope. And that was before what happened in '82,' he said. 'We didn't come up here at all after that. Place always gave me the creeps... no offence.'

'None taken,' Andrew replied with a smile. 'You should try living here.'

As much as Oliver was happy his client was being friendly with the help he had pulled together, he didn't like the way the conversation was going. Maybe it was natural for a place like Perron Manor, but he wanted the whole thing to be a positive experience for the family that lived here. Given the start date had slipped a little due to design complications, Oliver now aimed to exceed all expectations and didn't want anything else to sour the service he offered. He worried Steve's wandering mouth could do just that.

'Forget all that,' Oliver said. 'I think we can agree we're all too old for ghost stories, anyway. Some of us more than others, eh, Steve?' Oliver prodded Steve in the ribs before turning back to the house. 'First, we get started on the strip-out. Careful as we go, of course. All the iron we rip out goes in that skip.' He pointed to the large, blue metal container that had been placed on the gravel drive. 'Everything else, in the other one.' The other was a faded yellow container, roughly the same size as the first.

One of the ways Oliver was able to get his price low was by knowing he could sell all the waste iron from the pipework, radiators, and the furnace itself. Given the size of the house, he anticipated there would be a lot of metal, and it was something he could fetch a good amount of money for when weighing in at the scrapyard. The client was well aware of this, and the man seemed too astute to be taken advantage of—not that Oliver would ever try. Mr. Shaw had actually been impressed at Oliver's ingenuity in pricing and finding a way to drive his cost down.

'Okay, then,' Andrew said. 'I'm taking the girls out for a little while today. We're going to pick up a few portable hot water tanks, then go to the park to spend a bit of time outside. Should only be a few hours, but I figure it'll give you guys some time and space to get started without us getting in your way.'

'Perfect,' Oliver said. 'Though you don't need to worry,

we'll be able to work around your family. We'd just need to coordinate when we need access to certain rooms.'

'We can work with that,' Andrew said. 'But you get a few hours' free rein, which should help anyway. And remember what I said about that room up on the top floor.'

Oliver nodded. 'Don't worry, we won't need to be in there today. Though we probably will need access in a couple of days to stay on schedule.'

'That's fine,' Andrew stated. 'There's just a *lot* to get through in there.'

'Left in a bit of a state, was it?' Oliver asked, and received a chuckle in response.

'Like you wouldn't believe.'

Less than twenty minutes later, the family had left, and Oliver and his team were alone at the house.

The team Oliver had gathered were all self-employed, but people he knew and trusted enough to bring on board.

There was Steve, who had been doing this longer than Oliver had, even working on a few commercial-sized projects such as hotels and care homes for larger contractors.

The other three were Cal Wilks, Ashton Mitford, and then the youngest among them, Art Steward.

All competent enough, but Oliver intended to watch them all as closely as possible, especially the more inexperienced Cal and Art, just to make sure there were no hiccups. While work had been steady recently, it hadn't exactly been booming. However, if the client here had the kind of connections in the construction industry that Oliver suspected he did, then who knows what kind of other opportunities the job could lead to.

First, though, he had to impress.

While gathered in the entrance lobby, Oliver gave out his instructions.

'Right, this morning is going to be a tour of the building so I can show you what we have ahead of us. The more you know of the house before diving in, the better prepared you'll be. So, we walk around and get the lay of the land. Okay?'

'Fair enough,' Steve said, taking a long drag from his cigarette before blowing out a cloud of yellowy-cream smoke. Oliver coughed.

'Put that stinking thing out before we start,' he said. 'We'll make our way down to the basement first, see the furnace, then work our way up.'

'What's the deal with the room upstairs?' asked Cal—a stocky, good-looking lad in his mid-thirties.

Oliver chuckled. 'Think the previous owner left something of a mess up there, from what I understand. Lot of junk that needs sorting through. We can ignore it for now; the client has it locked up anyway.'

Oliver had already seen the space, and could attest that it *did* need clearing out, but he wouldn't necessarily call it 'junk,' despite what he'd said to the others. Some of it looked potentially valuable, if a little macabre. He knew the client intended to catalogue it all and get it checked out before any of it was removed. Apparently, someone was coming out the next day to look it over.

But he had labelled it all as junk merely to downplay any interest the lads might have taken in it. Though he trusted them, you could never be too careful. And he didn't want anyone wandering off to rifle someone else's belongings. Even if the area had been locked off by the client, wandering hands could always find a way.

Oliver led his band of merry men through the side corridor, which was devoid of any windows or natural light, and into the great hall.

'Hell of a place,' Steve said. 'Like something off one of them Victorian shows the wife watches on T.V.'

'Victorian shows?' asked Art.

'Yeah, where they all prance around like lords and ladies in big houses, dressed in fancy suits and gowns. You know the type of stuff.'

'Can't say I watch it,' Art replied with a grin.

'Me either,' Steve was quick to clarify. 'Like I said, the wife does.'

'Sure, sure,' Cal added with a smirk. 'You just happen to always be there while she's watching it, huh?'

'Ah fuck off, the pair of you,' Steve shot back, shaking his head.

'This way,' Oliver said, keeping the focus on the job at hand. He led them through a side door and into a small area where stone steps ran down into the dark basement below.

'No lights?' Art asked.

Now it was Steve's turn to smirk. 'Are ya' scared, lad?'

'No!' Art shot back. 'Just don't want to tumble down there and break a leg.'

'Lights are at the bottom,' Oliver stated. 'Wait here.'

He then began to descend the steps, feeling the temperature drop as the darkness overcame him. The existing heating system had already been switched off, but houses like this were funny beasts. The thickness of the stone walls usually retained heat quite well, but they were a bitch to get warmed up in the first place. The ground-floor had actually felt relatively comfortable, but in walking down here, there was a noticeable dive in the temperature. He could also detect an ever-so-slight breeze, which was odd.

He reached the bottom and held out a hand, feeling

along the stonework wall beside him while he searched out the light switch.

A quick skittering noise from deep within the black void drew his attention, one that sounded heavy but quick on the stone floor. Oliver shuddered.

That sounded like a big fucking rat!

And as much as normal creepy-crawlies didn't bother him, rats were different. Horrible, disease-ridden things.

His fingers eventually found the metallic fixture and Oliver flicked the switch. There was a quick strobe effect as the lights in the basement slowly flickered to life, causing a dancing of shadows that confused Oliver, giving the impression of movement close to the furnace.

As if something had ducked behind it.

But he knew it was just a trick of the brain as his eyes adjusted. Within moments, the bulbs settled into a steady stream of light, and they cast a dirty orange hue over the area.

Oliver could see the form of the old cells, as well as block pillars used to support the floor above. The furnace was at the far end of the space, and Oliver could also make out the piles of coal and wood that were used to fuel it.

The sound of footsteps behind him indicated the others had started their descent, and soon the group of five spread out into the large area, all eyes on the archaic metal furnace.

'Jesus,' Steve said, running a hand over his head. 'Never seen anything like that before. How old is it?'

'Who the hell knows,' Oliver replied.

'Going to take some heaving out of here, though.'

'It will, but I figure we strip it down first and take it out in chunks.'

'We got time for that?' Steve asked.

Oliver nodded. 'I allowed a few days for it.'

Then Cal cut in. 'How are the clients going to live here with no heating and hot water for so long? Don't they have a little 'un?'

'There are fireplaces all over the house,' Oliver replied. 'So they're going old-school.'

'And the hot water?' Cal asked. 'How will they bathe?'

'He's getting a few portable hot water tanks. They'll fill them up, plug them in, and use them to heat up water. They'll do for bathing and washing up and the like for a little while.'

'So... slumming it,' Art said.

'For a little bit, I guess,' Oliver told him. 'Which is why we need to work as fast as we can.'

Oliver then gave the group a quick tour of the next floor up, then finally the top storey—at least, as much as they could get access to. By the time they were done, it was a little past midday.

'Everybody happy?' Oliver asked with a clap of his hands.

'It's a *lot* to strip out, Ollie,' Cal said with a frown. 'The pipework alone will probably be a nightmare. If we go over the agreed time, I'm gonna have to bill you extra, mate.'

Oliver gave a dismissive wave of the hand. 'It'll be fine. Besides, I can come in on weekends on my own to keep things moving. You don't worry about anything, just concentrate on doing a good job. If we do run over, I'll see you're looked after. So, I ask again... everybody happy?'

The crew looked to one another, each searching for guidance. It was Steve who finally nodded his consent.

'Aye, Ollie, we're all happy.'

'Good. You guys go eat your lunch. I'm gonna go down to the basement and figure out how to take the furnace apart.'

23

THE PUZZLE LOOKED solvable to Oliver.

He'd carefully inspected the furnace, and could certainly see areas where dismantling the unit could work. He also knew where to start.

Disconnecting the protruding pipework would be job number one, and then the heavy-looking top section could be unfastened and lifted off—a job that would likely take all of their combined strength. But, from there, it seemed like the metallic beast could be further stripped down, reducing it to handleable chunks.

Now he needed to figure out if the furnace should come out first, and then work up, or if it was best to disconnect the radiators and work back down. Given a good portion of the top floor was currently off-limits, that essentially made the decision for him.

Oliver had eaten his sandwiches while he planned out his approach, as having lunch on the go was normal for him. He wanted the lads to have more structure, and dedicated breaks, even if they hadn't truly gotten going yet. Though he was self-employed, and usually had no people working under him, Oliver knew that a well-fed and appro-priately rested workforce was a happy one. He'd learned that pretty quickly when working on building sites as a youth.

So, he gathered up his sandwich wrappers, and prepared to go up and brief the others.

The lights above him suddenly blinked out.

Great, Oliver thought to himself. Perhaps a power-surge had tripped the circuit board switches—the only explana-tion for all the lights down here going out, rather than a single bulb.

The lights then flickered again; they were still function-ing, apparently, but not at full power. There was a strobing effect that carried on for a few moments, quickly flashing the area in light before cutting it back to brief darkness, over and over again.

Then, a prolonged darkness once again settled in. Oliver could hear the buzz of electricity flowing above him, but for now the lights remained off, and he could see very little besides the glow from the light at the top of the steps.

At least he could follow that to make his way out.

'For the love of God,' he muttered, agitated. This was *not* the start he needed.

'*Help.*'

Oliver's body locked up, and he twisted his head.

It took him a few moments to realise that what he'd heard was a voice. Meek and quiet, almost wheezy, coming from a space ahead of him, over near the furnace.

But it couldn't have been.

His first thought was that perhaps one of the others had come down to mess with him, but none were particularly light on their feet, and Oliver was sure he'd have heard them descend the stone steps.

Or maybe he'd heard nothing at all, which was the more likely explanation.

Going mad, old man.

But the 'old man' soon heard it again, uttering a different word this time.

'*Please.*'

A foul odour then drifted over to him, one that vaguely reminded him of barbecued meat, though this had a sickly, sour tinge to it. Oliver then heard wheezed and ragged breathing off ahead. It was faint, but definitely there.

'*It... hurts. It... always... hurts.*'

'Who's there!' Oliver demanded. No response. 'Cal? Art?'

Still nothing.

There was a long sound of squeaking metal, like an old door swinging on its hinges. The only thing it could be, Oliver knew, was one of the doors on the front of the furnace.

He grabbed for his phone, which he could use to at least cast some light on the situation. However, he had been more panicked than he thought and snagged his thumb on his pocket while pulling his phone out. The device slipped from his grip and skittered off across the stone floor, into the black.

Shit!

There were a few more moments of silence, followed by a shuffling sound, and more of that sharp, ragged breathing. Oliver took a step back, feeling genuine fear start to course through him.

It has to be one of the lads. They've snuck down here to try and frighten me.

'Stop fucking around!' he yelled sternly. 'I'm serious, otherwise you're off the job. The lot of you!'

The voice returned, and though it still sounded pained,

like the act of speaking was a struggle, it had a more sinister, threatening tone to it. *'It'll... hurt... you... too.'*

There was another flicker of the lights. Just before he was again thrust into darkness, Oliver saw something struggling towards him, walking with stuttering and awkward movements, like a hideous marionette, and he would have screamed if his voice hadn't gotten lodged in his throat.

Its skin was a mesh of charred black areas that had crisped over, along with weeping and angry red flesh where open wounds bled freely.

Misshapen fingers were fused together, and some of the meat from the arm that had been reaching towards Oliver had been burnt away to the bone. Though Oliver was sure this... thing... was male, given its rough form and voice, there were no distinct sexual organs dangling between the legs; instead, there was just a melted and twisted mound of skin.

And then there was the head and face: mouth hanging loosely and pulled down to one side, the lips stripped away to reveal teeth and gums behind, and a single, sagging, milky eye. The other was missing, replaced by a congealed pocket of black flesh. In addition, there were no ears that Oliver could see, and only a few strands of hair in with the seared red and black skin of the scalp.

The lights then cut out once again.

'I'll... take... you... through... the... door,' it wheezed in the dark, and something approaching a cackle escaped it. *'Come... through... with... me.'* It laughed again.

Oliver let out a whimper and began to back up quickly, moving away from the shuffling thing and toward the faint glow of light from the steps. As he did, he felt his heel clip on a raised section of stone slab, and Oliver fell hard to the ground, hitting the back of his head against the hard surface.

He let out a grunt. The shuffling sound before him suddenly grew quicker, and the wheezing more frantic and excited. Suddenly, the thing was on him, and Oliver felt a searing pain around his wrist as a hard and scabby hand took hold of him.

A bellowing scream erupted from Oliver, one that had been building since he'd first laid eyes on... whatever the hell this was. The smell was now overwhelming, causing him to gag and heave.

'Ollie?' someone called out from the top of the stairs. 'You okay?' Even in his fear-stricken mind, as Oliver fought against the impossibility that lay on top of him, he was able to hear Steve call down to him.

'Help!' Oliver screamed desperately. 'Help me!'

He then heard multiple feet quickly thunder down the steps. And, as they did, the weight above him, as well as the smell and the horrible breathing, vanished. The lights blinked back on, and Steve and the others came into focus, all wearing looks of confusion and worry.

'What the hell is wrong?' Art asked. 'What happened?'

Oliver took a few moments, trying to get his breathing back into a regular rhythm and calm his erratic heart.

'Did... did you see it?' he asked.

'See what?' Steve questioned, raising an inquisitive eyebrow. The man's eyes then widened a little. 'What did you do to yer arm?'

Oliver looked down and saw the skin around his wrist was angry and red, like a surface-level burn.

'Tell me you saw it!' Oliver screamed, feeling a sudden burst of despair run through him.

However, it was clear as the group looked at each other

in puzzlement they had no idea what the hell he was talking about.

Oliver suddenly realised that they wouldn't believe him, anyway. They'd think he was nuts.

But it *had* happened!

He'd seen that burnt monster come at him. Smelled its stench. Felt its touch. And there was also physical proof of that—the angry welt across his wrist.

The house, he suddenly realised. *It's true.*

What happened to his uncle all those years ago wasn't just a crazy story.

'Calm down,' Steve said. 'Your eyes look like they're gonna pop out of your head. Just tell us what happened.'

'You might wanna pull yourself together as well,' Cal said, frowning. 'Mr. Shaw's car just pulled up, think the clients are home.'

Fuck the clients!

How could he work here now, after having seen and experienced *that*?

Oliver pulled himself up to his feet, and took a moment to himself, as his legs felt like jelly. He looked over to the furnace. One of the doors was now open, though he was certain it had been closed when he'd first come down.

'The hell with this!' he spat, then pushed Steve out of the way, grabbed his phone from the floor, and quickly ran up the steps.

∿

∿

∿

Andrew went around the back of the car and pulled open the boot, looking at the portable water tanks they had just bought. They sat beside a brand-new coffee machine Sarah had insisted on getting. The next few weeks were going to be rough, he knew, but worth it for the luxuries the new heating system would bring.

Movement from the doorway of the house caught his attention, and Andrew saw Oliver storm from the house with a wild-eyed look etched on his face.

Chloe, who had just lifted Emma from her car seat, turned to the engineer. 'Hi, Oliver, how are you getting on?'

But Andrew could tell from the man's quick pace, set jaw, and balled fists that something was definitely wrong. He seemed extremely agitated.

'I'm leaving,' Oliver stated through gritted teeth, and quickly strode over to his van and pulled open the door. The members of Oliver's crew appeared at the front door as well, looking just as perplexed as Andrew felt.

'Excuse me?' Andrew asked. 'And *where* are you going?'

'Away from here!' Oliver shouted, surprising Andrew. 'I'll not set foot in that blasted house again. Ever.' He then turned to his colleagues. 'You lot coming?'

'What do you mean you won't set foot inside?' Andrew asked, raising his own voice and taking a step forward. 'You're under contract.'

'Fuck your contract!'

Andrew stopped short and raised eyebrows in shock.

'Ollie, what the hell's going on?' Art asked. 'What about the job?'

'Job's off,' he replied as he got into the driver's seat of his vehicle. 'Now get in, or I'll leave you here.'

Andrew strode up to the van and put his hand on the open door, preventing Oliver from closing it.

'I think you owe me an explanation. If you don't finish what you've signed up for, you know I can sue, right?'

Oliver leaned over to him, and Andrew saw something in the man's eyes that was beyond mere agitation, or even anger. It was fear.

'Then fucking sue me,' came the snarled reply. Oliver shoved Andrew back and closed the door. He leaned out through the window. 'I'll get the skips picked up, but I'm not coming back. You do what you have to do. I don't care.' He then cast a worried look back to Perron Manor. 'I'm not going back.'

Eventually, Oliver managed to get his dumbfounded colleagues into the van as well, and he drove off, leaving Andrew confused and furious.

'Erm, what the hell just happened?' Sarah asked.

Andrew had no idea how to answer.

24

'FUCK!' Andrew snapped, and threw his mobile phone down onto the kitchen countertop.

'Still not picking up?' Sarah asked, feeling the anger radiate from him.

'No. What the hell's wrong with that man?'

'I don't know,' Chloe replied. 'I understand you're angry, but can we please stop the cursing in front of Emma.'

Andrew nodded, looking a touch embarrassed. 'Sorry. Won't happen again. It's just... I don't get it. He seemed over the moon when I gave him the job. And now he quits and doesn't even have the courtesy to tell us why?'

'But he's under contract,' Chloe said. 'You said so yourself. Isn't he bothered about being sued?'

Andrew shook his head and shrugged. 'No idea. Though, in fairness, the contract just protects both parties against losing money. Like if he wrecked the house, then he'd have to pay for it. Considering he didn't even start, and isn't asking for any money, we can't really claim anything. We could try, but I doubt it would lead anywhere.'

Sarah took a seat at the table next to Chloe, and started

to play peek-a-boo with Emma, who was toddling around the floor, dragging a toy trailer along behind her. After getting back into the house after the altercation with Oliver, they had again gravitated to the kitchen area, despite Perron Manor having a dedicated living room, a study that doubled as a snug, and even a library, which they had barely used since moving in.

The kitchen had become the hub for their activity during most daytime hours.

She was as baffled as the other two as to why their engineer had abandoned them, but it wasn't something Sarah was going to lose her cool over. Yes, it meant they were stuck with that bloody furnace for a while longer, but it was hardly the end of the world.

However, she knew Andrew wouldn't see it that way, as it was the principle of the matter for him.

After a little while of playing with Emma, Sarah got to her feet, and then unpacked her brand-new coffee machine. She set it on the countertop and plugged it in, happy with the purchase. It wasn't often she indulged on material goods, but when she saw this thing in the store, it seemed like a no-brainer.

Andrew was still bemoaning the situation to Chloe and Sarah was beginning to feel restless. So, she grabbed the key for upstairs from the utility drawer and left her sister and brother-in-law to debate their options going forward.

But what options were there, really? They just had to find someone else to do the work.

That was the end of it.

Rather than get involved, Sarah wanted to go back up to the study on the top floor and once again look at the treasures within.

They had boxed away a lot of the items up there, which

had been a unique experience, especially seeing Chloe's face when handling a liquid-filled bottle that also contained a cluster of rodent foetuses floating within. Most of the belongings upstairs were ready for the arrival of an antiques dealer Andrew had found online.

The book and its display case, however, had been left as they were.

Once on the top floor, Sarah unlocked the door to the corridor and entered the study. It still looked cluttered, even though many of the books had now been pulled from the shelves and boxed up. Many of the artefacts were left out as they had been, for fear of damage, so the whole room had the feeling of a job half-finished. Looking at some of the strange objects, Sarah couldn't help but feel a sense of wonderment, and part of her ached to know the actual age of the things around her.

In one cabinet, there were amulets, sigils, a dagger that looked to be made of bone, and rolls of parchment. One of the sigils had a rather demonic-looking face etched into its metallic form.

Whoever Andrew had found to come and look through all of this stuff was likely to have a field day. Or a heart attack, depending on their disposition.

Sarah had never been one to have an interest in the occult, but she couldn't deny the appeal of the treasures this room held, especially up close. But there was one thing in particular that intrigued her more than any other item.

Ianua Diaboli.

After turning the small key in the edge of the cabinet's frame, Sarah lifted the glass top, then took hold of the book and brought it up to her face. She could smell the aged leather, and felt its substantial weight in her hands.

Open it.

She set it back into its cradle, then slowly and carefully opened the cover to the first few pages. The writing scribed in black ink was beautiful, but unreadable to her. Even so, she got the sense that the words here held power, through great wisdom and knowledge. The desire to learn its secrets was hard to ignore.

Sarah worked through the pages, searching for something—though she had no idea what. It wasn't until she saw the heading of *Impius Sanguis,* midway through the book, that she stopped.

She stared at the unintelligible text. There was no reason these pages should have held her interest so, especially when compared to the others, and yet she could not get herself to look away. Sarah found herself mouthing the words as best she could as she read through the text.

Enim sanguis clavis est.

When she eventually did turn to another page, Sarah noticed that it didn't hold the same interest to her. Neither did the next one. That pattern continued as she leafed through the book, even if some on the surface should have looked more interesting. Indeed, a page with a sketch of something covered in shadow was startling to look at, but it still did not hold the same mystery and sway as *Impius Sanguis*. And, when she flicked to the back and saw the title of *Claude Ianua*, something close to revulsion overcame her. She looked away and quickly closed the book.

Strange.

Sarah then closed the cabinet lid again and continued to look around, slowly walking over to the old writing desk that held a thick ledger. The cover was plain except for symbols drawn onto the leather, similar to those on the cover of *Ianua Diaboli*. Sarah opened the ledger and saw handwriting on yellow, lined paper. This time, the writing was very much in English, though the penmanship left a little to be desired. The first page had only a few lines of text written on it, and seemed to be an introduction of sorts.

These transcriptions from Ianua Diaboli *are as accurate as I can make them, given the use of 'Old Latin' in with the more classical use of the language.*

While the original author of the book remains unknown, its purpose, and the purpose of the texts therein, are very clear. They all pertain to a very specific phenomenon that is able to exist in our world, one that is very relevant to Perron Manor.

This house is special.

It is, I believe, alive. And Ianua Diaboli *could very well be a way to harness what exists here, for those brave enough to do so.*

- A. Blackwater.

Sarah pondered the name. A. Blackwater? From what she understood, the previous owner before her uncle was a man named Marcus Blackwater, who died in 1982. Could he have had an unknown Christian name beginning with the letter 'A'? If not, then this was written by someone else.

Suddenly, Sarah realised she had a way to make sense of *Ianua Diaboli*. She looked back to the book in the case, and a pang of excitement sprang up in her.

The ledger is a book of transcriptions!

Sarah then quickly shook her head. *Why is this rubbish entrancing me so much?* It was interesting, sure, but to actually make her excited...

'You okay there, Sis?'

The sound of Chloe's voice startled Sarah, who jumped and let the cover of the ledger fall shut. 'Jesus,' she said, looking to her sister. 'You scared the hell out of me. Why are you sneaking around like that?'

'I was hardly sneaking,' Chloe replied. 'And I've been calling you as well. Are you deaf? And what were you grinning about?'

Sarah cocked her head. 'Grinning?'

'Yeah. When I came in here you were smiling like a madwoman, staring off into space. You feeling okay?'

That took Sarah by surprise. 'I'm fine,' she said after a few moments.

Chloe narrowed her eyes, before shrugging her shoulders. 'If you say so. We're going to order food in again tonight, so I thought I'd check what you wanted.'

'Anything,' Sarah replied. 'Something spicy.'

'Spicy works for me.'

'So... has Andrew calmed down yet?' Sarah asked.

Chloe smiled but shook her head. 'Not really. But it is what it is, I guess. Strange that Oliver just ran off like that, though. Andrew still can't reach him. Seems like we'll just have to look elsewhere.'

'Yeah. It'll get sorted out, no need to stress or panic about it.'

There were a few moments of silence. Then Chloe asked, 'Why do you think the engineer bolted?'

Sarah shrugged. *How am I supposed to know that?* 'God knows. You have any ideas?'

Chloe chewed the side of her mouth for a moment. 'Well, can you remember when we first met him? He mentioned that his uncle worked up here way back in the day.'

The story did ring a bell with Sarah. 'Sure.'

'Apparently, Oliver's uncle saw something that freaked him out, and he ran. And with Oliver running out the way he did... I don't know, it just seems a bit strange. Maybe history has repeated itself.'

'So you think Oliver saw something that scared him?'

'Well... possibly. I mean, doesn't it fit? He looked terrified. Something had spooked him enough to give up the job entirely.'

'I guess,' Sarah admitted. What Chloe was saying did kind of make sense, but Sarah didn't like where the line of thinking would take her sister. If Oliver had gotten himself spooked over nothing, then fine, but Sarah didn't want Chloe to go down a path of believing there was more to it.

The incident of waking to find Chloe trembling in Sarah's own room, swearing she had seen an old woman had not been forgotten.

'But if that's the case,' Sarah said, 'then he's an idiot. It's an old, creepy house, and he shouldn't have let himself get so paranoid over nothing.'

Sarah maintained strong eye contact with Chloe.

Thankfully, Chloe seemed to grasp what had gone unspoken. 'You're probably right,' she said, then turned. 'I'm going to go back down, I'll catch up with you in a little bit.'

'Wait up,' Sarah replied, walking over to Chloe. 'I'm finished up here anyway.'

25

'No!'

Chloe's eyes snapped open, and she gripped the sheets of her bed with tightly balled fists. Her breathing was rapid and shallow—she was almost panting. She then batted a hand to the side of her head but found only air. Chloe got the distinct impression something had been close to her head, whispering in her ear.

It was a dream. Just a dream!

Even so, her body was locked rigid, and it took a moment for Chloe's aching muscles to relax.

Just a dream...

And it had been a dream. Looking round, Chloe could clearly see that she was no longer downstairs in that dark, horrible basement anymore. She remembered the feeling of biting cold on her back, as well as the extreme heat that flowed over her front as she had stood in front of the raging furnace. Something she could not see had been holding her from behind: something ancient, strong, and malicious. It whispered things into her ear that she could not under-stand, and she could smell its foul breath. The flames and heat from the furnace before her, with its open doors, had seared her skin.

The walls around the basement were no longer stone, and had instead looked like a horrible meld of skin and flesh, smattered with roving eyeballs and mouths that puckered and moved.

And a tall, pale man had been standing next to her. He'd been dressed in old clothing and had an almost skeletal face that wore a sinister grin. Wide and manic eyes without lids had watched as he held a squirming and crying infant in his grip.

Emma.

He had been reciting nursery rhymes in mocking tones, enjoying the panic in both mother and child.

Then, as Chloe screamed in desperation, the evil old man had thrown her child into the fiery depths of the furnace.

It was just a dream!

Even so, the panic that surged through Chloe was still intense, and she felt tears born of rage, helplessness, and failure bubble from her eyes.

Then she heard a voice on the baby-monitor beside her.

'Round... and round... the garden.'

Chloe snapped her head around, but the image she saw was just of Emma sleeping peacefully. Safely.

Her mind swam, still reeling. Was the voice simply another lingering memory from the nightmare?

She then cast a glance to her other side, where Andrew snored lightly beside her. She quickly rolled from the bed and stood, the feeling of the cool air pleasant on her sweaty and sticky body. Dressed just in her light-blue silk nightie, Chloe quietly walked from her room and into Emma's. She needed to see her daughter with her own eyes, just to make sure her child was safe.

Though the room was a touch cold, and that horrible odour from the old heating system was faintly detectable, all else was as it should be inside of the child's bedroom.

The wave of relief that washed over Chloe was palpable. The emotions were so strong that she had to take a seat in the rocking chair, and put her head into her hands, letting the feelings run their course.

Just a dream.

After sitting in the dark for over ten minutes, just listening to Emma breathe, Chloe decided it was time to go back to bed and try to get some sleep. However, that seemed unlikely, considering how awake she now was thanks to the adrenaline that pumped through her.

She stood to her feet and took a breath. The house felt oppressive. Heavy. Smaller than it should, considering its size. In truth, for reasons she couldn't explain, it had started to gradually feel smaller day by day, ever since that night when she and Sarah had heard the banging on the door.

And despite what her sister had insisted, Chloe couldn't completely ignore the possibility that there was something wrong here. Things she had previously passed off as just being in her head now seemed entirely possible.

Especially in the dead of night, surrounded by nothing but shadows, all of which felt like they were watching her.

Chloe felt guilty about dragging her family out here and insisting that living in a place with a such a history could actually work.

Another breath.

Don't let your imagination run away with itself.

Despite how she currently felt, part of Chloe knew that, logically, Sarah was probably right. She just hoped things would seem different when the sun rose, and she could think things through in the warm light of day.

Chloe walked from Emma's room and gently closed the door behind her. After making her way back towards her own bedroom, Chloe stopped short, detecting movement from the other side of the long corridor opposite her door. She gasped, and the image of a naked woman slowly walking towards her sent a chill up her spine.

Just as she was about to scream, however, she focused on the woman. The scream settled, retracting back down her throat. Confusion now overshadowed the fear she had been feeling.

'Sarah?'

Her sister did not answer, just continued her slow and steady walk, eyes half shut.

She's sleepwalking! Chloe realised.

Sarah stopped midway along the hallway, held her position for a moment, then turned her head to the side. Her body followed, and Sarah then began to ascend the stairs up to the top storey of the house.

Chloe let out a long sigh. She had no idea Sarah was prone to sleepwalking, though she was glad the figure had only been her sister, not something else.

While Chloe had heard that you weren't supposed to wake someone who was sleepwalking, she didn't want to just let Sarah wander around naked and possibly hurt herself, so she decided to retrieve her sister and get her back to bed.

She padded her way to the bottom of the steps and got there just in time to see Sarah turn from the top and move further into the darkness. Chloe climbed the stairs as well, surprised at the increasing pace. When she reached the top, the door that was usually locked now hung open.

Wasn't that locked?

Chloe caught a glimpse of Sarah as she disappeared into the study that Chloe detested so much.

'Oh for the love of God,' she said with a sigh. Chloe really didn't want to go back in there so late at night.

Regardless, Chloe followed, and she found Sarah standing before the display case again, hands on its glass surface, staring at the book inside through half-closed eyelids.

'Sarah,' Chloe said quietly, using as soothing a tone as she could muster. She didn't want to startle her sister, but still aimed to get her out of here quickly. She walked over to Sarah and took hold of her arm, which was surprisingly warm—even hot—considering the girl was totally naked. 'Come on,' she whispered.

Chloe was able to gently pull Sarah away from where she stood. Thankfully, Sarah was compliant. Chloe then guided her from the room and carefully back down the stairs to the storey below. Though it took a little while, the pair eventually reached Sarah's room.

Once inside the room, Chloe noticed discarded shorts and a tank-top on the floor. She realised Sarah had gotten undressed before leaving for her little expedition.

Still, what did it matter? People were prone to doing strange things when sleepwalking, Chloe knew, and she was just thankful she hadn't found her sister peeing in a cupboard or something. As Chloe laid Sarah down, she quickly cast a look over to the cabinet opposite the bed. Apprehension filled her, but there was nothing in the reflection except the two sisters.

Thankfully.

Chloe then pulled the covers over Sarah and tucked

them in tight before leaving the room. Once back in the hallway, she allowed herself a moment.

What a night.

The thought of sleep seemed even more elusive, and the idea of just lying in bed, listening out for noises within the house did not seem appealing.

However, a cup of hot chocolate certainly did. It was her go-to staple when unable to sleep, and the warm, tasty cocoa was usually enough to help relax her body and mind.

That meant going downstairs alone, of course, which was another unappealing thought. But, if she was going to make Perron Manor a success for them all, she would need to get over the fear she was developing about the house.

She thought again of that horrible old man tossing Emma...

Just a dream!

With a renewed sense of determination, Chloe quickly ducked back inside her room and retrieved a robe to help ward off the night chill. She then headed downstairs and made her way to the back of the house, towards the kitchen.

Perron Manor at night was a strange and unsettling beast. The silence seemed to have an oppressive weight to it, and was punctured only by intermittent creaks in the huge structure, and even the slight rattle of old pipework.

In addition, the feeling of being watched made Chloe increase her pace until she finally reached her destination, though she couldn't help but glance back over her shoulder once or twice en route, fearful she was being followed.

But no one was there, obviously. It was just her mind playing tricks.

Again.

Chloe could have used Sarah's new coffee machine to make her hot chocolate, but instead she boiled the kettle and used jarred powder. She was used to the taste of this brand, and wanted familiar comforts at the minute.

Once the drink was prepared, she took a seat at the table and cupped her hands around the warm mug. The lighting in the kitchen had the same dirty feel to it as most of the other old lights in the house, which were a far cry from the energy-efficient lighting they had left behind in their previous house. However, the lighting here felt a little warmer to Chloe—less clean and clinical.

The yellow light spilled out through the two windows in the room, both of which looked out the side of the house. There, she could see a little of what was beyond the glass, but the majority of what Chloe saw was the light bouncing back and the reflection of the kitchen that was cast in the glass.

It took her eyes a few moments to determine exactly what was outside, and what was just a reflection.

Ever since Chloe had seen that... thing... reflected in the cabinet in Sarah's room, she had always felt at least a little apprehension when looking through windows or into mirrors. Thankfully, this time there was nothing out of the ordinary, which went some way towards soothing her mind.

She took another sip and tried to enjoy the peace and quiet. The gentle tick-tick-tick of the wall-mounted clock, which read three-twenty-two, was the only thing to break the silence.

Her drink was close to half-gone when she started to feel relaxed again, even sleepy. She looked forward to climbing back into bed again.

Bang, bang, bang.

Chloe's body seized up at the sudden noises from the back door.

26

CHLOE DIDN'T WANT to go and look.

All she wanted to do was flee back upstairs. Those dull reverberations from the glass of the rear door were identical to the banging she and Sarah had heard months ago.

She didn't want to go through the same kind of fear again. Especially not alone.

Chloe couldn't help but consider who was making the frantic noises. Was it truly someone obsessed with the house, toying with them? Or someone—or some*thing*—a little more... unnatural?

Both options terrified her.

She could just cut through from the kitchen straight to the dining room, given there was an adjoining door, and then make her way back to the staircase that way. It would negate the need to move through the great hall, where she would be forced to look at the back door.

However, another part of Chloe refused, and was ashamed at her own cowardice. She was a mother, and had a duty to protect her family. Given how close Chloe was to the source of the knocking, then she had to at least look to see what she was dealing with.

Bang, bang, bang.

She gasped.

Chloe wasn't certain if the banging was loud enough to wake Sarah or Andrew upstairs, but she knew she couldn't wait for them to come down and help her.

And she refused to just hide away in the kitchen.

So, Chloe got up, which caused the chair legs to screech loudly on the hard floor as it slid back. She then timidly moved over to the kitchen door and rested her hand on the doorknob, the feeling of the brass cool to the touch.

But Chloe hesitated.

Fear played a part, but she also wanted to wrench open the door at the exact moment she heard the knocking again. That way, whoever it was would have no time to hide.

After a wait which seemed to stretch on forever, the sound returned.

Bang, bang, bang.

Fighting through the hesitation and anxiety, Chloe quickly pulled open the door.

The large space of the great hall was dark, which only accentuated the glow of the external security light that came in through the rear glazed door. Something had tripped the sensors. And yet, despite Chloe opening the kitchen door the instant the banging sounded, she could see no one outside at all.

Impossible.

Chloe's breathing got quicker, but she still took a determined step into the hall and flicked on the light. Then, she made her way over to the glass door, forcing herself to inspect further. But, as she was midway across the hall, the security light outside powered down, plunging the external area into darkness.

The light was on a timer, and would not stay on very long without movement to keep its sensors activated. Now, Chloe could see a little more through the glass door than pockets of the reflected area she stood in.

She waited, unsure of what to do next. Even squinting to focus her vision, Chloe was unable to see anyone lurking outside.

After a few moments, the light clicked back on. But again, no one was there.

In amongst the reflection of the great hall, Chloe was now able to see the stone paving of the courtyard outside, as well as the two protruding wings of Perron Manor that enclosed it. However, there was nothing out there that would have caused the light to turn on again.

She waited, still holding her breath, slowly walking forward. Eventually, the light cut out once again.

Chloe saw herself in the glass face of the door. She could also see the reflection of the great hall behind as well. She felt like something was playing with her, toying with her fear. She wanted to call out, to demand this all stop, but didn't dare. The utter silence was almost overwhelming, and a creeping sensation made its way up her spine.

Almost predictably, the light came back on again, illuminating the area outside.

This time, however, someone *was* standing there, right on the edge of the light spill. However, the person—who appeared to be male—was mostly hidden by the darkness of night, and he was absolutely motionless.

Chloe's breathing sped up yet again, and she began to hyperventilate. A tiny whimper escaped her.

Once more, the light went out, and she was unable to see

the strange man anymore. Chloe wanted to take a step back-wards, then sprint upstairs, but she couldn't move. Her legs felt like dead weights.

Then, the moment she had been dreading. The light came back on. She let out a gasp and began to shake.

The man was now directly outside of the door, close to her.

In an instant, Chloe noticed many of the tall man's details as he stared at her with a wide—almost manic—gaze. Pale skin, bald head, and one eye surrounded by bloody and tattered flesh with no eyelids, making the eyeball appear to bulge from the socket. His expression was blank. Whoever he was, the stranger was dressed in dark, basic-looking robes, almost monk-like, that hung down to the floor. His arms were folded at the abdomen, hands hidden within the interlocking sleeves, and the light from outside somehow seemed to pass through his form.

Chloe's heart hammered in her chest as unrelenting panic rose inside of her.

It had taken a moment for her vision to adjust when the light blinked on, and she had taken in all the details in an instant. But now, Chloe realised the man was not standing outside the courtyard and looking in.

Rather, she was looking at a reflection of someone standing behind her.

_____

27

CHLOE COULDN'T HELP the scream that erupted from her.

She instinctually clasped her hands over her eyes—unwilling to look on this horror any longer—and survival instinct kicked in, allowing her to take control of her limbs once again. She spun, then ran blind towards the rear wall, feeling the cold sensation suddenly increase, as if she had passed through a chiller. By the time she reached the door to the hallway, guiding herself by peeking through her fingers, the cold blast had faded.

Panic-stricken, she pushed the door open and fled from the room. However, she could not help but give one last glance back over her shoulder into the great hall. In truth, despite being so overcome with panic, she had expected the figure to be gone, given what had happened previously in Sarah's bedroom.

But he wasn't.

Chloe screamed again as the spectral monk simply stood stationary. However, he had now rotated his body and was glaring directly at her. He stood directly beneath a light fitting that shone down over him like a spotlight, and Chloe could make out the horrible detail of the damaged area around his left eye: angry, red flesh and torn skin.

Chloe bolted through to the entrance foyer, then thundered up the stairs to the floor above. The whole way, the feeling of someone right behind her, gaining ground, was palpable. It was almost overwhelming, to the point she just wanted to drop, curl up into a ball, and scream. However, each time Chloe cast a tentative look back, she saw nothing.

She followed the corridor to her room, terrified and panicked in equal measure, and feeling the blood pumping through her veins as her heart slammed against her chest. But just as she reached her room, Chloe stopped, and another cry fell from her mouth.

A figure stood in the corridor that ran perpendicular from her room.

As before, it took a few moments for her to realise it was Sarah. Again, she was naked. Just as she had been earlier.

The door behind Chloe opened, and she almost fell into her room, but instead dropped back into someone's grasp. Her body tensed and she expected some unknown thing to spin her around so she could stare into its undead eyes.

Instead, the arms that circled her were warm.

'What's going on?' she heard Andrew say.

Chloe spun around in an instant. She had to see his face. She had to *know* it was *him*.

Andrew was dressed in a plain white t-shirt and baggy blue boxer shorts. His eyes were still sleepy, but the frown on his face was one of concern. 'Are you okay?' he asked.

Chloe didn't answer, she simply buried her face into his chest and cried.

'Jesus, Chloe, what's wrong? What happened?' After a few moments, he added, 'Is that Sarah?'

Still sobbing, Chloe twisted her head, still pressing

herself into Andrew's form and his strong embrace. She saw that Sarah was once again making her way upstairs to the top floor and disappearing from view.

Chloe felt firm hands grasp her upper arms, and Andrew slowly moved her away from him, just enough so she could make eye contact.

'Tell me what's happening, Chloe.' His voice was low, but firm. 'Is it Emma? Is she okay?'

Emma.

Chloe quickly broke from his grip and ran to her daughter's room, terrified of what she would see standing over the child's bed. She burst into the room and flicked on the light, braced for whatever may be waiting. Other than Emma, however, the room was empty. The baby rolled from her front to her back and blinked her eyes in surprise.

The light was flicked off, and Chloe felt herself pulled from the room.

'What the hell is going on?' Andrew asked in a hushed but stern tone as he held onto her arm.

'I... I...'

But Chloe didn't know how to answer.

Should I tell him the truth? But he'll think I'm crazy.

A weird man dressed as a monk appearing in the kitchen? She could just imagine the look of surprise that would cross his face, immediately followed by a sceptical frown. And she didn't know if she could bear that right now.

But she didn't have a choice. It *had* happened. She was certain about it.

'I saw someone downstairs,' she said.

Andrew's eyes went wide.

'What? When?'

'Just now, in the great hall.'

She saw his body tighten up. His jaw clenched. 'Watch Emma,' he said. 'And get your phone and call the police.'

He turned and pulled away from her, but Chloe held on tight, gripping his t-shirt.

'Don't go!'

Andrew placed his hands on her shoulders. 'It'll be fine. Call the police.' He then released himself from her grip.

Chloe panicked. This wasn't like a normal intruder. It was something else. Something much more... unnatural. And, in truth, Chloe didn't want to be left alone again. But Andrew moved too quickly, and before she could try again to stop him he was jogging head-first into the unknown.

Which was absolutely stupid of him.

'Andrew!' she called, but he had already turned the corner and was out of sight.

28

OTHER THAN THE light being on in the great hall, Andrew could see nothing out of the ordinary. Certainly no intruders in the house. He went on to search the entire ground floor, looking in every room and cupboard, and checking that all doors and windows were locked. He even had a quick walk around the courtyard outside, as well as the area outside of the front door.

The initial rush of adrenaline that had run through him began to wane with each area he searched. The living room was the last room he checked downstairs; however, even before entering, he'd already resigned himself to the fact Chloe had somehow been mistaken.

There was no one here in the house with them.

Throughout his search, Andrew still wasn't able to shake the image of Sarah heading to the top floor, naked as could be.

He made his way back upstairs, feeling the chill in his bones from being outside in so little clothing. He found Chloe sitting on the floor with her back pressed against the door to Emma's room.

She looked pale and was still trembling. Whether anyone had actually been downstairs or not, *something* had clearly freaked her out. He sat down next to her and put an arm over her shoulder, pulling her into him.

'Emma's asleep again,' Chloe whispered. 'I keep checking on her, but she's okay.'

'She's a good sleeper,' Andrew said and kissed Chloe on the top of the head. 'Just like her old man.'

There was a moment of silence between them, before Andrew asked the question that was on his mind. He tried to keep all scepticism from his voice.

'What was it you saw, Chloe?'

She didn't answer immediately, taking a few beats before speaking. 'I... don't really know. I could have sworn there was someone standing in the hall.'

'All the doors and windows are still locked,' he replied. 'No one has broken in. What made you go downstairs in the first place? Did you hear something?'

She shook her head. 'No. I just... I was awake and couldn't sleep. Bad dream. So I went down, rather than just lying in bed. That's when I...' She trailed off.

'Did you call the police?' he asked.

Another pause. 'No.'

In all honesty, Andrew was relieved. It would have been a wasted trip.

He then heard movement on the floor above, and he felt Chloe immediately tense up.

'Sarah,' he said. 'What the hell was she doing?'

He felt Chloe relax a little. 'Sleepwalking,' she told him. Her voice sounded quiet, almost distant.

'She sleepwalks?'

'Apparently.'

'Naked?'

'Apparently,' Chloe repeated. There was a tiny hint of amusement in her voice, which was a good sign. She went on, 'I saw her doing it earlier, just after I got up. She went up to that horrible study, so I brought her back down.'

'Sounds like she's back up there. Should we go get her?'

Chloe seemed hesitant. But whatever had frightened her *must* have been imagined, or at least something normal that had been twisted in her head.

'I'll come with you,' he confirmed. 'But you'll need to dress her, or cover her over with something. I've already seen too much. She'll never be able to look me in the eye again if she finds out.'

'Okay,' Chloe finally said.

Andrew got up, and pulled his wife to her feet as well. He cupped her face before gently kissing her. She still looked scared, but also embarrassed, and she cast her eyes down and away from him.

Regardless of what she may or may not have seen, Andrew didn't want her feeling bad about this. His wife did so much for them, and put so much pressure on herself, that he refused to add any more burden to what she was feeling.

'We'll get a dressing gown from her room,' Chloe said. He nodded and led the way. Chloe reached inside of the room and grabbed a fluffy blue robe from the back of the door. They then made their way to the stairs, but Chloe hesitated at the bottom.

He stepped up first and took hold of her hand. 'It's okay,' he said, and gently pulled her along. Chloe came tentatively, and they headed up to the study.

Inside, in the dark, Andrew could see Sarah standing before a display case, her hand on the surface. She was mumbling something that sounded like gibberish.

'Go cover her up,' he whispered to Chloe. 'Then we'll take her back down.'

It took a gentle nudge from him to prompt his wife to step into the room, but she quickly hurried over to Sarah and draped the garment over her sister's shoulders. Chloe then took Sarah's hand, and Andrew heard a gentle, 'Come on.'

Sarah allowed herself to be led away, and Andrew followed the two of them back downstairs, where Chloe put Sarah back to bed while he waited out in the hallway. After closing the door behind her, Chloe looked sheepishly to Andrew. He smiled, rubbed her upper arms, then brought her in for a hug.

'Weird night, huh?'

'I'll say,' she quietly replied.

'Come on,' he said, taking her hand. 'Let's go back to bed.'

∽

Though Andrew slept soundly beside her, Chloe simply could not drop off. The vision of what she'd seen downstairs still plagued her thoughts. It had seemed so *real*.

But Andrew had found nothing, and now she was battling with herself, simultaneously doubting her own sanity and also feeling an overwhelming need to get out of the house to save her family.

She was also scared to think how Andrew, and particularly Sarah, would react if she told them the *whole* truth about what she had seen.

With her covers pulled up to her chin, Chloe kept checking the baby-monitor that sat on the nightstand beside her, and then looking over to a particular dark corner of the room close to the window. She needed to make certain Emma was safe, but her gaze was also drawn each time to the deep shadows at the room's edge. She could see nothing there, but for some reason it gave off an ominous aura, and she half-expected some spectral form to suddenly lurch out of the black, pale hands outstretched and ready to grab her.

That didn't happen, though she still couldn't help but constantly stare, certain something within the pool of darkness was looking back at her.

She didn't sleep much more that night.

29

SARAH FELT EXHAUSTED, like she hadn't slept a wink all night, and she was plagued by the memory of her strange dreams.

Plunging down through a hole that seemed to stretch on forever, surrounded by earth and rock, which eventually turned to... flesh, meat, skin. Within these seemingly living surroundings, she saw wandering eyes, moving limbs, and gaping mouths. An abstract nightmare. And the farther she fell, the worse the horrible screaming sounds became.

She thrust a forkful of warm eggs and toast into her mouth, savouring the salty flavour and trying to forget those horrible visions.

Something else was troubling her as well. *Why the hell have I woken up stark naked?* She certainly hadn't gone to sleep that way.

The smell of frying bacon filled the kitchen. Chloe was working frantically, insisting she make everyone a slap-up breakfast. She looked exhausted as well, with her usually immaculate hair just pulled back into a messy ponytail, and heavy bags under her eyes. Chloe turned and put down a plate stacked with thick, fluffy pancakes.

'Hun,' Andrew said. 'This is too much. We won't be able to eat it all. Come on, you sit down and eat some yourself.'

'I'm okay,' Chloe replied. 'I just want to keep busy.'

But it was clear to Sarah that her sister was definitely *not* okay. She was close to being manic.

Emma, who was seated in her high-chair next to Sarah, handed her aunty a blueberry from her own plate. She smiled, clearly pleased with her attempts at sharing.

'Thanks, kid,' Sarah said, taking the berry and popping it in her mouth. She chewed it loudly, making an exaggerated show of rubbing her belly. 'Mmmmmmmm.'

Emma laughed and picked up another blueberry. 'Again,' she demanded.

As Sarah pacified her demanding niece, she kept an eye on Chloe. Without knowing what had happened, she could only guess that perhaps she and Andrew had fought during the night.

Chloe wasn't making eye contact with anyone, though Andrew was. He kept sneaking awkward glances at Sarah, only to quickly look away again when caught.

'Okay, what's going on?' Sarah demanded. 'Have you two been bickering?'

Andrew sat up straight, and Chloe turned around, looking confused.

'What do you mean?' she asked.

'Something's out of whack this morning. You are running around like a madwoman, Andrew keeps looking at me weird, and I could cut the atmosphere with *this*,' she said, holding up a spoon.

Andrew looked at Chloe. 'I think we should tell her,' he said. Chloe frowned angrily and shook her head.

'Tell me what?' Sarah asked.

'It's nothing,' Chloe said.

Sarah rolled her eyes. 'Well, clearly it's not noth—'

'You were sleepwalking last night,' Andrew interrupted.

Sarah's mouth hung open a little bit in shock. 'I was... I was what?'

'Sleepwalking,' Andrew confirmed. 'You did it twice. Kept going up to the top floor, to that study.'

She didn't know how to respond. 'Really?' she asked.

He nodded, then his cheeks flushed a little. 'And you were... erm... not fully dressed, shall we say. Well, that's not quite accurate. You weren't dressed at all.'

'I was sleepwalking naked?'

Andrew nodded. Sarah's eyes went wide, and she pointed at him. 'Did you see anything?'

He shuffled in his seat. 'Not much, honestly. Chloe covered you up. But... yeah, it seems you like to walk around in the buff while you sleep.'

'Well shit,' was all Sarah could say. 'I didn't realise.'

'Has it happened before?' he asked.

Sarah shook her head. 'Not that I know of.'

Chloe still wasn't looking at either of them, having gone back to cut up more fruit. Sarah was confused as to why it was such a problem for her sister. Maybe the whole sleepwalking thing was a little odd, but certainly nothing to cause an issue between them. Hell, if anything it was funny.

'Is there something else?' she asked, staring past Andrew to Chloe.

After a silence, her sister turned. She was still frowning, and cast a scowl towards Andrew.

He shrugged apologetically. 'I was only going to mention the sleepwalking. That was it.'

Sarah was growing tired of the whole charade. 'What else happened last night?' she demanded.

Chloe chewed the side of her mouth for a few moments before sighing. 'I thought I saw someone. Out there,' she hooked a thumb over her shoulder, 'in the great hall.'

'Someone was in here?!' Sarah asked, incredulous, rising to her feet. 'Why the hell didn't you tell me sooner?'

But then, Sarah considered the way Chloe had worded the statement.

She thought *she saw someone.*

And Sarah also remembered the night Chloe *thought* she saw an old woman's reflection, as well.

'I looked,' Andrew said, 'but couldn't find anyone.'

Sarah kept her eyes on Chloe. 'So what happened?' she asked. 'Was there someone here or not?'

'We don't think so,' Andrew confirmed, but the cloud of anger that formed over Chloe's face indicated she wasn't on the same page.

'Who did you see?' Sarah asked.

Chloe's jaw was set, and her top lip curled a little. She set down the knife she was holding and began to walk from the room. 'I need to use the toilet,' she snapped, bringing everything to a close.

But that wasn't good enough for Sarah; she wasn't going to be left in the dark. So, she got up and followed Chloe out of the room, leaving Andrew to look after Emma.

'Hey,' she called as she and her sister paced through the great hall, Sarah a good few steps behind. Chloe ignored her, so Sarah repeated herself, louder this time. 'Hey!'

Chloe stopped and quickly turned around. 'What?' she asked curtly.

Sarah kept walking until she was close to her sister. 'Just tell me what happened last night. What's gotten into you?'

'Nothing,' Chloe snapped, rolling her tired-looking, red-rimmed eyes. She tried to turn away again, but Sarah quickly shot out a hand and grabbed her by the upper arm.

'Talk to me!' Sarah insisted.

Chloe stared back angrily. 'Would you please just let me go for a piss.'

'You don't need to pee,' Sarah shot back. 'I'm not an idiot.'

Chloe took a deep breath. Eventually, however, the tension in her jaw eased, and her features softened a little. She then began to talk.

'Honestly... I'm not sure I know. I swear I saw someone down here, standing roughly where we are now. So I ran. But, like Andrew says, when he came down he couldn't find anyone. And there were no signs of a break-in.'

'And what did this person look like?' Sarah asked.

Chloe shrugged. 'Just a person.'

'Man or woman?'

A sigh. 'It was a man.'

'Good. And what did the man look like? Short, tall, big nose... what?'

'Why does it matter?' Chloe asked, throwing her hands up in the air. 'He apparently wasn't even here to begin with.'

'Tell me,' Sarah insisted.

Chloe looked away for a few moments, but finally went on. 'He was tall. Bald. And wearing some kind of robes, or a cloak. He had a weird injury over one of his eyes. And... he kind of reminded me of the guy we saw on that security footage a little while ago.'

'Did he do anything?' she asked.

Chloe shook her head. 'No, just stood there, staring at me.'

Now Sarah was worried. Not because there could still be

an intruder loose in the house or anything like that, but because she feared for her sister's sanity.

'You know there was no one standing here, right?' Sarah asked. Chloe looked hurt at the statement, but Sarah continued. 'It was just like when you thought you saw that old woman in my room. None of it really happened.'

'This was different,' Chloe replied, but her tone was hardly convincing. 'It wasn't just a reflection. I *saw* him. He was real.'

'Okay, then answer me this, and be truthful. Do you think he broke in just to stand and look at you in plain sight?'

Chloe shook her head and turned again, but Sarah caught her arm for the second time. 'Answer me,' she demanded. 'Do you think someone broke in here last night?'

A moment's pause. 'No,' Chloe admitted.

'So, that means no one was standing here in this room, doesn't it?'

Sarah knew what her sister really meant, and what she really thought this strange man was. Not an intruder, but something else.

It was ridiculous. An impossibility. Sarah wouldn't let her sister—regardless of any stresses she was going through—be weak-minded enough to believe in such things.

But she wanted Chloe to realise it on her own. Hopefully, that would be the first step in getting past this nonsense.

'Do you agree no one was here?' Sarah repeated after not receiving an answer.

Chloe looked up and stared Sarah dead in the eye. 'No,' she stated. 'Someone *was* here.'

Sarah shook her head in disbelief. 'Is that so? Okay, so

no one broke in, but someone *was* inside the house. Explain that to me, please. Did they have a fucking key?'

'You know what it was,' Chloe said.

'I want you to say it.'

'Why?'

'So you can hear how stupid it sounds!'

'It isn't stupid,' Chloe insisted, yanking her arm from Sarah's grip. 'You weren't there.'

'So the house is haunted? And you're okay believing rubbish like that?'

Chloe strode away from Sarah and yelled back, 'Just leave me alone.'

But Sarah would not, and called after her, 'Careful no ghosts get you while you're taking a piss.'

Chloe didn't turn around, just raised a hand and flipped Sarah the bird. 'Fuck you!'

There was venom in her voice—real, seething anger. Chloe disappeared from the room, and it wasn't until after she was gone that Sarah started to feel bad for pushing so hard. And she was confused as to why she felt the need to do so.

'Shit,' she said to herself. *Nice going, dipshit.*

Then, the doorbell sounded.

30

ANDREW OPENED THE FRONT DOOR, Emma cradled in one arm, and was greeted by a short man who looked to be in his sixties. He was wrapped in a green farming jacket and wore a flat cap, burgundy trousers, and loose-fitting moccasins. Grey hairs protruded from under the cap, and the visitor stood with a straight back and strong posture, his chin tilted upwards. A scuffed leather satchel was slung over one shoulder.

'Hello, can I help you?' Andrew asked.

The man cocked a bushy eyebrow. 'I should hope so. *You* asked *me* to come.'

Andrew paused for a moment, then realisation dawned on him. 'Mr. Mumford?'

'The very same,' the man replied with a half-smile. He then held out a hand. 'But you may call me Isaac.'

Andrew shook, but was a little hesitant. 'Mr. Mu... sorry, Isaac. You are a little early.'

'Nonsense,' Mr. Mumford said with a wave of his hand. 'We said ten-thirty. I hardly think five minutes before that classifies as *early*.'

'It wouldn't, normally,' Andrew agreed. 'But we said *eleven*-thirty.'

The man shook his head dismissively, and Andrew had to keep from letting his small pang of annoyance grow into something more.

'No,' Isaac replied. 'Ten-thirty was the time. Am I to take it you are not available for our appointment, then?'

Isaac's grey-blue eyes—one of which looked to be slightly off centre—stared expectantly at Andrew. He had a good mind to tell the man to get lost, but thought better of it.

'I can accommodate you coming early,' Andrew said, stepping aside. Isaac made as if to argue the point, but Andrew cut him off. 'Come on in. I'll take you up to the study.'

Isaac stepped inside, put his satchel down, and then removed his coat, thrusting it into Andrew's free hand. He had a thick, green, wool jumper on underneath, with the collar of a white-and-burgundy-check shirt protruding out from the neck. 'Is there anywhere you can put the little ankle-biter while we do business? Best if we can concentrate unhindered on the job at hand.'

Andrew's jaw dropped. *Ankle-biter*?

'Everything okay?' Sarah said, appearing in the room. She walked over to them, and Andrew noted Chloe wasn't with her. He guessed the conversation between them hadn't gone too well.

'I think so,' the visitor said, and held out his hand. 'Isaac Mumford. I've come to inspect the items you inherited, to see if any of them are worth anything.'

Sarah shook his hand but cast Andrew an amused smile.

'Pleased to meet you,' she said.

'I take it you're the wife?'

Sarah's eyes widened, as did her amused smile.

'I'm the sister-in-law, actually,' she told him. 'And I also have a name. It's Sarah.'

'Delightful,' Isaac replied, not sounding the least bit interested. 'Would you kindly watch this one?' He pointed squarely at Emma, his finger inches away from the child's nose. 'Children tend to get in the way. Things will go much more smoothly if he isn't bothering us.'

'*She*,' Andrew corrected, sternly.

Isaac took a closer look at Emma, narrowing his eyes. 'Really?' he asked, then shrugged. 'If you say so.'

Andrew's fists balled up, and he turned to Sarah, with his eyebrows raised in disbelief. Sarah, in turn, looked like she was fighting the need to burst out laughing. But what could Andrew say? It was *he* who had found this strange man and arranged the appointment in the first place.

Andrew just hoped this Isaac Mumford knew his stuff as much as his reputation online seemed to indicate.

'Tell you what,' Sarah replied. 'Since I'm one of the inheritors, how about I come up with you and listen to what you have to say. My sister, *the wife*, will want to be there as well. I'm afraid you'll just have to put up with the child.'

Isaac let out a sigh. 'If you insist.' He then turned to Andrew. 'Would you keep it quiet, though, old chap?'

Andrew gritted his teeth together. He was about to respond, but at that moment Chloe walked into the room.

'Chloe, this is Isaac Mumford,' he said. 'He's here to look at the stuff upstairs. He's early, but that's okay, we can accommodate. Let's go and get this over with.'

'No need to sound so curt,' Isaac said, hooking his satchel over his shoulder again. 'And I *wasn't* early.'

∾

Sarah watched Isaac slowly walk around the large study as he took everything in.

'You packed a lot of the items away, then?' he asked, gesturing to the full cardboard boxes piled up on top of each other.

'We had to make a start,' Chloe said. 'They had been cluttering the room for long enough.'

'Cluttering the room?' Isaac asked, incredulous. 'If these things are authentic, then they are far from clutter.'

Chloe's expression was flat. 'I don't care,' she stated.

Isaac shook his head. 'Unbelievable.'

He then continued with his inspection, peeking inside boxes, studying the tomes that lined the bookshelves, and gazing at the various artefacts still on display.

Sarah could feel anger radiate from her sister. Some of it likely directed at her. She tried to make subtle eye contact to draw Chloe's attention, but to no avail.

Why the hell was I so hard on her?

Chloe was clearly stressed out and struggling with things at the minute, it was written all over her face, and Sarah *knew* that. Normally, she'd have discussed things rationally with her sister... but that hadn't happened back in the great hall.

'Anything of interest?' Andrew asked.

'Possibly,' was Isaac's one-word reply.

Moving at his own leisure, the man finally settled on the book in the display case. It was the most obvious item in the room, given its placement, and one it seemed Isaac had deliberately left until last.

'My,' he began, and lifted up the glass lid. He then let his fingers run over the book. 'This looks interesting. Very old.' He opened it, nipping the front cover between his fingers.

'Seems to be wooden bindings wrapped in leather. Could be medieval... or older.'

Sarah, Chloe, and Andrew all gave each other a look, and Andrew's eyebrows raised up. Sarah knew what he was thinking, as something that old would clearly be worth a pretty penny.

Isaac put his satchel down, then opened its flap, pulling out some white, cloth gloves. He slipped them on and then began to carefully flick through the pages.

'Hand-written,' he said. 'And in Latin. Not my area of expertise, but it seems to be authentic, whatever it is. Certainly an original.' Isaac quickly flipped the cover over again and read the title out loud. '*Ianua Diaboli*. Hmmmm, not something I've heard of. But I can certainly look into it.'

He slipped off his gloves and delved back into his bag, retrieving a notepad and pencil he used to scribble some notes. He then brought a digital camera from the satchel and snapped a few pictures. The flash was so bright that Sarah's view swam with motes, and she had to blink repeatedly to clear her vision.

'I assume I'm okay taking pictures,' he said without looking at them, then shot off a few more.

Sarah couldn't decide if she detested this man or absolutely loved him. He reminded her of a senile uncle who had no filter... or manners.

'So,' Chloe began, 'do you have any idea if this is all just junk?'

Isaac chuckled and shook his head. 'Define *junk*,' he replied. 'You may think all of this is rubbish, but someone else would value it highly. And the things I value, you might just disregard as clutter. It's all in the eye of the beholder.'

Sarah saw Chloe clench her teeth. 'Then tell me, does any of this have monetary value?'

'Possibly,' he said. 'There is a lot here. Most of it seems to have an inclination towards the occult and the dark arts, which isn't surprising considering the house it's stored in.'

'You've heard of this place?' Andrew asked. 'I thought you lived a few towns over?'

'I do,' Isaac replied. 'But that town isn't situated under a rock. A house with a history like this... of course I know of it. I'd also heard of the museum of the occult that was rumoured to be kept here. Until now, I didn't know if that was true.'

'You have an interest in this macabre crap too, then?' Chloe asked.

Another chuckle. 'Heavens no. Not my field, really. But I know people who can help, if I feel any of these items have merit. Which... I believe they might.'

'What *exactly* have you heard about Perron Manor?' Sarah asked, wanting to pull the conversation back to something that sparked her interest. 'And what did you mean by a *museum of the occult*?'

'Well,' Isaac began, as he continued to look around. 'This place has quite a history, as I'm sure you are aware.'

'Yes, we know what happened in '82,' Chloe said.

'And the rest,' he replied. 'That is just the tip of the iceberg. This house, it is said, often drew people to it who have a fondness for the darker things in life. That begs the question, why do *you* wholesome folks live here, hmmm?' He waggled his bushy eyebrows and laughed to himself.

'The owner of the house in the late eighteen-hundreds was a man named Alfred Blackwater. He had a similar profession to mine, and traded rare artefacts. However, it was well known he had a certain interest in things like this.' Isaac cast his arm around the room.

'And he used his quite successful business to fund his

acquisitions. When he had the chance to buy Perron Manor, which he viewed as the biggest occult artefact one could own, he snapped it up and continued building his collection. After his death, the house was passed to his son, Timothy, who left it empty but kept it in the family name. And when *he* died, it was then passed to Marcus, Timothy's son. Marcus had very similar tastes to Alfred, and continued his grandfather's work. And word spread of his collection, but no one was ever certain if any of it was true.'

'And what was your take on what happened that night under his ownership?' Sarah asked.

'Do we *have* to go over that?' Chloe asked with a sigh.

'Yes,' Sarah said, surprising herself at how curt she sounded. She then turned her attention back to Isaac.

'No one knows for sure,' he said. 'Just a lot of dead people. Butchered. If you ask me, the survivors had to have been in on it. How else do you explain the whole thing? I mean, look around.' He gave another gesture to the items in the room. 'The kind of people that own and collect these kind of things... is it such a leap to think they could have been swayed to act out some kind of ritualistic killing, or some such nonsense?'

Sarah saw that Chloe was shaking, and her fists were tightly curled, the knuckles white. Sarah could understand why Chloe was upset, as the man was unwittingly implicating their parents.

'The police didn't seem to think that was the case,' Andrew said, though Sarah could tell it was more to appease Chloe than anything.

'Bah,' Isaac responded with a flippant wave. 'Useless flat-foots. Especially in the eighties. Couldn't join the dots between two points to save their lives.'

'You don't buy the stories that the whole thing was somehow... supernatural?' Sarah asked.

She knew she shouldn't have said anything, but she wanted Chloe to hear it from someone else. It would no doubt cause another fight, but so be it.

Isaac's bellowing laughter at such a suggestion was all Sarah needed, and she saw Chloe's cheeks turn a deep red.

She felt an instant pang of guilt. *Why are you pushing this so hard? What's wrong with you?*

'Good God no,' the man said, wiping away a tear. 'A little too old for fairytales, I believe. And not so weak of mind as to fall for nonsense like that. Although, people *do* believe in that kind of thing, and I know that can lead them to do strange and horrible things. Like what happened in '82, in my opinion. Or that Chelmswick fellow, in the nineteen-thirties. You know of him, right? Killed a bunch of children in here, supposedly singing nursery rhymes at them as he did. It's true there have been a lot of... unpleasant... tragedies happen at Perron Manor down the years, but considering the age of the building, is that so surprising?'

Sarah looked over to her sister, expecting Chloe to have a face like thunder. However, Chloe's expression was... something else. Worry? Shock? Sarah wasn't quite sure.

'Are you about finished, Mr. Mumford?' Chloe asked, not hiding the annoyance in her voice.

'Not really,' he replied, continuing to nose around.

'Then allow me to word it differently,' she said to him. 'Get the fuck out of my house. Now.'

Everyone in the room paused in shock. Isaac's expression was the most surprised of all.

'Excuse me?!' Isaac asked incredulously, his face turning red. 'How dare you—'

'Shut up! Just shut up and get out now. You've been

nothing but a boor since arriving, and I'm sick of listening to you. We don't want to do business with you, so go. And don't come back.'

'Listen here, missy,' he replied.

But Chloe, it appeared, was in no mood to listen at all.

'No!'

She marched up to him and got right in Isaac's face. 'I have zero problem throwing you out of the house myself, if needed.'

Sarah immediately felt a flush of guilt. The exchange, and Chloe's outburst, was all her fault. Why had she pushed it so much?

Isaac's frown wavered, and the prospect of Chloe following through on her threat clearly ran through his mind.

'Fine,' he eventually said and started to pack up his things. 'Heathens, the lot of you. Good luck getting any money for what you have here, because make no mistake, I will blackball you to the local dealership community. *No one* will deal with you.'

'Less talking,' Chloe said. 'More hurrying up and getting the hell out.'

Isaac slung his satchel over his shoulder and stomped from the room like a child, muttering to himself the whole way back downstairs as the others followed him. Andrew handed him his coat, which Isaac snatched, then opened the door for him. Isaac moved to the threshold, then turned back to Andrew.

'Your wife is a rude woman,' he said. 'You should keep her on a leash.'

That was the last straw.

Chloe charged the man with a roar, and was far too quick for either Sarah or Andrew to stop her. She shoved their guest, and a look of complete shock registered on the old man's face as he toppled backwards, trying—and failing—to keep his footing. Isaac fell backwards, landing with a thud, inches away from the stone steps.

Chloe was over to him in an instant, standing above him.

'Leave it!' Andrew shouted, but Chloe just glared down at the grounded man, who held up a defensive hand and turned his face away.

'I will *not* tell you again, little man. Leave!'

Isaac looked as if he were going to say something again, clearly unused to not having the last word. Thankfully, however, he thought better of it. Instead, he gathered himself up and hurried away.

They watched him go, and Sarah saw Chloe was breathing heavily, hands still curled into fists. Finally, Chloe turned and walked back towards the house. She stopped at Sarah, and the look she gave her was one Sarah had never seen before. Almost like Chloe wished death upon her.

Sarah broke eye contact and looked down to the ground.

31

CHLOE SAT on her bed and sobbed. She wanted out.

Perron Manor was done to her now. Finished. Her dream of the idyllic mansion with its beautiful grounds had been shattered.

She felt bad about it, given she had been the driving force to get people together to live here in the first place. It was *she* who had put the idea to Sarah that selling the house wasn't the right thing to do. That it would make a perfect place to live.

She'd also spent no small amount of time and effort convincing Andrew, who had gone along with it out of his love for her and nothing more.

So, she would have to bear the brunt of tearing it all down. Andrew may well be happy with the situation, but she had a feeling Sarah would react differently.

Though, in truth, she did not care in the slightest how her sister took the news. Not now.

Fuck her.

Chloe used to think she could talk to Sarah about

anything. But after trying to share her recent experiences... Sarah just seemed like a different person.

Granted, they were pretty fantastical events, but Sarah's attitude had not just been disbelief—she had tried to belittle and humiliate Chloe.

Chloe couldn't remember a single time in her life where she had ever been this angry with Sarah.

But whether her sister believed her or not, Chloe just didn't feel safe here. Even now, alone in her bedroom during daytime hours, she still felt on edge, as if someone were watching her. Part of her just wanted to go back downstairs and join the others, if only to feel a little safer.

But she couldn't do that. At the moment, Chloe needed time and space. And facing Sarah again now would just result in an argument.

Chloe was feeling angry and hurt and scared and ashamed... and a million more negative emotions. So, for now, she just needed to pull herself together in her own space.

She remembered what Isaac Mumford had said about the man who killed children in the house. That story, regardless of anything else that had happened, probably scared her the most. The event in '82 was horrible, but as far as Chloe knew, the victims were all adults. But this...

There was also the comment about the killer reciting nursery rhymes to the poor children he slew. She remembered the previous night, and the thing she'd heard on the baby monitor after waking.

The thing she had convinced herself at the time was nothing but her imagination.

Round and round the garden.

There was a light tap on the door, and immediately Chloe tensed up. She imagined the tall monk standing outside of her room, rapping on the door. But a voice soon followed.

It was Sarah.

'Sis, it's me. Can I come in?'

'Go away,' Chloe replied. She was in no mood to talk with anyone, least of all her sister. The door opened anyway, and Chloe let out an audible sigh. 'Are you deaf?'

Sarah closed the door behind her, but didn't make eye contact. She seemed almost meek, which was a new look for her.

'I'm sorry,' she said, fidgeting with her hands and picking at the nails. 'I really am.' Sarah finally looked up, and her blue eyes settled on Chloe. The expression she wore was an earnest one.

'I don't care,' Chloe replied. Sarah didn't deserve to have her apology accepted. Not yet. Things were still too raw.

'I understand,' Sarah added. 'I deserve that. But I wanted to say sorry anyway. I overreacted. And, honestly, I have no idea why. Don't get me wrong, I don't believe there is anything wrong with the house like you do. But that was no reason to push you and try and embarrass you like that. I don't know what came over me and... I'm sorry.'

Whether intended or not, the line about still not believing Chloe stung, and didn't help her feel any less crazy. But the apology was welcomed, even if Chloe didn't want to admit it.

'I just don't get why you went at me so much. You've never done that before.'

'I know,' Sarah agreed. 'It's just... and don't get angry here... I felt that it was weak to think like that. To let your imagination run away with itself. And it made me angry, even though it shouldn't have. I don't know... I guess I've just been feeling tired a lot lately, and it's all getting to me.'

'Maybe all the sleepwalking is interfering with your rest,' Chloe offered. 'Like that isn't strange enough, anyway.'

'Don't,' Sarah said, closing her eyes and raising a finger. 'It's not a big deal. Don't make more out of it than it is. How many people in the world sleepwalk? Do they *all* live in haunted houses?'

Chloe stopped. She *did* think that Sarah's nighttime strolls the previous evening were strange, but couldn't really argue the point her sister had made. She was right. Lots of people did it, and it didn't usually mean anything.

Usually.

But that didn't change anything. Chloe's mind was made up. She should have really spoken to Andrew first before having this out with Sarah, but she proceeded anyway.

'I'm not going to live here anymore,' Chloe said. 'I can't. I'll speak to Andrew, and we are going to leave.'

Sarah's face fell. 'What?! You can't be fucking serious.'

'I am. I know you don't believe me about this stuff, and that's fine. But I know what I saw. And I'm not prepared to stay here and put my family in danger just because you think it sounds a little farfetched.'

'A *little* farfetched? Jesus Christ, Chloe, it sounds abso-lutely fucking insane. And now you're going to jump ship because of it? After *you*,' Sarah jabbed her finger at Chloe, 'were the one to persuade everyone to live here in the first place.'

Chloe had fully expected Sarah's response. 'I know. But it is what it is.'

Sarah had come here offering an apology, which was good of her, but Chloe knew there was another fight incoming.

And Chloe was fine with that.

'You selfish bitch!' Sarah snarled. 'I gave up my life for this. For *you*. And now you're running away?'

'*What* life?' Chloe asked—and immediately regretted it.

Shock, then hurt, registered on her sister's face. Sarah's top lip curled and her teeth clenched together in an angry grimace. She then took a step forward, and Chloe genuinely thought her sister was going to punch her.

Instead, Sarah marched right up to Chloe and dipped her head down, so they were eye to eye, with Chloe still seated on the bed.

'Fuck you,' she said in a low, nasty tone. 'Go. Fucking run away. You're nothing more than a pussy who's scared of your own shadow. You've always been the same. An utter. Fucking. Coward.'

Chloe jumped to her feet, and the two sisters stood toe-to-toe. The rage that surged through Chloe felt uncontrollable—almost unnatural. How had things so quickly spiralled to this?

'Get out,' Chloe said, trying her best to control the bubbling anger.

Sarah simply looked at Chloe like she was shit on her shoe, then shook her head and left the room.

Chloe was shaking, and she sat back down on the bed, breathing deeply. She tried to push down a rage she had never felt before, especially towards Sarah.

She needed to speak to Andrew and get him on board. Then they could look at getting out of this place as quickly as possible.

Sarah could do whatever the hell she wanted.

But despite all that, Chloe still felt a need to prove she was right, that she *wasn't* crazy. And in order to do that, she needed to know more about what was going on.

She needed that reassurance for her own sanity.

Even though her mind was made up, a small, lingering doubt remained. Who the hell could she turn to for that kind of help? Who would believe her?

Then, a name popped into her head. Someone who *would* believe her. However, it was someone she would need to apologise to first.

David Ritter.

32

'I DIDN'T THINK I'd hear from you again,' David Ritter said as he approached Chloe. She was seated in *Hill of Beans*—the same shop where Chloe had so quickly berated David for simply telling the truth.

Emma, who was seated in a highchair next to Chloe, looked up at David and pointed. 'Man!'

Chloe offered David a smile. 'I think I owe you an apology.'

'So you said in your message,' David replied and scratched at the back of his neck. He was dressed in loose-fitting jeans, scruffy trainers, a grey t-shirt with the Atari logo branded across, and a charcoal-coloured hoodie. Standing above them, he looked awkward and hesitant.

'Please... take a seat,' Chloe said, gesturing to the empty chair opposite.

David looked around at the coffee shop first. There were only a handful of patrons, and Chloe could tell he was more than a little uncomfortable.

Probably trying to think if anyone here recognises him from when I publicly embarrassed him.

Thankfully, David sat down.

'Can I offer you a drink?' Chloe asked.

He smiled and shook his head. 'No, it's fine—'

'I insist,' Chloe stated. She got to her feet. 'I'm getting one anyway. What do you want?'

'Coffee. Black,' he conceded. 'Thank you.'

Chloe stood up and approached the counter, which was only a few steps away. While waiting for the barista, Chloe considered again if the whole thing was crazy.

After her argument with Sarah—once she had calmed down—the first thing Chloe had done was to seek out her husband and lay everything out for him. Andrew had been shocked, and she could see the doubt plastered across his face when she told him everything. He didn't believe her, she knew; however, he did say he would support her if she wanted to leave. Which wasn't surprising.

One thing he had said, though, was that Chloe should smooth things over with Sarah before firming anything up.

But Chloe wasn't ready for that.

Next, she had looked up David Ritter online and found an email address through his paranormal research company website. He had responded soon after, and a meet up for that afternoon was arranged. David had been hesitant in his initial response, but Chloe had pressed the urgency of the situation, promising to explain it all.

Too late to back out now.

She just hoped that David was capable of providing some answers. After all, he had been to the house and claimed to have experienced some kind of paranormal phenomena himself.

Should have read his book, she thought to herself.

A barista approached with a big and friendly smile. After placing her order, Chloe moved back to her seat.

'They'll bring everything over as soon as it's ready,' she told David. 'I've ordered some cakes and biscuits as well, so feel free to dig in.'

'You didn't have to do that,' he said, and she noticed he had tucked his hands into his jacket pockets.

'No, it's fine. It's the least I can do after going off on you last time we were here.'

He offered a closed-mouthed smile.

Chloe went on. 'Look, David. I'm sorry for the way I acted. I had no right. For whatever reason, I was angry at what you were insinuating, and I just lost it. I shouldn't have. And again, I'm sorry. I really am.'

'Appreciate that,' David eventually said, and she saw his body visibly relax a little. 'I know the kind of things I was saying are hard to believe, so I don't blame you for thinking I'm nuts.'

'Well, that's just it. I *don't* think you are nuts. Not anymore.'

He frowned, then his eyes widened in realisation.

'Oh,' was all he could manage to say at first. After a few moments, he followed it up with, 'Is everyone okay?'

'For the moment,' Chloe replied. She appreciated that his first question was checking her wellbeing, rather than asking what had happened.

'But you have experienced something?' he followed up.

Chloe nodded. 'Yes. Though I wish I hadn't.'

A waiter approached the table—a young man with fluffy, wispy stubble and messy hair. He set the drinks and cakes down, and the smell of coffee along with the sweet food made Chloe's stomach growl loudly in anticipation. Too loudly, it seemed, and David looked up at her with wide eyes.

'Sorry,' she said with an embarrassed grin. 'I haven't eaten much today.'

David took a sip of his drink as Chloe grabbed a slice of caramel cake and bit into it. The taste exploded on her tongue, and she couldn't help but let out a small moan of appreciation.

'Mine!' Emma insisted.

Chloe turned to her and saw that her daughter had her arm outstretched, waiting for some of the delicious food as well. Chloe didn't normally like giving her daughter too much sugar, but couldn't very well deny her now.

Once the waiter had left them alone again, David leaned forward, placing his elbows on the table. 'Can I ask what happened?'

She nodded, then told him everything she could think of, starting with the events of the previous night but also her strange dreams of being pulled down through a hole in the ground—falling into an eternal abyss—as well as seeing the old woman in Sarah's room. She even told him about the hidden study. It felt good to unburden herself of it all.

At the mention of the room upstairs, David's eyes widened. 'I had no idea about that,' he said. 'The area was locked off when we carried out our investigation.'

'Well,' Chloe said, 'it really is something to see. But I think that pretty much brings you up to speed. So, tell me, do you think my family and I are in danger?'

She held her breath. The last time she'd met David, his word had been worth nothing to her. Now she was waiting for his judgment on the whole situation, ready to take his response as gospel.

'Quite possibly,' he replied. Chloe felt her stomach drop.

33

'THESE THINGS ARE COMPLICATED,' David went on. 'I've studied paranormal phenomena all my life, experienced some things I would have scarcely believed, and I still can't understand it all. But, after what I saw in Perron Manor, there is one thing I am sure of: that place is evil.'

'One that you want to investigate again, though,' Chloe cut in. 'So can it be too bad?'

'I have my reasons,' he replied. 'And I'd like to think I would be prepared enough to be safe. But the difference is, you and your family are living there, and are therefore in the house pretty much all the time. Given what I know about the history of the building, that kind of exposure never ends well.'

'Do I dare ask you to expand on that?'

'If you want to. It's all in the book I gave to your sister.'

'I didn't read it,' Chloe said. 'Though I might now.'

'Well, the important thing to note is that the cycle of tragic events has been repeated over and over for as long as Perron Manor has stood.'

'But my uncle lived there for many years, and nothing happened to him.'

'That's true enough,' David admitted. 'Like I said, these things are hard to explain and comprehend. I believe that these... spirits... for want of a better word, work on energy. It flows and pulses. Sometimes the power is stronger, and other times it isn't, so the manifestations are less potent. I have a theory that their actions are all tied to the living people they can draw on from the house. Maybe your uncle just wasn't a good fit for them.'

Sounded like a pretty flimsy explanation to Chloe. 'And the rest of us are?'

'Possibly,' David said. 'After all, you *are* experiencing heightened phenomena, are you not?'

Chloe stuffed a slice of shortbread into her mouth and chewed it quickly, considering David's words. They sounded ridiculous when spoken out loud, but it was the best she had to go on right now.

'Can we stop it?' she asked after she'd swallowed.

He hesitated in his response, looking uncertain. 'Hard to say. Normal hauntings can be tricky enough to cleanse at the best of times. Perron Manor is anything but normal. For example, I don't just think you are dealing with ghosts. I think there is something... darker... behind it all.'

Chloe hesitantly asked, 'What do you mean?'

David took another long sip of his steaming coffee. 'Well, towards the end of our investigation we saw something. And this was after already witnessing supernatural phenomena, and even seeing some spirits, which was a first for me. But things didn't stop there... they only got worse. At the end, we caught a glimpse of what I believe is the centrepiece of Perron Manor. The thing which was the puppet master to all the trapped souls within. A demon.'

Chloe just stared at him, unsure what to do with that information. On the one hand, it terrified her, but on the other just hearing the term *demon* sounded ridiculous.

'Stupid question, but having a demon... that's bad, right?'

David nodded. 'Extremely. Spirits can be bad enough, but this is a different level. Some believe demons have the power to twist and bend the souls of the dead to become their servants, to an extent, so those unfortunates are trapped in their own kind of eternal purgatory.'

'To an extent?'

'Yeah. There are differing views on this kind of thing, from a paranormal academic point of view.' *Paranormal academic*—those were two words Chloe would never have put together. But she let him continue. 'One school of thought is that demons are able to poison the souls of the dead and control them, but when left unchecked the tainted spirits act on their own free will. It's kind of like a warden controlling patients in an asylum. If not watched closely, the inmates run free.'

'Brilliant,' Chloe said. 'So, how do we get rid of the demon?'

'I'm afraid that is complicated. From what I understand, it isn't an exact science, and there are no guarantees. But I think an exorcism is the best bet. That could possibly banish the entity and free the souls of those trapped inside the house.'

Chloe slumped in her chair, feeling like she'd walked into a bad horror film. 'And how does one go about getting an exorcism performed?'

'You need to contact a vicar or priest to start the process. But it is a slow one. I know one local priest, Father Janosch, fairly well, and he has a little bit of experience in things like this. But ultimately, all he can do is verify the claims and then move the case up his chain of command, so to speak.'

'And how long does that take?' Chloe asked, but David's hesitant smile told her everything she needed to know.

'How long is a piece of string? I'd say months, at the very least.'

Great. We'll be dead before that happens. 'So I need to get my family out of there,' she stated.

'That might be your only option. At least for now. If you want, I can speak with Father Janosch and try to get things moving?'

Chloe paused.

Her instinct was just to go, flee, and leave the house to rot. But that would then mean they'd need to sell it, and that could be... difficult. Plus, Sarah didn't look like she would leave, anyway, and getting both Sarah and Andrew to agree to having an exorcism performed seemed unlikely. They would both think Chloe was losing it if she even suggested such a thing.

She closed her eyes. Her chest started to feel tighter. Chloe had never suffered panic attacks before, though she had an idea this could be the onset of one.

Everything seemed to be happening too fast and was spiralling out of control. It didn't seem too long ago that she was as happy as she'd ever been, looking forward to their new life in the perfect house. And now... now she was in a position where arranging a fucking exorcism seemed like a sane and reasonable step.

'I... I need to talk to my husband and sister about it,' she told him. 'They aren't exactly as open to this whole thing as I am. In fact, Sarah pretty much gave me the same treatment as I originally gave you.'

'I see,' David replied. 'Then you need to convince them.

This isn't a joke, and the longer it goes on, the worse it will all get. Especially given you already have a history with the house.'

Chloe cocked her head. 'What do you mean?'

'Well, you spent a little time there when you were young, right?'

'Yeah.'

'And you were there in '82?' Chloe nodded, and David went on, 'So the house, and the demon... it knows you. You got away once. It won't want to let that happen again.'

'Are you serious?!'

'Afraid so,' he replied. 'I've heard cases where demons can latch on to people instead of places, and they are relentless. Once they have contact, it can be hard to break, until the person is, well...' He trailed off.

'Dead,' Chloe finished for him. 'And I've walked right back to it.'

David gave a nod. 'Yeah. I could be wrong about all of this, of course. Like I keep saying, it isn't an exact science. But, considering these events started happening relatively quickly after you moved in, when sometimes they can take years to manifest, it stands to reason that whatever is there is using you to draw from. You mentioned your sister is acting a little strange, and sleepwalking. Could be that she is susceptible as well, and the demon is targeting her to get to you.'

Chloe leaned back in her chair. If her head had been spinning before, now she was completely reeling.

'So... this is all my fault?' she said, with a horrible realisation. Because *she* had brought her family in harm's way.

'Don't say that,' David quickly replied. 'You didn't know —how could you? It's just one of those things. You aren't to blame.'

But Chloe knew she *was* to blame. Regardless of whether the demon was focused on her or not, it had still been Chloe who had railroaded the others into coming to Perron Manor in the first place.

She had been the catalyst for the move. And now they were all going to pay the price.

'Can I ask?' David went on. 'What do you remember of your time there as a child? And do you remember much of *that* night?'

'Not a lot,' Chloe answered. 'I was six. How much can you remember from being six?'

'Not a great deal,' David admitted. 'But, with respect, I never went through what you did.'

'I wasn't even awake for most of that night,' she said. 'I have a vague memory of being outside with my uncle, and then my parents showed up, but I just seem to remember their panic at the time. Nothing more. I didn't actually see anything. While growing up, the whole thing was kinda hidden from me, never spoken about. I only really learned what happened after I looked it up myself. So, as bad as that night supposedly was, it never really affected me. That is why I was so comfortable going back there to Perron Manor. To me, it was just ancient history. Gruesome, yes, but it didn't change the fact I had inherited an absolutely beautiful house and didn't have to pay a penny for it. In my head, it was more foolish to turn it away. I never dreamed that it would be...'

She couldn't complete the sentence out loud, but her inner voice finished things up for her.

Haunted.

She contemplated her situation, trying to determine the best course of action. All roads seemed to point back to fleeing.

However, before that could happen, Chloe needed to have a long conversation with her husband and sister. Even then, it wasn't likely they could just leave straight away. She looked up to David.

'I have to ask,' she began. 'Given you know so much about it, even wrote a book, what is with your obsession with Perron Manor?'

David hesitated—taking another drink—and then lifted up a biscuit from the plate. 'I dunno,' he said. 'This kind of thing has always fascinated me. And since I'm local to the area, Perron Manor was probably the first place I became aware of that was rumoured to be haunted. I was only young at the time, but the stories always stuck. So, having such a fantastic location so close to me, which I was never able to access for the longest time, made it a bit of a 'white whale.' Even if only half the stories are true, I would say it's still the most haunted house in Britain.'

'Brilliant,' Chloe said, deadpan. 'And I'm living in the fucking thing.'

34

Sarah's lungs burned, and her feet were sore from pounding the tarmac. She would be back at the house soon but felt like she still had too much negative energy to burn. With gritted teeth, she pushed her jog into a sprint.

Anything to help snuff out the anger inside.

In truth, just getting outside again had helped a little. She had avoided Chloe after their fight, where at one point Sarah was close to taking a swing at her sister. Thankfully, Chloe left to go somewhere, which afforded Sarah space. Still, Sarah wanted to focus her anger into something at least semi-productive. So, she'd changed into her sportswear —a tank-top with a thin, cotton jacket over the top, lycra sports leggings, and a pair of running shoes—and went out for a long run.

The route had taken her down long and winding country lanes, before skirting the fringes of the town of Alnmouth. Finally, she was working her way back. It had been close to an hour and a half already, and Sarah was enjoying once again pushing herself physically. Ever since she'd moved in, her fitness had been neglected and taken something of a nosedive.

The scenery, too, was a welcome change to the relative gloom of Perron Manor. The beautiful sky above was beginning to burn orange at the onset of dusk.

While it felt good to be out of the house, she still had no intention of leaving it permanently. If Chloe was going to run, then she was a fool.

Sarah turned back into the driveway to Perron Manor and saw those distinctive three peaks at the head of the front elevation. She also saw Chloe's car was back.

She jogged up the steps in a few long strides, then stopped at the front door, checking her pulse. Sarah glanced at the brass knocker again: the frowning lion's head with a circular ring dangling from its mouth. She hadn't been overly enamoured with it upon first laying eyes on the thing, but it had certainly grown on her and helped add to the charm of the house.

Once inside, Sarah made a beeline for her room straight away, not wanting to see or interact with her sister. She showered, and as she was changing Sarah heard a gentle rap on her door.

'Sarah?'

Closing her eyes, she tried not to clench her teeth together too tightly. Chloe's muffled voice from the other side of the door was *not* welcome right now.

No doubt she just wanted to talk again about how she was going to run away, like a coward. Sarah didn't want to hear that. What she wanted to do was grab Chloe and shake her, and tell her she *had* to stay. She belonged here at the house.

They all did.

Sarah felt like she *had* found herself here, especially over the last few days. She knew where she needed to be.

Force her to stay.

Sarah had a sudden resolve to make Chloe see things the same way. Her sister called out again.

'Sarah, can we talk?'

Perhaps speaking with Chloe right now wasn't such a bad thing.

'Come in,' she called back, slipping on a powder-blue wool jumper, one that wasn't too thick or heavy.

Chloe entered the room.

Sarah had expected her to be ready for an argument—a frown and set jaw, shoulders square, ready for combat. But the half-smile Chloe wore was almost apologetic.

'What is it?' Sarah asked firmly.

'I spoke with Andrew,' Chloe replied. 'Went over a few things with him.'

'And how does he feel about his wife believing in fairy-tales?' Sarah asked, her tone thick with sarcasm. However, the point was ignored, and Chloe continued on as if Sarah hadn't said anything.

'We're going to look for another place,' she said. 'Both permanently and something in the short term. We might even rent. And we're going to try and find a hotel or bed and breakfast that can fit us in for tonight. Andrew is making some calls right now.'

Sarah's jaw hung open. 'You can't be serious.'

'I'm not sure if we will find anywhere close enough on so little notice, but I want to try. I just don't feel safe here anymore. And I... want you to come with us.'

A humourless laugh escaped Sarah before she could stop herself. 'You've lost it,' she said. 'Absolutely lost your

Goddamn mind. I'm not going to follow you while you scamper away like a gutless coward.'

Sarah thought the barb might have at least angered her sister a little, but instead Chloe just stepped forward, hands clasped together at her belly.

'Please,' Chloe said, 'just consider it. Even if it's just for a night at first. Get away from this place and clear your head.'

'No!' Sarah shouted. 'I'm not leaving. And you shouldn't either. Jesus Christ, Chloe, just think about what you're doing.'

'I know it's hard to believe,' Chloe told her. 'I get that. I also know I'm asking a lot. But, well, I'm not just asking. I'm *begging*. I spoke with the guy who wrote that book you read—'

'Who?' Sarah cut in. 'That whacko you yelled at in the coffee shop? *You* spoke to *him*?'

'Yes,' Chloe answered.

'And he got you believing this place is haunted, didn't he.'

'*He* didn't, Sarah. The things that happened to me made me believe it. But David did tell me it's dangerous to stay here, that the house wants me after I got away from it when I was little. And, without an exorcism—'

'Exorcism?' Sarah asked, bringing her hands up to her head in disbelief. 'Are you fucking for real?!'

'That's the only way to release the souls that are trapped here...' Chloe paused, then shook her head. 'Never mind, none of that is important. But, we need to leave.'

'Enough!' Sarah snapped, thrusting her fists down to her sides and gritting her teeth together.

Within moments, Andrew appeared at the door, Emma in his hands. He gave Sarah a half-smile, and it occurred to

Sarah that she'd not spoken to him properly since all of this madness started.

'Can you believe this?' she asked him, pointing at Chloe. He didn't answer, so she pressed further. 'Tell me you don't believe this rubbish as well?'

'Look, Sarah,' he said, defensively, 'there's no need for you guys to fight. We need clear heads here.'

'Clear heads?' Sarah asked, incredulous. 'Clear heads do not believe in ghosts, Andrew.'

He looked away, almost embarrassed. Sarah knew he didn't really believe his wife either. And yet, he was still going along with her crazy demands.

'Sarah,' Chloe began. 'Please. Just come with us tonight.'

'Actually,' Andrew cut in, 'about that. I haven't been able to find anywhere with any space on such short notice.'

Sarah saw Chloe's face fall. Was she really so scared to spend just one more night in the house? If so, it was pathetic.

'There has to be somewhere,' Chloe said, but Andrew just gave an apologetic shrug.

'I'm sorry.'

Sarah folded her arms across her chest. 'Okay,' she said with a smirk. 'How about this. We stay *here* tonight. If something happens, and I see it, then I'll believe you. If nothing happens, then you consider the fact that whatever *is* happening could all be in your head, and you are upheaving all our lives for no reason.'

'No,' Chloe said softly, shaking her head.

'Chloe,' Andrew began, 'there isn't any other option for tonight, we need to stay here. Unless you want us to sleep outside. But I don't think Emma would thank you for that.'

The muscles in Chloe's jaw tensed, and then she stormed out of the room.

'You obviously can't be that scared if you're happy enough to go off on your own,' Sarah called after her, and Andrew shot her a scowl. 'Oh come on, Andrew, why are you humouring her here? Is it just so you can get your way and get out of this place? It's all clearly bullshit and you *know* it. You're just using it to your advantage.'

'I'll tell you what I know,' Andrew said, with a surprisingly stern tone. 'I know that my wife—your *sister*—is really struggling at the moment. No, I don't think the things she is saying are physically true, but I can see something is weighing on her. I've never seen her like this before, so I'm worried about her. And, given how close you two always were, I'm surprised you can't see it, either. Or do you just not care anymore?'

Sarah's mouth was already open to fire back when she caught herself and paused, considering his words. Her body relaxed a little, and her posture slumped as guilt washed over her.

He was right.

Regardless of what Chloe was saying, it was clear something was very wrong. And instead of helping her sister, as she normally would have, Sarah's reaction had been to try and mock her, shame her, and beat her into submission. Sarah's defences had come up straight away, as if any slight towards Perron Manor was somehow aimed at her as well.

It wasn't like her, especially when it came to Chloe, the person she was closest to in the whole world. Sarah felt nauseous as the realisation came over her, and she started to leave the room.

'Don't,' Andrew said. 'Another fight isn't going to help anything.'

'We aren't going to fight,' Sarah replied. 'I promise.'

She then went looking for Chloe, searching the middle

floor. And finding her in Vincent's old room surprised Sarah.

Chloe was seated on the end of the bed, looking at the floor, and had tears running down her face. Her hands gripped the bedsheets so tightly that her knuckles were white.

Seeing her sister like this, almost broken, only served to increase the shame Sarah felt.

'Hey,' she said, her voice little more than a whisper.

Chloe didn't look up. 'Hey.'

Sarah didn't know where to begin with her apology, but she sat on the bed next to Chloe and put an arm around her. Thankfully, Chloe leaned in.

'I'm sorry,' Sarah said. 'I don't know what's been wrong with me lately.'

'Well, I'm sorry for fucking this all up for us,' Chloe replied. 'You're right. I *was* the one who persuaded everyone to come here, and now I'm the one who wants us gone.' She sniffed, then wiped the back of her hand across her face, smearing tears across it. 'What the fuck is wrong with me?' Chloe asked, and she broke down again, her shoulders shaking as she sobbed.

'Nothing,' Sarah insisted, then hugged her tightly. She then turned Chloe to face her. 'Listen to me, Sis. If you want to go, then we'll go. Tomorrow, we'll find somewhere to stay, then leave.'

'But... you don't want to. You don't believe any of it.'

That was true, but what was really important here had suddenly been brought into focus: Chloe's wellbeing.

Screw the house.

'I believe that you need to be away from this place, for whatever reason. So, we'll do it. I'll come with you, and we can figure the rest out from there. I know we'll need to stay here for tonight, but come tomorrow, we're gone. All of us.'

The sounds of the pipes within the walls suddenly beginning to rattle startled them both, and Sarah heard a faint screeching that sounded like expanding metal. However, everything soon settled into silence again.

Sarah then saw that Chloe had tensed up, so she smiled mischievously at her sister.

'Guess the house doesn't want us to go, huh?' she joked.

Thankfully, Chloe smiled as well. 'I guess not.' Then Chloe added, 'Are you sure you're okay coming with us?'

'Of course,' Sarah replied, happy to see the relief on her sister's face. 'Are you gonna be okay staying here for one more night?'

Chloe shrugged but was still smiling. 'Looks like I'll have to be.'

35

It had just turned nine o'clock in the evening, and darkness had set in outside.

Chloe, Sarah, and Andrew were all gathered together in the living room. Emma was up in her room, asleep. Chloe hated that her daughter was alone, and it made her even more on edge.

They had tried to keep the child downstairs with them, to placate Chloe, but Emma had refused to sleep with the others in the room. She just thought it was playtime. The child fought against her obvious tiredness and, eventually, her weary yowls turned into a full-on screaming fit. It was then Andrew suggested that they put her to bed, but keep a close eye on the monitor. Given he didn't really believe there was any danger, his primary concern at that point was that his child get the sleep she needed.

Chloe didn't want to agree, but Sarah had assured her that they would all be close by, and at the first sign of trouble all three of them would be able to get upstairs quickly to help. She had explained everything in a kind and gentle manner, with no mocking or condescension. Chloe appreciated that, though she still felt like a child being talked down to by the grown-ups.

That only served to make Chloe question her sanity even more. Was she just losing it? Had the events of the previous night actually been perfectly explainable but she had just twisted them out of all proportion in her own, tired mind?

Previously, she had been certain of what she had seen. No question. But now...

Instead of concentrating on the film on the television with the others, Chloe spent most of her time looking at the baby monitor, watching Emma sleep soundly, clouded in the blue hue of night-vision.

Andrew had managed to get the fire in the room going, which kicked out a lot of heat and a pleasantly smokey smell. He was seated next to Chloe, with an arm draped over her and her head rested on his chest. Sarah was on the sofa adjacent to them, wrapped up in a blanket.

On any other occasion, it could have been a wonderful and cosy night in for them all.

But for Chloe, it was simply a case of counting down the minutes until she could go up to bed. She was seriously considering sleeping on the floor of Emma's room tonight, though she knew Andrew would likely not be happy with that.

It was hard not to replay the events of the previous night, and also to call her memory into question. *Was* there a way it could have been explained?

Emma let out a moan, and Chloe fixed her eyes on the screen. However, the child was just shuffling about in her sleep. Perfectly safe.

Sarah let out a yawn from her place on the adjacent sofa.

'Sorry, Andrew,' she said, 'but you have the worst taste in films.'

'This is a classic,' he protested.

'It's garbage,' Sarah replied.

Chloe actually found their playful bickering nice. Like a small return to normality.

'Back me up here,' Andrew said, prodding Chloe in the ribs. She jolted a little and smiled.

'Sorry, hun,' she said, turning to him, 'but I'm not a fan.'

'Bah,' Andrew huffed, making a show of throwing up his free hand. 'You're both heathens.'

Chloe chuckled, then turned back to check on the monitor again. Emma was still safe.

In fact, even after the film finished and the three of them decided to go up to bed, nothing untoward happened. Chloe and Andrew bid Sarah a good night—Sarah even hugged Chloe tightly—and then they quietly checked on Emma.

Still safe.

Chloe and Andrew then readied themselves for the night and climbed into bed. The monitor, as ever, was positioned on the nightstand, not far from Chloe's head.

With the lights off, Chloe lay motionless, just watching the dark shadows in the room and feeling the stresses of the day catch up with her. But all was well... or as well as it could be. Nothing was happening. And that was enough.

Eventually, Chloe fell asleep, knowing that this would be her last night ever in Perron Manor.

36

CHLOE WAS HELD DOWN, unable to move. Everything was dark around her. The voice that came from above was vile and inhuman, sounding like the purest form of hate she could imagine. A smell followed it—a disgusting stink of rot and death.

'We are going to kill your baby.'

Chloe fought with everything she had. Large, cold hands grabbed her head. She still could not see. Her neck twisted and then began to snap as she was killed in absolute darkness.

She woke with a gasp, gripping the sheets of her bed, her body locked tightly.

That voice, and the smell, was still with her. A feeling of cold emanated close to her ear.

'Kill... your... baby.'

Chloe quickly managed to regain control of her body to turn her head in panic, but saw nothing beside her, only the blue hue of the monitor.

Just a dream. Another horrible fucking dream.

Her breathing was rapid, and she couldn't help but take short and shallow breaths as anxiety gripped her. The sheets around her felt damp with sweat. Andrew snored loudly beside her.

Calm down, Chloe told herself. *Control your breathing.*

She tried to do just that. Eventually, her body relaxed.

Another horrible dream.

But in the end, she knew it was just that—a dream, and nothing more. Chloe wiped a little of the sweat away from her forehead and turned her body so she could squint at the monitor. Emma was seemingly in a deep sleep, lying blissfully unaware of anything except her own dreams. The digital clock next to the monitor showed the time was a quarter past three in the morning.

Chloe rolled over to her back and let out a sigh. *Get a grip on yourself.*

She then allowed her eyes to close again, hoping she could relax enough to fall back to sleep.

However, a noise from the corner of the room—a faint and brief clicking sound—drew her attention.

The only light afforded was the dull glow from the baby monitor, as well as the faint bits of moonlight that managed to penetrate the thick, dark curtains. Most of the room was heavy with darkness, and Chloe's vision could scarcely stretch over to the far wall. There was one corner in particular, however, that seemed much darker than the others, where the shadows were heavier.

Chloe could not see where the walls met, but it was where the sound seemed to have originated.

She squinted, but couldn't make anything out. Then there was another sound, one that made her body lock up again: a long and loud exhale, coming from the same place.

Chloe lifted herself up to her elbows, eyes wide, and

tried to process what she had just heard. Could it be that someone was standing in the corner of the room, lost in the shadows?

She didn't know what to do, so when she whispered a faint, 'Hello?' she immediately felt stupid. Did she really expect some kind of response?

And yet, that is exactly what she got.

The response was a hoarse whisper, male, and sounded almost pained.

'*Chloe...*'

Her heart seized. She wanted to elbow Andrew hard in the back and scream his name, just so he could witness this. But she couldn't find the strength to move.

Then, she saw something emerge slightly from the black. It was the form of a man, though she could see little more than his facial features, the body below still hidden.

Chloe gripped her sheets tighter. She struggled to breathe while gazing at the smiling face that was framed with dark, brushed-back hair. The man's eyes were bloody and mangled holes. Tendrils of blood ran from the wounds, lining the face like horrible tears, even streaking his exposed teeth. His jaw was square and chiselled, and the throat beneath had a yawning slash across it which opened up the flesh. Blood ran freely from that wound as well.

Though she didn't know how, the man's face seemed familiar, somehow.

'*We've... missed... you,*' he said. Each word seemed to be a struggle, though his mouth never moved. Blood pumped from the open neck wound.

Go away, go away, go away, Chloe begged.

This couldn't be real. *Couldn't be!*

And yet, she could see it. No matter how much she

willed the horrifying image to disappear, it simply would not. The man continued to smile and stare.

A noise escaped her throat, but it was barely comprehensible—neither a word nor a scream. More like a mewl.

Then, the man retreated in one swift and fluid motion, once again disappearing into the darkness.

Chloe fought to try and push her fear back enough that she could move, or at least scream.

However, another noise came from beside her, and was enough to force Chloe to turn her head. She looked to the baby monitor. The sound was crackly, but sounded like a heavy breath.

'No!'

The word fell out of her, an instinctual reaction to the thing on the screen. It wasn't her daughter anymore, but a face so close to the camera as to be washed out in white.

She could make out a set of cracked and misshapen teeth, given the mouth was so close to the camera. Thin lips were pulled back into a hateful smile as the mouth tittered. The skin was pulled tightly over the skull beneath it, but the eyes were out of the frame.

And then, words spilled from the monitor in strained and breathless tones.

'*Round... and round... the garden...*'

Finally, the fear that held Chloe prisoner was broken as sheer panic that exploded within. Whatever that thing was, it was in there with Emma.

'Andrew!' she shouted and jumped out of bed. In her peripheral vision, she saw her husband start to stir, but she was out of the room before he'd fully woken up.

Please be okay, please be okay, please be okay, Chloe repeated the mantra over and over again as she burst into the hallway, praying for the best. The thought of her defenceless and innocent daughter alone in her room with that... *thing* embedded a new level of terror inside her that she didn't know was possible.

She thrust the door open and hit the light switch, illuminating the room. Emma's fuzzy head started to move, and the child rolled over with a look of surprise on her little face.

Chloe's eyes darted around, first looking to the camera, then checking everywhere else. She was scared, more than she had ever been in her life, and confused beyond belief, but the need to protect her daughter made her fight through the fear. She quickly checked under the bed, in the wardrobes, and even behind the curtains.

But she found no one.

'Chloe?' she heard Andrew call in a tired and confused voice. 'What is it?'

She didn't respond but instead scooped Emma up out of her cot-bed, then checked her over. Other than being a little disgruntled at being woken, Emma seemed fine, and she rubbed at her eyes with small, chubby hands. But Chloe's heart still hammered in her chest, and she knew she had to get the little girl out of that room.

Hell, out of the house.

Then, Chloe saw Emma look past her, over her shoulder, and Chloe felt an intense cold radiate from behind.

Emma pointed.

'Man!'

Spinning around, Chloe let out a shriek. The thing that towered over Chloe, blocking the door, was indeed a man, but not the one she had seen in her bedroom. This one was different: thinner, older, and much, much taller.

The stranger's skin was the colour of ash, and his eyes were milky, with small pupils dead centre. There were no eyelids, so the stare he gave was a manic one, with his eyes almost bulging out of their sockets. His face was almost skeletal, and his bared teeth were cracked, chipped, and misshapen. Wispy and patchy white hair jutted out from his cranium at wild angles.

In addition, she saw that the man was dressed in a dirty and ragged black suit, one that looked to be from a different era.

A horrible stench wafted over Chloe, like rotten meat, and a large and pale hand reached out for her.

37

SARAH'S MIND swum back to consciousness, and she sat upright in bed. Everything was confusing. Shards of abstract images—leftover fragments of her dream—replayed in her mind.

Tania. The bomb. Sarah bathing in what remained of her friend, grasping the sloppy remains and rubbing the glistening red flesh over her own body. *Such... pleasure.*

However, screaming had pulled her from the dream. She lifted her head from the pillow and felt something like a breath on her face. Not just a breath, however, but a spoken word.

Dede!

She shook her head again, and it did not take long for her waking mind to fully take over and push the horrid dream away, banishing it to a vague memory that quickly dissipated. A sudden feeling of urgency brought Sarah's senses back to full alert.

Though the screams sounded far off, they were still very audible.

Chloe!

She quickly scrambled from her bed, planted her bare feet on the floor, and ran from the room, dressed only in the white tank top and grey shorts she had been sleeping in.

The corridor outside felt cold, as if all the windows on the floor had been left open during the night. She saw Andrew appear from his room, and the two made brief eye contact. He looked as confused and panicked as Sarah felt. He stopped at Emma's room, the source of the screaming, and Sarah then realised that she could hear Emma crying as well.

Her heart dropped.

Please God, don't let anything have happened to her.

Andrew frantically tried to open the door to Emma's room but was met with resistance.

'Chloe, what's happened?' he yelled and banged his fist against the thick wood. 'Let me in!'

The only response was another scream, so he began thrusting his shoulder into the door in an effort to force it open. Andrew threw himself at the door again and again, but it did little more than rattle its hinges. Emma continued to wail.

Sarah was next to Andrew a few moments later and pushed him aside.

'Chloe!' she screamed. 'Let us in!'

She tried to force the door open as well, and kicked against it, thrusting the sole of her foot hard against the weak point where the handle and latch were. The door shook. Another kick. And another. Then, with a scream, Sarah flung herself shoulder first, again aiming for the weak point.

Nothing.

Andrew began to help, and the two of them hit the door with their bodies, one after the other, in quick succession.

The wood of the door dented and cracked, and it was forced open ever so slightly.

They kept going, yelling out for Chloe, but getting no response. Andrew looked inside through the small gap they had made, where the door met the frame.

'Jesus, someone's in there with her,' he exclaimed, and Sarah pushed her head in to see as well.

A large figure, easily over seven feet tall, loomed over Chloe, who was sitting on the floor with her back pressed against the far wall, Emma clutched to her chest.

The man who was slowly approaching her, almost gliding, suddenly turned and gazed at Sarah and Andrew as they peered in. Sarah let out a gasp at those wide eyes and their dead stare. She knew instantly that the thing was not human.

Chloe was right!

All along, Chloe had been right.

'Leave her alone!' Sarah screamed, but was not able to sound nearly as commanding as she wanted or needed to be.

Keep going, a voice inside told her, the one she relied on when she needed to face dangerous situations.

'I'm coming, Chloe!'

Of course, Sarah had no idea how to help when she finally got into the room, given what they were facing, but still she had to get to Chloe and Emma. Sarah backed up, tensed herself, and again thrust a strong kick into the door.

Thankfully, this time, the door opened, as if whatever force had been holding it shut instantly disappeared.

Sarah just about fell in the room, with Andrew close behind. Chloe was still on the floor, sobbing, and pressing herself against the far wall. Emma wriggled and cried in her arms.

But Sarah could see no-one else. She looked around the room as Andrew ran over to his wife and child. Checking the wardrobes and under the cot-bed yielded no results. Whoever—or *what*ever—had been in here, was now gone. Sarah then rushed over to her sister and niece and dropped down next to Andrew.

She locked eyes with Chloe, who looked defeated and terrified in equal measure, with tears streaked down her face. Sarah put a firm hand on Chloe's shoulder, knowing they were not out of the woods by a long shot. She didn't pretend to even remotely understand what was happening, but she knew they were still in danger.

'Sis... we need to go. We need to get you and Emma out of here. Now.'

38

EMMA WAS PRESSED TIGHTLY to her chest, but Chloe didn't dare relax her grip any. They were running down the main stairs, with Andrew on one side of her and Sarah on the other.

No one was talking, only panting frantically as they moved.

Given what had happened up in Emma's room, Chloe didn't need the others to admit they believed her now. They had seen the entity with their own eyes.

The thought of that dead man still terrified her, and she could not shake the feeling of his icy touch from when his hand had lain on her shoulder. At the time, Chloe had turned away to shield Emma, but the sound of the door to the room being kicked open had quickly drawn her attention.

The tall man was gone, but Sarah and Andrew had emerged. They came to her. Soon after, they all ran.

Sarah was holding Chloe's upper arm tightly as they turned onto the half-landing, guiding her. They then thundered down the remaining flight of stairs, towards the entrance door.

A horrible banging sound erupted from all around, like something was trying to break through the very walls of the house. Chloe felt thick reverberations in the steps beneath her feet.

So sudden was the onset of violent sounds that she jolted, and Emma almost slipped from her grasp. Her reactions were quick, thankfully, and she managed to keep hold of the child. But the close call still made her heart race even more, if that was possible.

Emma's cries only made the frantic situation they found themselves in even worse. The child was confused and scared—the same as the rest of them. Chloe felt like a failure in every respect.

When her foot made contact with the marble floor, the continuous crashing sounds ceased instantly, though they still echoed in her ears. Then, the front door slowly creaked open on its own.

The fleeing group drew to a quick halt as the door finished its swing. There was no one outside. All Chloe could see was the front steps leading down into the night.

Who the hell opened the door?

'What do we do?' Chloe asked, her voice a scared whisper.

'We run,' Sarah replied, sounding determined.

Chloe didn't have time to argue, as Sarah again grabbed her and pulled her along. Andrew followed, and they all quickly moved towards the now-open door. Chloe didn't like it, though. Something was very wrong.

Her concerns were quickly realised when a bloody hand appeared from outside. Its fingers curled around the side of the door frame, taking hold from its position close to the ground. The group stopped again and Chloe shrieked. She heard a low moan, and a dry sliding sound as a disfigured *thing* pulled itself into view.

It was once a man, but the head had been brutally battered and misshapen. Large, tumour-like bulges protruded from one side, and both eyes were covered over with a stretch of solid skin.

It was his mouth that drew Chloe's attention first, with the jaw completely removed. Blood ran freely from the ripped and jagged flesh at the sides, and another pained groan came from him. The horrific entity pulled itself farther into view. One arm was cut and lacerated, but the other was just a deformed and withered stump from the elbow.

'This can't be happening,' Andrew said, wide-eyed in sheer terror. He took a step back, pulling Chloe with him. The rest of the monstrosity at the door came into view, though there wasn't much more to see given it was cut off at the midsection. A severed spinal cord was dragged behind, wrapped up in spaghetti-like entrails.

The crawling monster reached out towards them with its good hand, and its tongue lolled and writhed like a snake.

Chloe screamed. The three turned and ran, ducking into a side corridor.

'The back door,' Sarah commanded, breathless, sounding distinctly less determined than before.

39

CONCENTRATE ON GETTING OUT. Nothing else matters.

The things Sarah had witnessed were enough to drive her insane. But she knew that if she gave in to that line of thinking, then it was all over for them. So, she pushed the need to rationalise everything completely out of her mind.

Just focus on the next step.

The next step was getting to the great hall, and then getting the hell out through the back door. Then they could escape.

Unless something else was waiting for them there, of course.

Sarah led the others through the corridor safely, and out into the great hall. It was dark, so Sarah switched on the lights upon entering. They flickered a few times before hitting their full strength.

A shriek from Chloe drew Sarah's attention, and she looked to the glazed rear door. Sarah felt her body freeze.

Standing in front of the door—perfectly still and blocking the exit—was a woman. She was dressed in an old, black dress with a high collar. White hair was pulled up into a loose bun.

The woman looked ancient and had sagging, wrinkled, and ashen skin. Black teeth were revealed as her cracked lips spread back in a menacing grin. Where her eyes should have been were instead black pits that ran with blood. The muscles in her throat moved, and Sarah heard a croaked, vile-sounding chuckle.

The woman lifted up her arms to them, and Sarah saw that the fingers were skeletal, with only small patches of dark and decayed flesh on the bone.

Shit.

Then the banging noises started again, accompanied by horrible wails and screeching. It sounded similar to when they started the furnace, only amplified in intensity.

'We can't go that way!' Chloe exclaimed, stating the obvious.

Sarah was always prepared for a fight if the situation called for it, but how the hell were you supposed to fight *those* things?

A pressure built in her chest and Sarah realised her focus was waning. Fear was taking over.

'Back the way we came,' Andrew instructed. However, even before they turned, Sarah felt a blast of icy-cold air across her back.

Someone was directly behind them.

When they spun, Sarah saw a young, blonde-haired man, who was completely naked, his stomach cut open from navel to breast. He was only a few feet away, and intestines ran out from the stomach wound over his gesturing hands. The man looked at the group through milky, blank eyes, with an almost confused expression.

'*Help*,' he whispered.

The banging continued around them, getting louder and louder. The group sprinted away from the staggering man, who shuffled after them, still holding his rope-like intestines.

'This can't be real!' Sarah shouted, desperate to cling to sanity. But she was finding that difficult.

Only one exit seemed to be unobstructed, and they moved towards it—the door down to the basement. Sarah pressed her palm to a nearby wall as they ran, in an effort to keep her balance as Chloe fell into her. As Sarah's hand touched the wall, she felt something warm and wet. Glancing at her hand, she saw it was streaked red.

Blood was trickling down the wall.

'What the fuck...'

Chloe looked as well, then let out a cry of fear. The walls were actually *bleeding*. And what's more, Sarah was certain that she saw texture beneath some ripped wallpaper that didn't seem right. Was that... *skin?*

'We need to keep going,' Andrew stressed, but it was clear he was as scared as the rest of them and looked close to tears. Through it all, Emma continued to cry.

Even through her panic, Sarah knew they should try and loop around again towards the front door, as the basement offered no way to escape. However, the half-man they'd seen at the entrance was dragging himself through the other door that led to the front entrance, his tongue trailing across the floor as he moved.

The door to the basement hung open, inviting them in.

'There!' Andrew said, pointing to it. 'That way!'

He ran ahead, pulling Chloe and guiding them towards it. Chloe, in turn, pulled Sarah.

No, she thought. *This isn't right. We're being shepherded.*

She tried to stop them as they crossed the threshold into

the small room that housed the steps, and pulled at Chloe's hand. However, something cold and firm grabbed her from behind.

Sarah didn't even see what it was, but it caused her hand to slip from Chloe's.

Her sister looked back, confused, and then the door between them slammed shut.

She was then spun around, and the thing that held Sarah pushed her hard up against the now-closed door.

'Sarah!' she heard her sister call out from behind. But as Sarah stared into the demonic yellow eyes before her, she knew it was hopeless.

'Chloe! Run!'

40

'WE NEED TO GO,' Andrew urged, breathless. He pulled Chloe along with him towards the steps that led down.

'But what about Sarah?' Chloe argued. 'We need to get her!'

Andrew shook his head without making eye contact. 'We *need* to keep moving. Whatever those things are, they'll be through soon.'

Emma's crying was relentless as Andrew guided Chloe over to the top of the steps. She didn't know what to do. Leaving Sarah like that didn't seem right, but then, she needed to get Emma away from danger.

They descended, Andrew leading the way. It occurred to Chloe that it should have been pitch black down in the basement, but she could see a faint and flickering orange glow.

The farther down the steps they got, the more Chloe could make out the distinct crackling of a fire. It was only when they reached the bottom that she saw it: the furnace at full blaze. All of its front doors were open and the flames within were roaring. They stopped in their tracks.

'Andrew, we need to go back,' Chloe cried.

Over the noise of the fire, Chloe could hear something else as well, something coming from *inside* the inferno. Cries of pain. She also saw movement—a black form that writhed within the fire and moved to the front of the furnace.

It was a man. Hideously burned, with blistered, blackened, and melted features.

'*Help!*' he cried, reaching an arm through one of the openings. Chloe saw that the fingers of the hand had been fused together, one of his eyes had been melted away, and there was a sickening smell of cooking meat suddenly around them.

She turned around and pulled Andrew with her, but both quickly stopped.

Someone was standing on the stairs behind them. And Chloe immediately recognised the face and brushed back hair—as well as the gouged-out eyes and slashed throat. It was the man she had seen in her room earlier, the one who had peeked out from the shadows.

Once again she had the impression she vaguely recognized him.

Andrew let out an involuntary cry of panic, and the two backed up. The man on the stairs laughed. He was dressed in a dark suit with a black shirt beneath. The chest of the shirt was wet with his own blood, which spilled freely from the yawning hole in his throat.

'*Hello... Chloe,*' the man said in a strained voice.

Seeing his fine—if ruined—clothing and hearing his voice again, though distorted, ignited something in Chloe's memory. From a time when she was very young.

She knew who this man was now. *Marcus Blackwater!*

He took a heavy step down towards them, emitting an insidious chuckle.

Chloe and Andrew continued to backpedal until Marcus —or what *used* to be Marcus—stood in the basement with them, barring the only exit. Emma writhed in Chloe's arms, still crying. Chloe didn't know what to do. She felt the heat from the great furnace behind her.

She then jumped as Andrew let out a fierce roar, and he charged at the entity blocking their escape. Chloe didn't even have time to call out his name before her husband reached Marcus. The grinning monster held up its arm, and planted its palm directly into Andrew's oncoming chest.

Andrew let out a pain-filled cry, and his body was thrown back like a rag doll, landing over ten feet away. He crumpled to the ground and rolled over, ending up in a motionless heap.

'No! Andrew!' Chloe cried out, unsure if her husband was even alive.

Marcus Blackwater just continued to cackle.

The screaming of the man trapped in the furnace suddenly ceased, and that alone was enough to draw Chloe's panicked attention. She quickly turned her head to see that the burned figure was still inside the roaring fire, but now seemed unconcerned with the searing flames. He peeked out through one of the holes, focusing on her with his one good eye, seemingly unconcerned by the heat and fire that continued to ruin his body. He reached a hand out again and curled its fused fingers inwards in a beckoning motion.

'*Give me... the baby.*'

Horrible, mocking laughter burst from the unmoving mouth.

Chloe ran over to Andrew, unsure what else to do with Marcus blocking the stairs and the horrible burnt thing in the raging furnace. Emma continued her desperate screams.

Chloe touched Andrew's arm. It felt ice cold, but he was still breathing.

'Get up, Andrew,' she begged, but he was unresponsive.

She then felt cold hands grab her by the shoulders—although 'hands' wasn't the right word. The fingers were long and sharp, more like talons, and the tips pierced her skin. She screamed, but whatever it was held her firm, easily overpowering her. The cold and the stink that flowed from behind Chloe was overwhelming.

A shadow fell over her front. She looked up to see someone standing before her, looming over both her and Emma, while she was held from behind.

'*Ring... a ring... o' roses...*'

It was the old man in the filthy suit. The one with the wide, lidless eyes, and almost skeletal features.

And he plucked Emma from Chloe's arms.

41

SARAH OPENED HER EYES, and it took her a moment to realise where she was: still in the great hall, but sitting on the floor with her back against the door that had cut her off from her sister.

She twisted her head both left and right, but the thing that had grabbed her was now gone. However, its ice-cold touch still lingered on her skin.

Sarah realised she must have blacked out, but *why* exactly, or for how long, she had no idea. She could not shake the image of the face, twisted and inhuman. Or its burning yellow eyes.

It had been different than the other entities she'd already seen. Something ancient and evil.

A demon.

Sarah's heart pounded violently in her chest, and she couldn't help from shaking. As cowardly as it made her feel, she wanted to flee. The idea of staying here to help her family caused her stomach to churn. Despite all the life-threatening situations she'd been in throughout her career, Sarah had never experienced fear like this.

Everything was just so unknown. The rules of engagement were non-existent, and the enemy seemed as unbeatable as it was unknowable.

Getting to her feet seemed like a herculean effort and left her feeling weak and exposed. Though she could see nothing else around her in the great hall, it felt like a million eyes were watching and waiting, ready to pounce when the time was right.

She knew she should run downstairs to help Chloe, Emma, and Andrew. However, Sarah couldn't bring her body to move. She remembered what her sister had said in their fight the previous day, something about the house wanting Chloe because she'd gotten away from it once before.

That was probably why it had stopped them from leaving. But it had her now. It had what it wanted.

Sarah looked to one of the doors that led to the front exit. Perhaps it was an opportunity for her while the house was busy. It shamed her beyond words, but that exit now looked *very* appealing.

42

THE HORRIFIC SCREAMING of his wife was the first thing to register in Andrew's mind as he slowly regained consciousness.

He opened his eyes, but his vision was spinning and blurred. He wanted to vomit.

What the hell is happening?

His body felt like it had been frozen, and an intense cold radiated out from his chest in waves. It took a moment for his memory to catch up, and he was reminded of the impossible things he and his family were currently facing.

The last thing he remembered was charging at the man with the slashed throat. Then, he'd been hit with a flash of cold so strong that he thought his heart had stopped. Weightlessness followed, then... darkness.

His vision began to clear, and he was met with a sight that threatened to stop his heart again.

Chloe was held captive by some dark, hideous abomination of vaguely humanoid shape, though twisted into something else entirely.

But that was not the worst of it.

A tall, old-looking man held his child, his poor baby girl Emma. He was carrying her towards the roaring furnace, where a burning man waited within the flames.

Hoarse whispers escaped from the old man, who glided slowly forward as Emma howled frantically.

'*A pocket... full... of posies...*'

Andrew tried to crawl forward, but he could barely move his limbs. His strength did seem to be returning, but far too slowly, and he knew he wouldn't be able to act in time.

The old man with his baby girl moved closer and closer to the furnace.

'*A-tishoo... A-tishoo...*'

'Noooo,' Andrew weakly cried out.

But the hideous old man kept going and finished his awful nursery rhyme. '*We all... fall... down...*'

43

CHLOE STRUGGLED for all she was worth, writhing her body as violently as she could against the inhuman grip. But no matter how hard she tried, it was impossible to break free. She saw Andrew was now moving, pulling himself forward, but his progress was incredibly laboured.

She sensed other bodies emerge from either side of her, feeling their cold. These spirits of the dead, with pale, expressionless faces, all watched on as the old man carried Chloe's daughter to the furnace. There was an old woman with her throat cut, the monk with the ruined eye, and a plethora of other horrors, including Marcus Blackwater.

All had come to watch the sacrifice.

Tears streamed down Chloe's face, and she screamed her voice hoarse. The old man was at the furnace now with her daughter. This was it. He pulled the child back, ready to throw.

'Noooooo!'

Chloe whipped her head to the side. The guttural cry had come from a voice she recognised. Rapid footsteps pounded off the stone floor, and soon Sarah broke through the darkness, sprinting for all she was worth, a feral and angry expression etched on her face.

She wove through the motionless undead crowd, and flung herself at the man holding Emma. Chloe's breath was caught in her throat as she watched Sarah grab Emma from the old man's clutches. In one fluid motion, Sarah turned herself mid-air and landed on her back, protecting Emma from the fall.

Demonic roars of outrage thundered from the gathered crowd. Sarah hauled herself up, holding the crying child protectively. She backed up and turned her body to keep Emma shielded from the spirits that had begun to slowly advance towards her as one.

Chloe felt the cold grip from behind release her. She quickly turned and saw that there was no longer anything behind her. Which meant she was free.

However, when Chloe looked back over to Sarah, she saw that something stood behind her sister, merging with the darkness and only partially visible. It was a tall and yellow-eyed demon, skin cracked and obsidian, and its facial features twisted and melded together to be more monstrous than human.

'Sarah!' Chloe screamed. 'Behind you!'

Sarah quickly turned, then scuttled backwards with a scream upon seeing the demonic thing that stood so close to her.

'Run!' Chloe ordered.

She was unable to get through the throng of bodies between her and her sister, but did see there was enough room in the basement to skirt around the mass of drifting apparitions.

Her sister noticed it too, and Sarah ducked to her side,

then sprinted towards the edges of the room. Sensing her chance, Chloe bent down to Andrew and pulled him.

'Get up!' she screamed. 'We have to run!'

He groaned and tried to move, but he was slow and sluggish. Chloe wrapped an arm over her shoulder, letting him brace his weight on her. She managed to get him to his feet.

'Just... go,' he said weakly.

'Come on!' was all she said in reply, and forced herself to backpedal with him away from the danger. He stumbled with her, his skin still cold to the touch, though warming slightly.

Chloe saw Sarah arc around the floating mass, and then make a beeline towards the pair. She quickly unloaded Emma to Chloe and took over supporting Andrew.

'Give him to me,' she said, her voice thick with urgency. 'And run!'

The relief that surged through Chloe at once again holding Emma in her arms was immeasurable, though she was very aware that they weren't safe yet. The three of them moved as quickly as possible back towards the steps that would lead them upstairs again, but they were greatly slowed by Andrew. Chloe could hear the groans and moans from the horrors that she knew were following but did not dare look back to see.

They reached the bottom step, but just as they did, the flickering light from the furnace cut out in an instant. This time, Chloe could not help but look back... and saw only darkness.

No advancing entities, no raging inferno, and none of the horrible sounds that had been ringing in her ears only moments ago. Just a dark and empty basement. The only noise was their own panicked breathing.

'What... what happened?' she asked, confused.

'It doesn't matter,' Sarah said and pushed Chloe forward. 'We just need to get out.'

Chloe led the way, running up the stone steps and holding Emma tightly, with Sarah and Andrew following closely behind.

44

WITH ANDREW'S weight on her, progress for Sarah was slow. Though the entities down in the basement had vanished in an instant, panic still flooded through her, and she was desperate to get out of the house.

The whole situation was maddening. They were being hunted by things that just should not exist. And on top of that, Emma had been so close to...

Sarah couldn't finish the thought.

She still felt eternally ashamed for even considering leaving her family behind when the opportunity had presented itself. She just hoped the well of courage she'd found would help see them through to an escape.

By the time they had reached the top of the steps, Andrew was moving more freely and holding most of his own weight. Whatever had happened to him was apparently wearing off, at least to the point where he could hold himself up. Sarah still let him lean on her, but by the time they had cut through the great hall and were into the connecting corridor, it was easier to let him move completely on his own again.

The whole time they were running, Sarah was on edge, fully expecting something to reach out of the darkness and grab them. But the house remained silent, and they ran into the entrance lobby. The closed door was only a few feet away now, and escape was within reach.

Why the entities downstairs had suddenly disappeared and let them go, Sarah didn't understand. Right now, she also didn't care. Just as long as they broke free of the house.

She let Chloe and Andrew approach the exit first, and Andrew released the thumb-turn lock. He pulled the doors open and saw that the way ahead was clear.

Andrew then pushed Chloe and Emma out first, then he followed, with Sarah close behind.

This was it. They were going to be free...

But no.

Just as Sarah was about to cross the threshold, she felt her body lock and something take hold. No matter how hard she fought against it, some unseen power held her still, like a statue.

'Chloe!' she managed to cry out.

As her sister turned around, Sarah felt herself savagely pulled back, and she shot through the air, rising higher as she went. She could do nothing but scream as her body slammed against the far wall of the entrance lobby, and she then hung in mid-air, over the half-landing. She was about eight feet above the landing, held by something she could not see.

Sarah could see Chloe outside, and she looked horrified. Then, Sarah's legs were forced together, and her arms pulled out to her sides, her body forming the shape of a crucifix.

Disembodied wails and roars then rose up around her.

45

CHLOE HAD no idea what she was supposed to do.

She had gotten Emma free, Andrew too, but now her sister was trapped inside Perron Manor, held above the ground by an invisible force while she screamed in agony.

'We... we need to go,' Andrew said, his voice shaking. 'I'm sorry, but we need to get Emma to safety.'

But Chloe couldn't do that. As scared as she was, there was no way she could abandon her sister. After all, it was Sarah that had saved Emma from those... things downstairs. She had saved them all, in fact, and Chloe would be damned if she was going to now leave Sarah behind in her time of need.

So, she thrust Emma into Andrew's arms. He had finally regained his strength and could carry the baby. She then grabbed his shoulders and looked her husband directly in his eyes, and they widened in surprise and worry.

'Go,' she instructed. 'Get Emma out of here now. Get off the grounds and don't stop until you are free of this place. Don't turn back.'

'But—'

'There's no time!' Chloe snapped. She loved that he was protective of her, but he needed to get their daughter away from danger. 'Do it. We'll follow.' She then grabbed his head and kissed him hard before pushing him away. He reached for her, but Chloe ducked away from him. 'I love you,' she said, then barked, 'now go! For Emma's sake.'

Chloe backed up, not giving Andrew the chance to argue further. She knew he wouldn't let anything happen to Emma, and even though it must have been killing him inside, he began to walk away.

Thank you, she mouthed to him, then turned around. Sarah was still inside, hanging in mid-air, and her screaming had increased in both pitch and magnitude. Still in the crucifix position, there was obvious tension in her arms and legs, as if they were being stretched out.

A protective instinct to save her little sister took over, and Chloe bolted back inside of the house.

However, once she had crossed the threshold, an army of ghostly entities revealed themselves to her. All motionless and standing watch.

They were everywhere, dozens of them, crowding around the perimeter of the lobby as well as up either side of the stairs. They had left Chloe a direct route up to her sister.

More of the rotted and twisted spirits watched on from the walkways above as well, peering over the edges. The cold that filled the room was intense, causing Chloe's breath to fog up the air before her.

'Go,' Sarah pleaded, weakly.

But Chloe would not. Instead, she began walking towards her sister, and the pale faces of the dead turned, following her movements as she went.

She was exposed and vulnerable, and Chloe knew that

at any minute the things could pounce and kill her. But she kept going. Not quite able to break into a run, she still managed to tentatively push herself forward.

When she placed her foot on the bottom step, Chloe fully expected to be swarmed. They could simply crowd round her now and box her in, leaving no room for escape. But they didn't, and instead let her climb the stairs.

What are they waiting for?

She reached Sarah on the half-landing, and her sister's bare feet hung down directly before her. Chloe looked up, and Sarah's face was etched in pain. She still groaned in agony, and Chloe could see a tension in her sister's arms and legs as they were being pulled away from her body. Something was ever-so-slowly ripping Sarah apart.

'Run,' Sarah again pleaded. 'It's doing this just to get to you.'

But Chloe didn't care. If Perron Manor wanted her soul, then it could come and take it. She was *not* leaving her sister. She grabbed Sarah's ankles and pulled.

'Let her go!' Chloe cried out.

The gathered dead *still* did not approach, and simply stood by as a mere audience. Whatever was holding Sarah was strong, and Chloe was not able to free her, but she continued to desperately yank at Sarah's legs anyway.

'Please,' Sarah whispered between cries of pain.

'No!' Chloe shouted back, to the house rather than her sister. 'Enough! You won't take her, you hear me? You can't have my sister. I'll burn this fucking house to the ground before I let you have her. Now... Let. Her. Go!'

Chloe pulled again, and to her surprise, Sarah fell, her body dropping hard onto Chloe. They both fell backwards and tumbled down the long flight of stairs.

The world was a spinning blur, and pain erupted as

Chloe bounced down the steps, hitting different parts of her body: her back, her knee, her head, even the back of her neck, which twisted a little at an awkward angle.

She hit the marble floor and rolled twice, skidding to a stop. Her mind reeled and body ached. Disoriented, Chloe tried to turn her head to seek out Sarah. Her vision was blurry, and there was a terrible pain in her neck and head, enough that she felt like vomiting. But she managed to find her sister, who lay close to her. She was moving, but slowly, and was groaning in pain.

Chloe also noticed through blurry eyes, however, that the souls of Perron Manor had disappeared.

It felt like the house was toying with them, dangling the promise of freedom as a false hope, ready to pull it away again. Chloe could see no other options—they had to run.

She grabbed Sarah's arm and heaved herself up, pulling her sister with her. Chloe felt like she could topple over at any moment, but adrenaline and sheer desperation drove her forward.

'Come on,' she said through gritted teeth, limping back towards the open door. She felt battered and bruised, the fall down the stairs taking more out of her than she'd initially realised. But her vision, while still blurry, was focused on the exit.

Sarah hobbled with her. The house was quiet except for their panting and occasional pained groans. The door grew closer, step by step until the threshold was upon them.

Please, Chloe begged to herself. *Just let it be over.*

She tasted the fresh air, even felt it on her skin as her foot passed over to the porch outside. Sarah was beside her the whole time... and then she wasn't.

Chloe's sister was suddenly thrown forward, pushed outside to the ground.

And instead of being flung with her, Chloe was instead held by something, and cold, sharp claws dug into the skin of her upper arms.

Chloe screamed and was then pulled back inside while her feet slid helplessly across the marble. Still upright, she came to a stop just before the bottom of the stairs again. She could feel a radiating cold from behind, as well as a gut-churning and sulphuric smell.

The demon had her. Sarah turned from her position on the ground outside and cried out for Chloe, who felt the large talons now take hold of her head and force it to twist around to one side.

But her body did not move in the same direction.

Perron Manor had her now, she realised in her last moments. Her neck was then slowly and deliberately broken.

46

FROM HER POSITION OUTSIDE, Sarah saw the life drain from her sister's eyes and turn into a blank death-stare. Her neck was horribly twisted to one side, and Sarah had even heard an audible *crack* as Chloe's neck broke.

She screamed.

The thing that held Chloe then dropped her lifeless body to the floor, and it fell into a crumpled heap. Chloe's face was turned towards Sarah, who continued her pained cries, unwilling to accept what her eyes were showing her.

Her brain hadn't fully registered the situation, but Sarah was quickly back on her feet, and she ran as quickly as she could back towards her sister. The demonic creature stood above the fallen girl, and its monstrous mouth was twisted into a grin.

However, before Sarah could get back inside, the doors of Perron Manor slammed shut, cutting her off from her sister. She banged on the door, repeatedly, desperately, kicking and punching the surface. But it would not open. Eventually, after throwing everything she had at the door, Sarah collapsed to the ground, hyperventilating. The overwhelming pain and sadness at seeing her sister's death was too much to take.

It can't be. It can't be. Chloe can't be dead.

And yet, as much as her mind refused to believe it, somewhere inside she knew it to be true. If Perron Manor did indeed want Chloe—the girl who had escaped all those years ago—it had her now.

Sarah cried, her heart broken, and she thought of Emma and Andrew. A mother and wife, the best of each, stolen from them by this house of evil.

Sarah sat in front of the door to Perron Manor for close to half an hour, sobbing and wailing, unable to let what had happened sink in. Then, the door behind her clicked open of its own accord.

She turned and saw Chloe's body lying alone on the cold floor. Everything was silent. Sarah rushed over to her, and took Chloe in her arms, hugging her, still feeling her lingering warmth. She could smell the lavender scent of Chloe's hair.

Sarah knew that the house could very well take her too, now, but she didn't care.

But nothing came for her. Eventually, the realisation dawned on her that she needed to go to Andrew and tell him what had happened. And that meant leaving her sister... which she just didn't want to do.

After another fifteen minutes of sitting with Chloe in the dark, Sarah gently laid her head back down, and got to her feet.

'I'm so sorry, Sis,' she whispered.

Sarah then slowly walked from the house. She began to trudge her way down the long driveway, feeling the harsh, painful stones under the soles of her bare feet.

After getting only a few feet from the building, a sudden

sensation washed over her, like she was being watched. Sarah spun and examined the house. The door was still open, and Chloe was inside as before, but nothing else looked out of place... until she looked up to one of the mid-floor windows. Sarah's breath caught in her throat.

Chloe!

But it wasn't the Chloe she knew. Even at this distance, Sarah could make out that the features were twisted and distorted, with milky eyes, sunken and pale skin, and matted hair. And her expression was one of pain and sadness.

This version of Chloe put a hand up to the window, pressing her palm flat against it. Though no words could be heard, Sarah was easily able to read what Chloe mouthed.

Help me!

47

---

2 WEEKS LATER...

The casket was one Chloe would have liked. It had been picked out by Andrew, and had a dark mahogany veneer to it with shiny brass handles. A few handfuls of dirt lay on the closed lid.

Chloe's body was inside.

Thankfully, the dark clouds above had not unleashed the torrent of rain they'd been threatening, with the worst of it being a mild shower at the start of the funeral.

It felt weird for Sarah to be back in her hometown again after so long away, and to see her extended family—none of whom she was close to.

She was just thankful that both her parents had passed, so they didn't have to see or feel this moment. It would have broken them—God knew it was breaking Sarah.

The graveyard was well kept and pleasant, and the traditional stone church stood large and imposing behind them. Chloe had not updated her will and testament since moving to Perron Manor, so as per her last wishes, she was laid to rest here.

But she wasn't at rest at all, Sarah knew. And certainly not at peace.

Sarah stood above her fallen sister, looking down and crying uncontrollably. She was supposed to be paying her respects, but Sarah couldn't focus on anything other than what she'd seen the last time she was at *that* house. The image of Chloe, upstairs and alone, begging for help.

While Chloe's earthly shell lay below Sarah, she knew without question that the essence of her sister was still back at Perron Manor. Trapped and suffering.

And would be for all eternity. Unless...

She felt a hand on her shoulder and knew instantly it was Andrew. He stood beside her, dressed smartly in a dark suit. His face was streaked with tears as well, and he offered her a sad smile. Emma was with his parents, who stood on the other side of him. The poor little girl had no idea what was happening.

Probably for the best.

Sarah returned Andrew's smile. She felt bad for him. More so for Emma.

The night Chloe died, Sarah had eventually walked to find Andrew, and explained what had happened. He had reacted angrily, which was natural. He'd said he needed to see her, and no amount of arguing could persuade him. So, Sarah had to stand in the night with Emma while he ran back to the house. Eventually, he returned with an armful of blankets, and his face was still full of rage. But the house had not taken him, and no harm had come to him. In fact, he claimed to have seen nothing.

He'd also told Sarah that he had called the police, as they couldn't just leave Chloe like that. Sarah had agreed, but asked how they would go about explaining what had happened.

In the end, they had lied.

They stated that Chloe had woken them all up during the night to the sounds of someone else in the house. They had tried to flee, and Chloe had tripped and fallen while running down the stairs. She'd landed on her head, and they heard a horrible crack.

Sarah hated herself for having to lie about the death of her own sister like that and pretend like it was some freakish accident. The police investigated, and advised they found no trace of a break-in, but they said they didn't discount it as a possibility. In the end, they accepted the cause of death as an accident.

A light breeze circled Sarah, carrying with it the smell of wet grass as the priest said his final words. It was time for them to leave. Sarah again looked down at Chloe's casket, and though she spoke no words, made a vow.

She would not let Chloe suffer for eternity.

Afterwards, Andrew had arranged for a get-together at a local country pub, where people could gather and drink and eat, like it was all some kind of party. Sarah didn't want to be there. She wanted to be getting on with things, with the job at hand, but felt obligated.

Sarah gave it a couple of hours, and right as she was getting ready to bid her farewells and leave, Andrew approached her with Emma. The child looked as cute as could be in a little dark dress and adorable big white bow in her hair. Earlier in the day, Sarah had heard the little girl asking for her 'Mummy,' and that had broken her all over again.

'You look like you're getting ready to leave,' Andrew said to her. 'You keep glancing over to the exit.'

'Sorry,' Sarah replied. 'I'm just not comfortable here. Not comfortable with this whole thing, to be honest.'

'Me either,' he agreed. There was a pause between them. 'Emma and I are going to be staying with my parents for a little while, until we find somewhere to live.'

'Okay,' Sarah replied.

'You are welcome to stay, too. Their place is pretty big.'

'I'll be okay.'

'Well, you're always welcome to come see Emma. Anytime you want. You know that, right?'

She smiled. 'I do. And thank you.'

Another pause, then he went on, 'I suppose it goes without saying that neither I nor Emma will ever set foot back in that place again. I don't want anything to do with it.'

'Of course,' Sarah replied, giving an understanding nod. Legally, in the event of any of them dying, the house was to fully transfer its ownership to the surviving sister, as per the stipulation in the original will. And, given they had no time to change any of those stipulations before Chloe had died, that meant Sarah was now legally the sole owner. 'I'll put it up for sale,' she said. 'And if I manage to sell it then you and Emma are getting half the money.'

'We don't need—'

'It's non-negotiable,' Sarah said, cutting Andrew off. 'And I can promise you, I'm never going back to that fucking place again, either.'

But that was a lie.

48

1 Week Later...

The hazelnut coffee Sarah sipped was piping hot and full of flavour. Chloe would have hated it.

The last time Sarah had been in this place—the *Hill of Beans*—was with her sister. The man she was now due to meet had received a tongue lashing, and all because he had delivered a warning they should have heeded.

David Ritter entered the coffee shop and quickly spotted her. He gave her a sad, sympathetic smile—followed by a wave—then walked over.

'I'm sorry to hear about what happened to your sister,' he offered.

Sarah just gave a tight-lipped smile and small nod in return, then gestured to the empty chair opposite. He took it.

'It was an accident,' Sarah told him, lying once again. She didn't want him to know the full details of the story, nor the full dangers Perron Manor actually posed. Not when she needed something from him.

'So it *was* the fall that killed her?' David asked, seemingly a little surprised. 'I'd heard that was the case, but thought maybe...'

'No, that much was true,' Sarah told him. 'But before the fall, things happened we didn't tell the police about.'

David gave a solemn nod, but one with no hint of an 'I told you so' smugness.

'So,' he started, 'you said in your message you wanted to talk to me about something?'

'Yes.' Sarah took another sip of her drink. 'Chloe and I got into a fight that day, before everything happened. She believed what you told her about Perron Manor, and I... well, I had a hard time with it. But she did let something interesting slip. According to you, the only way to free the souls trapped in there was... with exorcism?'

'Possibly,' David said. 'But it was more an educated guess, to be honest. Why?'

Sarah took a breath. 'After Chloe died, I saw her again in the house. Upstairs. And she was in pain.'

David just nodded. 'The house has her,' he stated.

That threw Sarah. She thought her revelation might have been more of a surprise to him. *Does he know more about that place than he's letting on?*

'I believe it does, yes,' Sarah continued. 'But I can't let it keep her. I won't allow it.'

David paused for a moment. 'So... you want the place exorcised.'

'That's right,' she said, then added, 'and I need you to help me do it. Will you?'

David didn't need to consider the question for very long. 'Yes,' he said enthusiastically. 'I'll help you.'

Sarah felt a wave of relief, then smiled. 'Good.'

I'm coming for you, Chloe.

The End

HAUNTED: DEVIL'S DOOR

THE STORY CONTINUES AS THE MASSACRE OF 1982 IS TOLD IN FULL...

Haunted: Devil's Door
Book 2 in the Haunted Series.

Halloween night, 1982: many people disappeared or were brutally killed at the Blackwater Hotel—formerly Perron Manor. The events have always remained a mystery.

Until now...

Ray and Rita Shaw, along with their daughter Chloe, move into the hotel to help with its renovation and grand opening. All under the watchful eye of the mysterious owner, Marcus Blackwater.

But as they move closer to that fateful date, things begin

to happen in the hotel that are unexplainable. And Rita herself begins to change.

Unbeknownst to the family, there are other plans afoot. Marcus Blackwater has his own agenda, one started by his grandfather many years ago.

The story culminates in a horrific turn of events that changes everything you think you know about the house... and its inhabitants.

Buy Haunted: Devil's Door now.

INSIDE: PERRON MANOR

Sign up to my mailing list to get the FREE prequel...

In 2014 a group of paranormal researchers conducted a weekend-long investigation at the notorious Perron Manor. The events that took place during that weekend were incredible and terrifying in equal measure. This is the full, documented story.

In addition, the author dives into the long and bloody history of the house, starting with its origins as a monastery back in the 1200s, covering its ownership under the Grey and Perron families, and even detailing the horrific events that took place on Halloween in 1982.

No stone is left unturned in what is now the definitive work regarding the most haunted house in Britain.

The novella, as mentioned in Haunted: Perron Manor, can be yours for FREE by joining my mailing list.

Sign up now.

www.leemountford.com

OTHER BOOKS BY LEE MOUNTFORD

The Supernatural Horror Collection
The Demonic
The Mark
Forest of the Damned

The Extreme Horror Collection
Horror in the Woods
Tormented
The Netherwell Horror

Haunted Series
Inside Perron Manor (Book 0)
Haunted: Devil's Door (Book 2)
Haunted: Purgatory (Book 3)
Haunted: Possession (Book 4)
Haunted: Mother Death (Book 5)
Haunted: Asylum (Book 6)

ABOUT THE AUTHOR

Lee Mountford is a horror author from the North-East of England. His first book, Horror in the Woods, was published in May 2017 to fantastic reviews, and his follow-up book, The Demonic, achieved Best Seller status in both Occult Horror and British Horror categories on Amazon.

He is a lifelong horror fan, much to the dismay of his amazing wife, Michelle, and his work is available in ebook, print and audiobook formats.

In August 2017 he and his wife welcomed their first daughter, Ella, into the world. In May 2019, their second daughter, Sophie, came along. Michelle is hoping the girls don't inherit their father's love of horror, but Lee has other ideas...

For more information
www.leemountford.com
leemountford01@googlemail.com

ACKNOWLEDGMENTS

Thanks first to my amazing Beta Reader Team, who have greatly helped me polish and hone this book:

James Bacon

Christine Brlevic

John Brooks

Carrie-Lynn Cantwell

Karen Day

Doreene Fernandes

Jenn Freitag

Ursula Gillam

Clayton Hall

Tammy Harris

Emily Haynes

Dorie Heriot

Lemmy Howells

Lucy Hughes

Dawn Keate

Diane McCarty

Megan McCarty

Valerie Palmer

Leanne Pert

Justin Read

Nicola Jayne Smith

Sara Walker

Sharon Watret

Also, thanks to my editor, Josiah Davis (http://www.jdbookservices.com) for such an amazing job as always.

The cover was supplied by Debbie at The Cover Collection. (http://www.thecovercollection.com). I cannot recommend their work enough.

And the last thank you, as always, is the most important—to my amazing family. My wife, Michelle, and my daughters, Ella and Sophie: thank you for everything. You three are my world.